THE RASMUSSEN DISASTERS

Books by James Leigh

The Rasmussen Disasters
Downstairs at Ramsey's
What Can You Do?

James Leigh

THE

1817

HARPER & ROW, PUBLISHERS

NEW YORK, EVANSTON,

AND LONDON

RASMUSSEN

DISASTERS

FIRST EDITION

LIBRARY OF CONGRESS CATALOG CARD NUMBER: 71-83634

To Phil and Fran Levine

I. SUNDAY, MONDAY, AND THEN SOME

ONE

Sunday morning moved west. Three-quarters of a billion Chinese faced the sun, and maids tidied the brothels of Saigon. A German tourist got up early, escaped his guide, and on the muddy riverbank behind the Taj Mahal found a dog eating a corpse. A child? Another animal? The tourist could not tell. He recorded the phenomenon with his Zeiss-Ikon and went back to his hotel for breakfast.

Sunday morning moved west, shining impartially on the counterrevolutionary beards of Russian rabbis, the suppliant forearms of devout Muslims, and the meager shanks of teen-age Jordanian boys, one of them, according to a famous North American seeress, destined to be mankind's next savior. The sun woke black South African gold diggers in their apart-hidden compounds, and blessed the prim roofs of the Dutch Reformed Church, and when a director of the Crédit Suisse sat down to breakfast before the crystal window of a chalet outside Geneva, a beam of sun discovered on the burnished silver lip of a coffee jug one small fly, rubbing its hands together as if anticipating a profit. Outraged as by an

error in bookkeeping or a visible flake of fiduciary sin on the
pure life of a trusted associate, the director nonetheless remained composed. He cleared his throat. *"Là . . ."* he said.
His wife rang for the maid.

Above the sunken temples of fabulous Atlantis, above the
Sargasso drifting like a madman's dream of history or a
riddle in seaweed for God to solve, Sunday morning moved
west to yet more fabulous and cryptic America, in whose
great Eastern cities churches and supermarkets were opening for business, and the fires of Saturday night still burned,
though some of the men who had set them were home sleeping. A woman opened her third-story window to water a
geranium, the sun flashed on the jelly glass in her hand, and
a young National Guardsman shot her dead from the street
below. "You fuckhead," his lieutenant said. "Think of the
image."

Sunday morning moved west, arousing America to hang-
overs and prayers, Bloody Marys and prefab hotcakes and
imitation maple syrup; to bracing dips in a thousand munic-
ipal plunges mostly integrated by law; to 4-H barbecues and
Boy Scout jamborees, film festivals and sports-car rallies,
love-ins and mass arrests, Dick Tracy and Peanuts in color,
the Game of the Day in color, Meet the Press in color, everything in living color except Mom, Dad, and the kids, looking
preoccupied and insubstantial next to the funnies and the
television screen.

Even unto the lower-left-hand corner of the continental
U.S.A.—held by some to be the spiritual source of all these
wonders—Sunday morning came, and, still playing no favor-
ites, brought its warmth and light to the largest city in the
world, never mind what the official figures say: vast Los Angeles, semiconscious beneath its own foul breath; subsumed,
unified perhaps by that permanent yellow-black pall of poison gas overhead, and if not by that then by nothing; justi-

fiably hopeless of ever equaling the sum of its parts, all those neoplasmic communities thrown up almost as fast as God is said to have created the world, though admittedly of less durable stuff—quick plaster and chicken wire, chipboard and Formica and Styrofoam and green pine—by credit magicians, builders of tracts and shopping centers, visionaries who think ahead now to bulldozing down the Sierra Nevadas for more subdivisions when the time comes, and it will.

Sunday morning came to every last part of greater Los Angeles, including a treeless southeasterly trapezoid, designated Westpark perhaps to keep its contents from thinking they lived in Buena Park or Woodland Park or Huntington Park or Baldwin Park.

Westpark, subtitled "A Dream of Modern Living" by its creators. Westpark, home of the Everlasting Gospel Bible College and the Bonanza drive-in movie theater (triple features, free car heaters, and a Kiddie Korner); home of the Westpark Super and the Westpark Bowl and the Westpark TV Mart, of two indoor movie theaters, the West and the Park; of five churches and two high schools and four liquor stores (Ace, Bud's, U Savo, and Westpark). All these plus several thousand remarkably similar houses, in each of which, according to the 1960 Census, existed 3.8 souls.

Sunday morning got to Westpark right on time, and moved on across the Pacific Ocean toward Midway Island and Monday, but for Rasmussen the damage was done: he was awake.

The pressure was there inside him when his eyes opened, but Rasmussen, sly by reflex, let his lids close again until he was sure that his wife Ann was no longer in the master bedroom. The pressure was still faint.

Tentatively half open again, his eyes hid in their deep sockets as his right hand plucked a Camel from the open pack on the bedside table, fit it into his skull, set it burning with the gas-jet lighter. The hand did this every morning without having to be told. After forty-five years it was one of the few things in life Rasmussen could depend on, and now, while the smoke complicated the morning foulness of his mouth, the same trusty hand crept swiftly and autonomously between his legs to sort out the loose mass of his genitals, melted together in warm sleep.

One, two, three: all present and accounted for. Rasmussen liked knowing they were still there.

In the back bedroom his son David, nineteen, was up to something in the same line. Having awakened to aching tumefaction from a clogged hot dream of a golden black girl named Rosanne Larkin, he considered how depressing it was still to be doing this at his age, but did anyway.

The certain foreknowledge that consummation would not match the deceitful promise of the urge spoiled his concentration on the accompanying color film in his head—a wide-screen pink-and-tan closeup of conjoined moving parts—but, with the help of an improvised sound track, *Oh David you some man! Aw you too much for me, baby, oh oohh,* and to the tempo of the batter his mother was beating loudly in the dining room, he paid the dues on his dream right into the Kleenex, the usual despairing spasms. "Ah shit," he exhaled. "Hotcakes again."

Hotcakes *and* bacon, which his mother arranged in a careful pink-and-white mosaic on the cold stainless-steel grill of her giant kitchen range, until only the bright steel rim lay exposed. She took a fresh white dish towel and ran a corner of it around the rim with a stiff accusing forefinger. The towel came away clean.

A large fly materialized loudly not two yards away. Someone had left a door open. With a single pointblank round from a tastefully slender pale-blue spray can, she hissed the fly dead in midair. Holding her breath until the poison vapor had dispersed, she squatted quickly to whisk the fly's corpse into a tiny dustpan. A moving film of clear cold water bore it, without actually touching the stainless-steel sink, down into the garbage disposal, where, at a touch of her finger on the switch, it presumably ceased to exist.

Now she drew breath, and let out a little sigh of satisfaction as she washed her hands. But her purposeful loud batter-beating had brought forth no slugabeds, and yet the fly had come from *somewhere*. . . . "Margie?" she called. "*Margie.*"

Her voice carried to where her twelve-year-old daughter lay supine on the blue chenille rug beside her bed, but Margie was thinking, in a manner of speaking, about something else. Eleven hours of sleep had so exhausted her that she had climbed from bed only to lie down once more at the opportune recollection of her gym teacher's advice: "Sit-ups, Rasmussen," Miss Glenn had said. "Sit-ups every morning," that sinewy breastless lady had said. "*And touch those toesies. Trim off all that baby fat pronto.*"

But once on the rug, Margie had found the floor not all that uncomfortable. From way down here, this was how it looked to little baby animals, clumsy puppies and furry kitties. She would much rather be a kitty, growing naturally svelte and graceful, never worrying about measurements like 29-29-33. Yawning, she let her head fall sideways, and saw how clean it was under her bed.

Meanwhile Rasmussen lay smoking. Sun yellowing the plastic Venetian blinds meant Sunday. That much he knew; otherwise his mind was only technically awake, a television screen showing a test pattern. The familiar pressure behind his groin meant something, too: he had got up only twice in the night. His average was almost exactly 2.5, something else he could depend on. It was a reason to get up now, and on Sundays he needed one.

Checking a groan before it could produce a cough, his body angled up and swung itself out of bed, and he carried his round anomalous little belly on scarecrow legs into the bathroom, where he fell in at attention before the toilet bowl. It always took several seconds.

Then he checked the faithful right hand before it could throw the Camel butt into the bowl, and saw, in the middle of a square of tissue floating centered on the surface of the pool, moored by its four corners to the gleaming white banks, a bright-red mouth gaping up at him, not smiling. A wide thick-lipped fish mouth, a lopsided bull's-eye. It had to be on purpose. Not like Ann not to flush, not at all. And there was the wastebasket polished and empty. Not like her at all.

Rasmussen built up as much back pressure as he could, took aim, and drilled it.

Ah, Sunday. It was all out there waiting for him. He took his time shaving, deep-soaking his tough beard with a scalding-hot towel and a heavy coating of menthol spray lather, sliding a new super-stainless blade from its plastic clip, checking the adjustment on his Adjustable. Rasmussen loved shaving the skin shrunk tight over his bony jaw.

Over the years—ten? thirty? he could not have said—the baffled sweats of a thousand irritations and blurred menaces had congealed into a skin tough as plastic, a two-way protective coating that deflected the soft endless bombardment of dissatisfactions while diffusing his reactions to them in a sort of organized inattention. It was this skin which he prepared so carefully each morning, like a soldier polishing his shield.

But he couldn't shave the top of his head, where the four

straight-back stripes of yellow-brown hair hadn't offered adequate protection for years, so he covered it daily with a Dodgers baseball cap of snug-fitting dark-blue felt. The shave, the cap, and a gray-green wool coat sweater with green suede front panels: inside this armor he could get through the day. On Sundays, with no saving rush to work and school, he needed it just that much more to shed those three presences while he poured his own first cup of coffee and, weather permitting, made it out to the patio with the Times, all five pounds of it.

Now, settled in an aluminum-and-plastic chair in the patio —every brick of it laid by his hand—Rasmussen ignored the sun's hot prickle on his freshly smooth face and addressed himself to the first news section. NEW PEACE TALK THREAT HINT, RECORD BOMB LOAD, TROOPS HUNT SNIPERS: they could have been last Sunday's headlines, last month's, or last year's, but their very familiarity was a source of comfort: the world was going to hell on roller skates, but hadn't quite got there yet.

Other sections of the paper reinforced this negative optimism: the Dodgers had lost to Houston last night, which meant they couldn't possibly lose both ends of today's doubleheader; the market had slipped eleven points in the past week, but had never *plunged*. Rasmussen went to one ball game a year, with his bowling team, and he owned no stocks, but he knew reassurance when he saw it.

Now he skimmed the paper, keeping his eye out for the longest feature story, a two-pager if possible. Once chosen, a finger keeping the place for quick reference at the first sounds of breakfast served, it would engross him dependably through eggs or hotcakes.

Rasmussen saw in this a positive contribution to the silence of breakfast, if not to its peace. Real peace was plainly not to be had at any price, but a silence broken only by the necessary gobbling and scraping of mealtime was not the worst of silences. Not by a long shot.

"Charley."

His wife's call to breakfast caught Rasmussen still uncommitted between NEW DRUG DISCOVERIES MAY HOLD ANSWER TO "FREAK-OUTS" and GM DESIGN EXPERT SEES RETURN TO CLASSIC BODY STYLES.

NEW DRUG DISCOVERIES had fewer pictures taking up space, so he began reading it as he went inside. David, he saw peripherally, was not there yet. Still in bed. So much the better. Two-to-one were hopeless odds, but three-to-one were worse.

He sat down in his place, buttered and syruped a hotcake, and forked the first wedge into his face without missing a word *as URC's Dr. Morton Schmolzer told conference members of a dramatic new antidote to the nightmare horror of psychedelic "freak-outs. . . ."*

Ann hadn't even wanted her first hotcake. She gave up on her second after one bite, drained her coffee cup, refilled it, and, as in the mildest of hallucinations, seemed to see her husband's skull inside the Dodgers cap floating free of his body, the eyes fixed to the page directly before them on the table, the jaw dealing slowly and efficiently with the bites of hotcake brought to it from the plate to its right, as if to make clear its greater concern with reading than with feeding.

About what might be going on beneath the cap, behind the downcast pale-blue eyes, she was not at all curious. Perhaps there was nothing in there at all but the words and the bites of hotcake, a sickening chewed-up mixture.

David came in. Ann pushed her chair back. "How many hotcakes?" she asked him. Rasmussen's skull went on reading and feeding.

"How many?"

"A couple."

That meant to Ann that he would eat four. She went out to cook them. She knew the warmer still held four strips of bacon, and things should come out even.

Wasted. Man, am I wasted. Across the table, David saw Pig Bird dreamily making roads in the congealing syrup on her plate in a way that seemed depressingly to correspond with the way he felt. He let his body slip slack down onto his chair, as if body or chair might fall apart on contact.

Wasted. Weekdays were bad, but Sunday was the end. Sunday the zombies sat around all day waiting for dark. And at dark, instead of going out to stalk victims and suck their blood, the zombies waited for bedtime.

And there in the Daddy Chair on his right, The Cap pretended to be reading about . . . what?

"NEW DRUG DISCOVERIES MAY HOLD ANSWER TO "FREAK-OUTS"

The Cap loved reading about that stuff even better than war or riot news, especially the parts about how kids went crazy behind "dope" and got underage girls knocked up: *the worst thing that could happen to anyone,* according to The Cap. Compared to *that,* getting zapped in a rice paddy was nothing.

Unforgettable, that man-to-man talk he had had with The Cap, and for dessert, a package of rubbers! Delivered fast, sneaky, hand-to-hand-looking-the-other-way, like laying a joint of marijuana on you. "Here, you better keep these handy, boy. Better be safe than sorry."

And had David blown that one! Instead of saying, "Gee whiz, Dad, thanks a million," he had tried to explain about the pill, how all the girls who'd lie down nowadays were on it. Blasted The Cap clear off his pad: didn't David see, for Christ's sake, how even if this so-called pill worked (The

Cap had his doubts), how even then you couldn't trust girls? *These* were the only way a man could stay in control. "So who wants all that control?" David had asked.

The End! "OK. OK. I could tell you a few things, wise ass, but you're way ahead of me. OK. But when you get a girl in trouble, don't come cryin to me. It's your baby!" (Not trying to be funny, either.)

Now there was this Cease-fire, and The Cap was easier to be around. As long as the paper got delivered, and nothing went wrong with the tube. Otherwise, look out! One day the pressure must build up and blow The Cap, top of his skull and all, through the roof like a tactical warhead. David didn't wish for it, as long as he himself was let alone. But it seemed to be exactly what the Cease-fire meant: "Mmm boy, one of these days . . . *pow!*"

David didn't wish for it, but still, for *anything* to happen would be a kind of blessing, around this zombie shelter. Even the ringing of the telephone, which Pig Bird now flew to answer, while The Cap went on reading about freak-outs.

"For you, Dad," said Pig Bird in a brought-down voice. "I think long distance."

That was a shocker. Who could want to talk to The Cap enough to call him long distance? David watched his father, clutching the folded-back newspaper, scuttle out of the room at that purposeful speed he reached normally only on his way to the toilet.

Here came Mrs. Clean with his hotcakes and bacon, which looked like something out of Family Circle, and would taste like Kleenex. "It must be his grandfather," she said. "You want coffee?"

"Milk," said David, and he had to smile: The Cap's grandfather! The idea had always been too much for him. He simply could not conceive of anyone that old. Like life on other planets.

"Bernie?" came The Cap's voice from the front room. "Bernie? That you, boy?"

"Oh my God in heaven," said Mrs. Clean.

Bernie? Fabulous Uncle Bernie? David listened ear to ear with his mother.

"Sure, well, ah, how's it goin, kid?" To Ann, Rasmussen's voice sounded on the run. He was getting ready to back down on something. As well he should, she thought.

"No, we're all about the same. She's fine. They're fine. What you been up to?"

Uncle Bernie, thought David. The family failure—which was saying something. Last seen nine or ten years ago, a lot of blond hair and a red face sweating booze and pot. A house-wrecking midnight battle beyond David's locked bedroom door, and curses, the best he'd ever heard. A few minutes later, a car crashing through the back of the garage.

"Well, good to hear your voice, Bern," The Cap said. "Drop us a card now an then, hey?"

The last one was from Tangier. The Cap got the atlas out and pointed. "That's where your Uncle Bernie is."

"Your Uncle Bernie the dope addict," Mrs. Clean had added, and was now thinking, along with worse things, as Rasmussen said, "Huh? Jesus, Bern, I don't know. . . ."

Here it came, whatever it was, Ann thought. His voice was backtracking at high speed now.

"Tonight? You kiddin me? That's pretty short notice, I mean. . . ."

A visit from Uncle Bernie, David thought. Oh goody! The idea of himself clapping his hands, jumping up and down for joy, made him smile.

"Weeell, OK, for a couple of days, I guess. Sure. That's it. Naw, we got a new couch, foam rubber. What time do you figure . . . A *bike?* From San Francisco? Oh. Yeah. Well, we turn in pretty early, you know. OK. Yeah. OK. See you tonight."

David normally managed to be looking the other way when The Cap came into the room; it saved arguments. But now he had to see: there came The Cap, wearing his you-want-to-make-something-out-of-it? face. "Bernie . . ." he said to no one in particular. "He's comin to spend a couple of days, while he looks for a place. Gettin in tonight, he said."

"On a bike?" said David.

"Motorcycle," said The Cap. No more than that and right on out into the patio without breaking stride.

"Marvelous," said Mrs. Clean. Then, to Pig Bird: "You and I are going to a motel while he's here."

"Which motel?" said Margie. "With a pool?" The idea of a motel made its own immediate space in her leisurely consciousness, having no more to displace than an unvisualized memory, or "memory," of Uncle Bernie. It sprang out, instantaneously clear and bright as a Polaroid photo on the prepared paper of her mind: in the center foreground a big swimming pool, shimmering electric blue, edged with red-and-yellow awnings and umbrellas; beyond, all brand-new and unslept-in, the sleek neat modern rooms where Cokes peeked from snowdrifts and the wall TV's hummed cool and blue.

But by then Margie was thinking of a new bathing suit, quite independently of her certainty that her mother would not buy her one. Indeed, only that knowledge permitted her to think of the bathing suit at all, since a bikini—the only fun kind to think of—was quite out of the question until she had more to put in the top part, and less bulking white beneath it. A bikini literally could not be thought of except on the lithe and permanently tanned figure which now stretched languidly inside her, waiting to emerge, perhaps next summer, from its pale padded cocoon.

"Can't I come, too?" said David.

"You can not," said Ann, a split second ahead of the realization that he had not been serious. She began to clear the table.

Margie heard the exchange with one ear, glad that David would not be along, and rejected a metallic-green bikini in favor of a red-orange one, the color of sweet-and-sour sauce. It looked better against the sun-hammered blue of the pool.

Back in her spotless, fly-free kitchen, Ann slammed the breakfast dishes into the washer rack just hard enough not to break them. Bernie Rasmussen! The thought of him made her want to vomit. No, worse, as if she had to vomit and couldn't. Why hadn't Charley told him a simple no? Even after so long, he could not have forgotten. Not Charley Rasmussen, with his total recall of every bad turn ever done him, real or imagined.

The last time. Charley drunk, Bernie drunk or full of God knows what kind of dope. *Bum! Fake! Dirty son of a bitch!* Lamps and chairs flying, a bottle through the front window, the French doors all splinters and jagged glass. *Bourgeois chickenshit bastard! Fascist!* On and on like that, Charley trying to kill Bernie, Bernie trying to kill Charley *and* wreck the house, setting the curtains on fire with Charley's lighter (*God damn thief!* yelled Charley, letting the curtains burn), and then running out the front door calling them all dead corpses!

And even that hadn't been enough. Because Bernie had taken the car keys with him, an old trick of his, and a little later sneaked back into the garage, put the car in first instead of reverse, wound up the motor like a jet plane, and drove halfway through the rear wall of the garage into the back yard.

In the bathroom trying to stick iodine up one bloody nostril, when the crash came Charley broke the glass applicator

off inside and ripped his nose open. And when the police
had finally got around to looking in on the party? "Sorry,"
said Charley. "My brother an I just had a few too many."
Snuffling blood into a perfectly clean white bath towel.
"Naw, nothin serious, just a little family row, you know. . . ."

That hadn't been the first time Ann had given up on
Charley Rasmussen, but she did it again to keep in practice.
As for Bernie, there had never been anything to give up on,
unless you counted all his loud filthy incoherent talk about
experience, and *reality,* and his *talent,* and the worldwide
conspiracy against it! Seriously, Ann wanted to vomit.

So of course she would take Margie to a motel, and let
the *men*—that was a funny one!—have a nice little stag party
for just as long as they liked. Maybe Bernie would bring
some dope, and some beatnik hippie girls, and they could
have a real orgy.

She pushed the dishwasher out of sight beneath the sink
and switched it on. Its muted watery rumble harmonized
with the grinding whir of the garbage disposal annihilating
the breakfast scraps. How often Ann had wished she could
deal as conclusively with the problems of her life: *wash*
Charley clean and new, or if not new, at least usable, to be
stacked in a dust-free cupboard of her mind; *dispose* of Bernie once and for all.

"Margie!" she called. It was getting late for church. Both
children had fled the dining room. She found her daughter
fused into an overstuffed chair watching Donald O'Connor
and Peggy Ryan doing a song-and-dance in cheerleaders'
costumes. "You pack your little bag," said Ann, "with your
undies and school things, and when I get back we'll pack
both our clothes in my big one."

"What say, gang?" said Donald O'Connor.

"Did you hear me?" said Ann.

"What?" said Margie.

"You heard me," said Ann. She went into the bathroom and took her gum massager from its plastic sheath. Her Sunday excitement began to mount, but she controlled it, and gave her gums their due; pyorrhea was no joke.

Howard Bunch, Sunday lunch, sang her pulse. The only poem she'd ever made up. Now, with the electric toothbrush, and her special extra-hard pale-green nib, she brushed long and hard, the vibrations reinforcing her own.

Ah, her teeth! If the rest of her looked forty-three-on-Tuesday, at least they did not. Thirty-two of them, all her own, and white, white, white. It always sustained her to focus on her mouth in the mirror and flex a grin. If there was no humor in that dependable white flash, still it was her best feature.

Forty-two-on-Tuesday. It was getting late. It *was* late. But Ann remade her mouth, blotted it on a sheet of tissue, and dropped it into the toilet. She touched up her hair, sprayed cologne in the sharp right angle of neck and shoulder where Howard, her Sunday husband, might kiss her before. She flushed, grinned hard at herself, and went out.

"I'm going," she said to the house, expecting no acknowledgment, and getting none.

In the patio, Rasmussen heard her leave and quit in midsentence, *Although Dr. Schmolzer holds out little hope for what he calls the "hard-core*

In his room, David heard her go, and went on reading Chapter LXVII of *The Playboy Philosophy.* He was smiling.

In the living room, Donald O'Connor shouted through his little megaphone: *"Don't give up, gang! We can still win the big game!"*

TWO

If Sunday was for Rasmussen the worst day of the week, a torporific marathon of exhausting inactivity, then Sunday-night supper was the blessed three-quarters pole past which he could coast toward bedtime, yawning more frequently and belching less self-assertively as beer and television worked their fuzzy magic upon him.

But not this Sunday-night supper, not a chance. Bernie was coming and Ann was going: all day long Rasmussen's mind had grappled sluggishly with those two promises as with a problem stated in a foreign language or a higher mathematics. As well he did not know that for Ann Sunday was the best day of the week, at least the hour straddling noon. If she revealed this in any way, Rasmussen was blind to it.

Nor were his worries relieved at all tonight when she served supper with her habitual punctuality, an achievement so delicately programmed that no one could sufficiently appreciate it. The kitchen clock was maddeningly invisible from the dining room, so that Ann couldn't even confirm it herself. The best she could do was leave the kitchen, bearing the main dish, at six o'clock minus two and a half seconds, *after* Rasmussen and David and Margie were seated. She had arrived at this interval by halving the average duration of a round trip. As a double check, she employed the eight steps she took one way as a countdown.

Eight-seven-six-five-four-three-two-one and as the pork chops en casserole touched down on the asbestos pad, the red sweep-second hand of the kitchen clock kissed the dot of 12 and became for an instant part of a straight black line bisecting the face of time like the judgment of God. Hypothetically, that is. Ann was left with only the tiny martyred satisfaction of watching the three of them commence to feed in total ignorance of her achievement.

Rasmussen took his first bite of chop. It was, as always, dry. As with most things Ann cooked, the flavor was in the gravy, if anywhere. Yet far from depressing him, this familiarity reassured him, and he blurted out a proposition he hadn't even known himself to be considering:

"If I absolutely guarantee he'll be out of here in two days, how about sticking around?"

Christ, what a damn-fool thing to have gone and said! What an opening to give her! Rasmussen slashed half his chop free of the bone, stuffed it in his mouth, and glared.

Ann didn't even stop chewing. But in a moment she would. Rasmussen chewed furiously, as if so long as one of them were chewing, neither could speak.

She swallowed. "How can you guarantee he'll be out of here in two days?" she said.

Rasmussen had no answer to that one.

"Does the fire insurance cover wrecking the furniture?" she said. "Or knocking down walls?"

"Just leave it to me," said Rasmussen, more and more foolhardy. She wasn't acting nearly suspicious enough; his head was full of alarms.

She chewed and swallowed. "Why do you want me to stick around?" she said. "I'd just be interested to know."

Well, he had gone this far. Might as well shoot his whole roll: "I'd just kind of like it to look like a family," he said. "While Bernie's here." In a way the riskiest thing he had said yet, exposing him to a fantastic range of recriminations, still it seemed momentarily to Rasmussen no more than the simple truth.

Looking at him as if he were some mildly curious freak, her eyes focused thoughtfully on the bill of his cap, Ann chewed and swallowed once more. "All right," she said. "Two days. But the minute he gets up to anything, we leave."

"*You mean we're not going to the motel?*" Margie sprayed particles of mashed potato at her mother. "But I'm all *packed!*"

"Mother's changed her mind," said Ann. "But you better just leave your bag packed, in case."

"But it's all *packed!*" said Margie. As indeed it should have been. She had spent most of the day packing, unpacking, and repacking the little blue vanity case. The betrayal cut deep. She reached for the potatoes.

"No more potatoes," said her mother. "What's the matter with your pork chop?"

"Nothing," sulked Margie. "It's delicious." She never made any other answer to such questions: it was what you said. When she had discovered this, watching television several years ago, Margie had done a much more impressive job of it, even to bouncing up and down in her chair and crying, "*Gee, Mom, this is dee-licious!*" But her mother had told her not to overdo it.

Now she picked at her chop, and wondered what it would be like to be a pork chop lying on a plate while somebody got ready to gobble you up. Margie would rather be a furry little kitty: nobody would stick a fork in you then.

Rasmussen exchanged fork for spoon, the better to scoop up the soup of potatoes and gravy, which didn't have so damn much flavor in it after all. Why didn't he feel better about having won? It had been too easy by a long way. The bill would be coming in. But what the hell, let him just get through two days with Bernie, and he would pay it. Still, there was something fishy about it. . . .

Ann felt unreasonably pleased with her whimsical reversal. Pressed to explain, she might have sheltered behind the myth of feminine changeability, but simply having done it was its own reward, augmented by her sense of the unease it created in Rasmussen, not to mention the bonus of his phrase, already filed away for future use, about "liking it to look like a family." Besides, or perhaps in the first place, she still felt half full of her Sunday, unsatisfied and ready for anything. Let it be Bernie and all the filthy catastrophes he could invent. Her awakened nerves craved action.

When the doorbell chimed, she reached it before anyone else had stirred. David and Margie sat waiting, and Rasmussen had only time to hope she wouldn't change course once more, and fling the door open, screeching, "You get out of here, Bernie!"

It was Viola from next door with a cardboard box under one plump golden arm. "No, we're just finishing," said Ann over her apologies. "Have some dessertandcoffee? Charley get Vi a chair."

"Aw no thanks," said Viola. "My waistline, you know." She gave one fleeting curved caress to the round of her belly and set the box on the chair Rasmussen fetched. "Just look at these darling babies," she said, displaying a furry black-

and-white salad of kittens on a bed of shredded newspapers.

Margie clawed greedily into the box and came up with a squeaking blue-eyed mite in each hand.

"Take all you want," said Viola. "I been meaning to bring em over for a week. Or Howard says into the bucket."

Rasmussen knew Ann would handle it, and went on spooning up potatoes and gravy, his eye straying only once to the rich dark cleft between Viola's breasts as she hovered over the box. Just another long-dismissed possibility. Impossibility.

"Well, thanks, Vi," said Ann. "I don't think we better."

"Aw, Mom . . . *please?*" David knew the tears ready in Pig Bird's eyes were real, because kittens really did turn her on. Didn't she know they weren't good to eat?

"*Please?*"

But it would be no deal: the time Pig Bird had brought the puppy home, Mrs. Clean had made herself forever clear on the subject of dirty little *animals* getting *into* things, tearing things *up*, making *messes*.

"They give me hay fever, Margie. Now you know that."

"But Mom, I'll feed em an take care of em an everything. Please?" David saw Pig Bird blink hard, trying to squeeze the tears out into plain view.

"No. Mother's sorry, but no."

"Well, if they give you hay fever . . ." said Viola.

"Just one?" A hard blink dislodged one real tear. "Mom, please, just one?"

"No. I said no and I mean *n-o.*"

Destroyed, Margie ran to her room.

"*Margie!*"

"Aw that's OK," said Viola. "You know Howard's the same way? Says they do dirt on things and—"

"*Margie bring those kittens back here this minute!*"

Margie marched in, face glazed stiff with tears, a kitten

in each fist. She dropped them on top of their brothers and sisters, and marched out again.

"Maybe I'll go try Hickeys'," said Viola, moving for the door. "You know the mama's still prowling round outside? They're still a long ways from weaned yet. . . ."

Why don't *you* try nursing them? thought Ann. With those big fat things of yours. "Well, good luck," she said, and closed the door. "She likes animals because she can't have children," she informed Rasmussen. The words just popped out, surprising her.

"Oh yeah?" said Rasmussen. "I wondered about that." He hadn't, but it seemed good safe neutral ground.

"That's right," said Ann. "Can't. She told me."

"Too bad," said Rasmussen. In fact, the news that they could not reproduce somehow augmented his vague disinterested approval of the Bunches. Bud Cronk said the Welfare actually paid the niggers for fucking, which was true in a way when you thought about it. But the Bunches were the cleanest niggers he had ever heard of. They minded their own business, gave no one any trouble. For weeks at a time he never thought of them at all, unless it was to mention to a sympathetic customer that he had some living next door and they seemed perfectly OK. Black Panthers were something else, of course. Rasmussen was of the opinion that concentration camps were too good for them.

"Now," said Ann. "Who wants pie?" She loved having Viola drop in.

"Frozen?" said David.

In the three years since the Bunches had moved in, Rasmussen's original muttering do-nothing disapproval had been marvelously transformed into a remembered good-neighborly tolerance: that they had turned out so well proved it.

"Homemade," said Ann.

"Not for me," said David. She made pies, he knew, because she liked making them, and cleaning up afterward. If he and The Cap and Pig Bird all preferred frozen, it made no difference to her.

"Charley. Pie?"

"Just a sliver." Actually, only Rasmussen's Tuesday-night bowling obligation had saved him from going with Ann to the sparsely attended first-and-last meeting of the Westpark Neighborhood Association. Those who did show up all felt vaguely out of line, except of course for Bert Hearn, Jr., and a couple of other gung-ho nut cases—Rasmussen always thought of them as volunteer types. Everyone was entitled to his opinion, sure, but Bert Hearn, Jr., seemed to think he was a cross between J. Edgar Hoover and the Lone Ranger. Lucky for the Rasmussens he lived three blocks away. It could as easily have been next door, where after all the Bunches had moved in, without incident, except for the package of dog shit somebody—kids, probably—jammed in their mail slot.

Margie slipped back into her chair, red-eyed but prepared to forgive the evening's double betrayal at least to the extent of eating a piece of pie. Rasmussen scraped the last morsel of butterscotch filling from its pallid gray rind, licked it off his fork, and drifted away into the living room. Nothing really good on TV until Bonanza, but chances were that Bernie would arrive in time to spoil that. Meanwhile he was less likely to disturb the peace in here, not that he ever did anything else after Sunday supper. Besides, Bernie would be here soon enough, and disturbing the peace was *his* specialty. He had the convictions to prove it.

But a worried mother sent her small, deaf-mute son to the Cartwrights for safekeeping when the boy's brutal stepfather broke out of prison. They kept the pitiful creature safe, put the brute back behind bars, and Rasmussen watched it all, interrupted only by his own periodic trips to refrigerator and toilet, all on the quarter hour. Beer did that to him.

The Saint became involved with a strange Italian cult which worshiped the glories of early Rome, fought for his life gladiator-style, and came out with every hair in place. Still Bernie did not come.

David emerged from his room a little after eleven and did his parents the favor of saying what was on both their minds: "Maybe he got in an accident."

"Not Bernie," said Rasmussen.

"No such luck," said Ann. "Not till he gets here. I'm going to bed."

Rasmussen watched the Late Show, something about a circus, until he'd finished his six-pack. He switched off the set, made sure the porch light was on, and went to the bathroom.

After a stiff workout with the electric toothbrush and a heart-constricting hot-and-cold shower, he went into the master bedroom and did something very strange indeed, tried to get into Ann's bed.

"Charley." Had she been a less rigorous mother, she might have taken just such a tone with a child who had just wet its pants.

That was all it took. Rasmussen slipped into his own bed not even disappointed. Had her rejection threatened him with real disappointment, he would never have risked it in the first place. Nothing ventured, nothing gained? Well, he felt he had ventured no more than he might have gained, and *that* wasn't much. Rasmussen went right off to sleep.

Not quite six hours later he was just burrowing back into his bed after his second necessitous passage of the night. At first the buzzing seemed to lull him toward sleep, but it became louder faster than he could get there, ending in a popping splutter and a clank next door at Bunches'.

Rasmussen came wide awake. A brief silence did not reassure him. Was that Bunches' doorbell? More silence. Those *were* voices, that *was* Bernie's voice. No mistaking that adolescent whoop thickening into a croak.

Rasmussen got out of bed and into his robe in a jiffy. Not hoping, not even thinking that he could steer Bernie in and silently to sleep on the couch without waking the house, nonetheless he stole on night-patrol feet into the living room and peeked out past the drape at the front lawn. Just in time to see, or rather to hear, his brother pound the door *and* ring the chimes. Too late to hurry now, but Rasmussen did anyway.

"Charley!"

Bernie embraced him before Rasmussen had time for a good look, and when he stepped back out of the bear hug, brushing at something which tickled, he got an eyeful.

"Baby listen, lemme get this bike in off the street, hey?" said Bernie. "I mean, it's borrowed, you know."

"Sure," said Rasmussen, staring. "Garage ain't locked." But it was he in his flapping maroon flannel robe who strained the heavy, weighted door up while his brother pushed the little Japanese cycle in next to Ann's blue Volkswagen. What was Bernie doing, dressed up like the funny papers?

"Hey, that's some groovy broad next door, hey?" said Bernie. "Gettin integrated round here an everything, man, that's beautiful. Wow, she's built up from the ground, that chick, what's her name, man?"

"Where'd you get that hat, Bern?"

"Fresno, man. I ran into this thing in *Fresno*, ain't that something? Or I wouldn't have been so late, you know. This cat was into the Indian thing, an he just made me a present of it. . . ."

Rasmussen saw Bernie's head turn toward the front step,

and looked there automatically. There they all were, on the small, lighted concrete platform, staring at Bernie, and from the blank surface of their wonder, disgust, smiling disbelief, Rasmussen's gaze rebounded once more to his younger brother.

If Bernie looked like anything nameable, it was Uncle Sam, after a three-month drunk on an Indian reservation: the domed black Stetson with its tall red feather sticking up brokenly behind; the eighteenth-century British red coat, chained and braided and brass-buttoned (or were those bells?); the Southern convict's blue-and-white stovepipe overalls tucked into surplus Army combat boots: a hallucination made flesh, although little enough real flesh was to be seen, thanks to huge round steel-rimmed blue spectacles, whose earlatches were lost in a thick tangled fall of blond locks like oily vines, which had overgrown the face as well, perhaps replacing the original beard as weeds replace grass.

"Wouldn't he like a bath?" said Ann.

"How you doin, baby?" said Bernie. "Hey, wait a minute." He reached among his undergarments—an olive-drab Army shirt and a pinto vest, to name two—and found a little wooden-handled bell. He tinkled it shyly, then admonishingly, in the direction of the front step and chanted a few strange words in a reedy singsong. "Blessing," he explained.

"Does he think he's in the Salvation Army?" said Ann.

"Still got a kind word for everybody, same as always," said Bernie. "Baby I might fool you. I might be the *real* Salvation Army, all you know."

Whether she had meant his clothes or his tinkle bell, Rasmussen had to admit that she had a point there. But now Bernie seemed to be seeing them all for the first time. He began slowly to nod in deep approval of what he made out through his blue glasses. The vines parted and he said, with an air of reverent discovery, "Yeah, man. Yeah, I really start to dig it now. *The family!* May not be my bag, but it's a whole *thing*. . . . Charley, you really got it all right here, you know that? The family, baby. Wow, you're beautiful, all of you. . . ."

Ann turned away, expressionless. David and Margie followed her inside.

"You want to come on in, Bern?" said Rasmussen. Would she count tonight as one of the two nights? What time was it anyway?

Shaking his head, jingling like Santa's sleigh, Bernie went in ahead of him. "Beautiful," he said.

THREE

In 1944 a University of Bologna *ragioniere*, deserter from the Italian Army, had offered PFC Charley Rasmussen the temporary use of "a young schoolgirl, virgin, no clap, no syph." Upon the changing hands of a certain sum, delivery was to be made at a point to be determined somewhere inside the walls of the pimp's alma mator.

"How do I know it's there, this place, where you say?" said Rasmussen, nobody's fool.

"It has been there one thousand five hundred years," said the pimp. "Look how she is beautiful, *che bella ragazza!*" He kissed the gathered fingertips of his left hand and showed Rasmussen a smudged photograph of his eldest sister, taken in her white confirmation dress the year Il Duce had come to power. "Her name," he intoned, "is Novella d'Andrea."

You couldn't really tell from a snapshot, although she looked pretty good, and certainly young. Rasmussen wanted to get laid badly enough; even in Italy he'd had his trouble. But the pimp wanted half the money down in advance, to bribe the girl's mother, he said. This sounded decisively too fishy to Rasmussen, and he told the fallen scholar to fuck off.

That was the closest he had ever come to seeing the inside of a university, a systematically missed opportunity he neither bragged nor complained of, ever. Like many who graduate from high school and no more, he perhaps valued his common sense more highly and less critically than independent laboratory tests would have justified.

But if asked to explain his latest welcome to Bernie in terms of common sense, or any kind of sense, Rasmussen wouldn't have had a prayer. His little brother had never, ever, been anything but bad news.

That dogged irrational affection of some fathers and mothers, elder brothers and sisters, for the most extravagantly good-for-nothing child; that helpless loyalty, confirmed rather than corroded by the worst outrages and betrayals: something on this order might have explained it, except that Rasmussen wasn't sentimental. Never had been. Bernie was the sentimental one.

True, their grandfather had done his muscular, repetitive best to pound certain rocklike verities into Rasmussen's skull. "Brother always sticks to brother" was one of them. But neither Charley nor Bernie had ever willingly heeded a single one of the old man's dicta, and this could hardly be an exception.

No, the contrary was to have been expected, if anything. Rasmussen's bride of three years had pointed this out to him shortly after his return from Europe. Ann used to read books in those days, some of them about psychology. "It's natural you should hate him," she said. "Didn't he kill your mother by getting born?"

So he had, if you wanted to look at it that way. But, if you looked at it that way, Bernie was perhaps to blame for their father's disappearance eleven months after his wife had died bearing her second son. And that was too fishy for Rasmussen to swallow. He preferred calling Bernie bad luck and letting it go at that. The Depression had sunk plenty of people without a trace, his father just happened to be one of them, it could happen to anybody. And who knows? Maybe he had not been sunk. Maybe he'd just had the common sense never to turn up again. In any case, blaming it on an eleven-month-old baby was plain crazy.

Since then—with the best reasons in the world—people had been trying to lay the blame on Bernie, and getting nowhere. He wasn't having any. That was his secret, Rasmussen thought.

In 1932, when their father had used the key to the highway, the old man took charge of them. He had a way with children, and Rasmussen never knew what to call it until he got drafted eleven years later and heard someone say, "There's the right way, the wrong way, and the Army way." He never met a sergeant who showed him much; not after being brought up by his grandfather.

But it didn't work on Bernie. When he got big enough to whip, he was still given to peeing his pants, or the bed he shared with Brother Charley, and you had to hand it to the old man: he knew his duty. He would whale away at the pretty blond toddler with the best will in the world, for whatever seemed to him the right length of time. Bernie would oblige with roaring red-faced tears, stop, eat his supper, and the next morning not only pee the bed but lie there in it, crooning happily until breakfast. You know who washed the sheet and hung it out to dry. Not Bernie.

Given his matchless talent for fucking up, apparently from babyhood on; given the near certainty of his daily whipping, and the limitation by two crutches of the old man's mobility, Charley was amazed that Bernie never made any special effort to evade punishment. Later he was to understand: Bernie could take any amount of punishment, because the blame that went with it rolled off him and dried up as quickly as his tears.

Of course, if you missed your whipping, you missed supper: therein lay the simple beauty of the old man's discipline. The easy chair in which he lived was deployed right in front of a locked three-story cooler with heavy screen shelves, which held, at all times, the entire company stores. Not so much as a graham cracker was ever to be seen lying around loose. Actually, the old man's unrelieved guard was mainly symbolic, since he kept the key to the cooler on a six-foot bathroom chain moored to his belt. That way he could delegate to Adjutant Charley the task of drawing rations, and spare himself the bothersome clamber up out of his chair.

The old man got his pension from the Spanish-American War, knew infallibly where and when to collect relief handouts, and brought in a few nickels and dimes, eggs and grapefruit, by fixing things: anything he could hold in his lap, if it wasn't electrical he could fix it. So no one ever went hungry for actual lack of food.

If he hadn't believed that an army travels on its stomach, he might well have augmented his discipline with the threat of bed without supper. But that wasn't his style. He preferred leaving it up to the men whether or not they had supper. Any whippings outstanding from the preceding twenty-four hours were dispensed promptly at sundown. Then they would eat. Miss your whipping, miss your supper.

Perhaps the earliest sure signs of Bernie's radical mysterious difference were the times—Rasmussen recalled several distinctly—when Bernie, age five, missed supper *when he had no whippings coming!* He just didn't get the idea, even though of course missing supper was itself a whipping offense. Perhaps the old man began to realize he was wearing his arm out for nothing. "Seems like he can't get his mind on it," he would say. He may have thought the dreamy good-natured child could understand *duty* only as his duty to himself. But time, Rasmussen would have said, had proved him wrong about that. Duty, including duty to himself, was a virus to which Bernie had been born immune.

Not to mention its subspecies: prudence, thrift, cleanliness, truthfulness, etc. As an adept of the Black Mass was to the Holy Sacraments, so was Bernie Rasmussen to the Boy Scout Handbook, and all long before he was old enough not to join Troop 4. Charley hadn't joined, either. One outfit was enough.

As second in command, of course, Charley was responsible for him. But when your only subordinate is a congenital fuck-up, and your CO as tough a disciplinarian as the old man, the middle is a bad place to be. And Charley not only caught hell for his inability to keep the troops in line, he caught all the leftover hell the old man gradually stopped giving Bernie.

Nor could he take it out on Bernie himself, the difference between twelve and five, fifteen and eight, being just too great to make revenge satisfying. Besides, Bernie would always tell the old man, who wouldn't stand for it. "Brother always sticks to brother," he would say, and *whop! whop! whop!* with what he called his "fly swatter," a two-inch leather strap worn by daily use to the pliancy of a lady's evening glove.

And there was still more to it than that. Part of Bernie's inverted genius expressed itself in making bigger boys mad at him. They were Charley's responsibility, too, and although the age gap was often an advantage here, Bernie wasn't discriminating among the big boys he offended. Rasmussen carried the proof of it with him to this day: a pivot tooth and a deviated septum.

So Basic Training in the spring of 1942 looked like a rest cure to Rasmussen, simply because the old man and Bernie weren't there. The twenty-one dollars a month, all his very own, was so much gravy on his new feast of independence as an infantry private. A personal future seemed possible, for the first time in his life, if only he made sure never to set foot again in Santa Fe, N.M.; never again to get within whopping distance of the old man; never again to be responsible for Bernie, who, at eleven, was beginning to hit his stride. Rasmussen had only to avoid getting killed, and for this at least his long service in the old man's outfit had prepared him: his central, peripheral, and autonomic nervous systems were coordinated perfectly against volunteering; he could not have volunteered for anything to save his life.

So it was a little hard to explain a year later that he rode a jammed train three-quarters of the way across the country to spend his last stateside leave in Santa Fe, N.M. Rasmussen didn't even try to explain. Maybe the lesson of ten years needed the one final reinforcement it got the minute he walked in and saw the old man in his chair, whopping a fly on one extended leg. "Charley," said the old man by way of greeting. "Go down to the police station and see about Bernie." Damned if Rasmussen didn't do that very thing, on the double.

"Kid this age," said the desk sergeant. "Painting prick-and-balls on every building for blocks around. He needs a good whipping."

Rasmussen couldn't think of anything to say to that, but the times and his uniform got Bernie loose in his custody. His teacher Miss Allen had big tits, Bernie explained. She said he had talent and ought to try bigger things. And if Charley told the old man that he, Charley, had given Bernie a whipping on the way home, maybe the old man would take it easy. . . .

"I thought he give up whippin you," said Charley.

"Well, since you been gone . . ."

The old man, of course, wasn't about to delegate that responsibility to anybody, not even an honest-to-God soldier in Uncle Sam's Army. But to Rasmussen's expert eye it was a halfhearted whopping he dealt out to Bernie at sundown. As if to make up for it, the old man rattled on all through supper about what a lot of cowards and sissies the men of the draft Army were next to the heroes of '98. Rasmussen knew better than to argue with his old CO, but mentally he kicked himself in the ass for having traveled two thousand miles to find out what he already knew better than anything else in the world.

And it worried him. What would he do after the war? What was to insure him against coming right back here again? He couldn't think of a thing except getting killed. But he was finely enough attuned to the exigencies of the situation to recognize a solution when it occurred to him: he would get married.

The only place to seek a short-order bride in Santa Fe, N.M., that year was the USO, where beneath bare white bulbs and red-white-and-blue paper streamers a troop of patriotic and unspoken-for local girls handed out free coffee and doughnuts and nonalcoholic fruit punch to any and all defenders of Western Civilization; danced with those who could dance, and made conversation or shared tense preoccupied silences with those who couldn't.

Rasmussen, clap-free survivor of three Georgia whorehouses, with marriage on his mind, put first things first. Identifying a number of girls as high-school classmates, he eliminated in advance all those known or rumored to have given up their flower before graduation.

He went to work on the remainder, starting, without hope, at the top of the list. But red-haired Sally Oakley was dancing almost every dance, and when she wasn't, a fast-talking wall of uniforms surrounded her. Rasmussen, no dancer, and not much of a talker, got halfway down the list before he got his first private words out of a prospect. They were: "What are you in? I like the Air Corps best."

A couple of tries later he got a plump dark girl, doubtless Mexican, to go outside with him, outside into a bare, well-lit asphalt yard. There was no one in sight, and Rasmussen seized the moment. "Let's get married," he said, clutching a large breast as a token of his seriousness.

"Whoa there!" said the girl, recoiling. "I'm engaged." She offered in evidence a diamond or rhinestone the size of half a grain of rice. Rasmussen took her back inside. In the future he would have to check for rings. The next girl he enticed outside had no ring, but before he could propose she said, "Rasmussen? Are you that nutty little Bernie's big brother? You sure don't look like him much." Rasmussen stuck his grabbing hand in his pocket, and called it a night.

The next night he got lucky. Chastened by his failure with known girls, he switched to complete unknowns. Nor did he waste time with the top of the list, but concentrated at once on the wallflowers, of whom a plentiful supply idled in overtalkative twos and threes between the refreshments and the dance floor, or drifted alone, unconvincingly bent on some vague, never-to-be-accomplished errand.

Or simply stood in a dream, expecting nothing, like the skeletal girl Rasmussen spotted near the door, as if protecting her route of escape from somewhere she didn't belong and would rather not be. He came up to her, but before he could say, "Hi," she looked at him out of blue eyes set close, opened her wide mouth, and said, "I can't hardly dance at all."

Something strange moved inside Rasmussen's chest, like a pain in an organ he didn't know the name of. "Want to take a walk then?" he said. The way she looked at him, there was no reason to expect she would do it, but she did; perhaps only too glad of an excuse for leaving, she walked with him readily enough across the yard and out through the gap in the wire fence where the sign said WELCOME SERVICEMEN. Half a block farther in the direction of nowhere, he told her his name. Hers was Ann Baldock, she said.

Rasmussen still had the pain in his chest. There ought to be a better way than this, he sensed, but if there was he didn't know it, and time was short. When he paused in a dark stretch between street lamps, so did she. He got an arm around her, and with his free hand began searching for a breast beneath the tired starch of her jumper. "Let's get married," he said.

She did nothing about his hand, perhaps because he hadn't yet found anything to speak of. He couldn't see her eyes when she looked at him. "You mean it?" she said.

"Damn right I mean it," said Rasmussen, too intent on his project even to be very disappointed in what his free hand covered with room to spare. Even the possibility of her acquiescence intoxicated him, and he told her the rest of it, forcefully, his voice high with emotion, not even wondering at the completeness of the plan as it formed itself now in his mouth for the first time.

Getting out of Santa Fe was the main thing. From that everything else would follow. She would get his allotment, move to Southern California, get a job in a war plant. And when the war was over . . . Rasmussen left her to imagine the joys to follow, having all too sketchy a notion of them himself.

They were walking toward the next street lamp then, as

two ideas fought for space in Rasmussen's skull: one, that her downstaring silence might mean she was getting ready to say no; two, that he should probably be doing or saying something more to convince her. And beneath these thoughts, faintly heard, whispered the promise of a girl in a seven-by-six raw pine cubicle, a black Georgia girl as rail-skinny as the one walking beside him now: *Sweetest meat next to the bone, honey.*

Beneath the street lamp they stopped again. A police car rolled by without slowing; they were the MP's problem. "It's sure fast like this," said Ann, looking off past him into the dark. "How do I know you mean it?"

"Try me," said Rasmussen. He'd heard somebody say that in a movie.

"I'm not eighteen yet," she said. "I'd have to get my father's permission."

Rasmussen hadn't counted on anything like that. Here he had already volunteered once tonight, and now it sounded as if he might have to do it again. But she only said, "Are you coming again tomorrow night?"

"Sure," he said.

"I'll tell you then," she said. It was only after she had stood there staring for another half minute, and then started walking briskly away from him, that Rasmussen realized he should have kissed her. But you couldn't think of everything. He had never kissed a girl in his life.

Twenty feet away, at the edge of the pond of light, she turned around. "You probably won't even show up," she said.

But he did. They took the same walk, and under the same street light she said she would marry him. This time Rasmussen did smash his mouth down hard on hers, and hugged her to him until her backbone cracked audibly.

"Ow!" she said as she broke loose. But she must have seen

the bafflement in his face, because for the first time she laughed, her face splitting open in a dazzle of perfect white teeth which Rasmussen, even in the confusion of his passions, duly noted. When she smiled she was actually pretty. It seemed a gratuity not to have been hoped for, and he heard the black girl whisper louder.

But getting out of Santa Fe, N.M., was the main thing, away from the old man, away from Bernie. Forever. So Rasmussen thought a month later as he crossed, newly married, to North Africa. A few complications had in fact attended his taking of the big step, but if not downright delirious afterward, he was well enough pleased with his new future not to think too hard about why his new bride had given herself away so readily. He could explain it well enough by the now proved fact that he was not hopelessly unattractive to woman; no, by God, not by a long shot. He didn't have to pay a girl to lie down under him; all he had to do was marry her.

Getting away was the main thing. Now he had done it. At least Rasmussen thought so, and that comforting untruth may well have helped him survive the war. For of course that wasn't to be the half of it yet, and had he known just how literally Bernie would interpret "Brother always sticks to brother" after the war, Rasmussen might even have overthrown his nervous system and volunteered.

And now, so many years later, there was no explaining the phenomenon of Rasmussen ushering that debauched and jingling Uncle Sam into his house. Unless it was that in some deep crevice of his being, he craved for *something to happen.*

You could count on Bernie for that.

FOUR

Uncle Sam, flying on instruments, moved straight through the dark house to the kitchen. Rasmussen, a puzzled but loyal John Q. Public, trailed the sound of jingle bells, while the other three witnesses went back to their beds, Ann with the tensely controlled not-quite-slam he knew so well.

Bernie's voice sounded in the dark. Did he say he wanted *pot?* Rasmussen, aghast, fumbled for the light switch, the blue-white fluorescent tubes flickered on, and by their clinical light he saw Bernie haul out a plastic bag ominously half full of a brownish substance. Above the broken red feather, the electric clock said nineteen past five.

"Cup of coffee, Bern?"

"Aw come on, baby," said Bernie. "That shit's really poison." He set the plastic bag on the blue Formica table and began casting around over the shiny uncluttered surfaces of the kitchen, taking in Rasmussen at last, the only stray object in sight. "With a good tight lid," he said. "Where she hide em?"

Rasmussen dug in behind his extra skin, as if not to notice his brother's felonies would exempt him from complicity. Narrowly watching Bernie make a clattering search through three cupboards, he tried feebly to recall which weed or vine or cactus or mushroom it was they cooked up and drank the liquid and went out of their mind.

Bernie came up with a small copper-bottomed saucepan. "Here you go," he said, and clashed the lid in place like a cymbal. What froze Rasmussen, however, was the simultaneous extrasensory certainty that Ann stood in the doorway behind him. He felt her furious prefatory exhalation like a cold draft at his back. And he didn't have his cap on, either.

"We eat breakfast at seven-thirty here," she said. "Until then we sleep."

"That's a groovy dress you got on, baby," said Bernie. "Got very free lines."

Rasmussen, caught holding the small drip coffeepot which electric-minded Ann had banished, said, "We'll clean up," but by then she had vanished, as if propelled backward by the jet force of her concluding sigh.

Bernie was measuring water into his saucepan with the care of a lab technician. "You know if she sleeps in a transparent thing like that, baby, it's a signal for you to fuck her more," he told Rasmussen. Without effect, for Rasmussen was remembering Dr. Schmolzer's grim warning of how easily LSD could be home-brewed by "anybody with a college degree in chemistry." He suspected Bernie of possessing the equivalent of a PhD when it came to concocting dope.

"What you makin, Bern?" he inquired mildly.

"Rice, man." Bernie poured a quantity of the brown substance into one cupped hand and dropped it into the saucepan. "How do you light the fuckin gas?"

Rice? It looked a bit like dirty rice. Rasmussen had heard of morning glory seeds and banana peels, but rice was a new one. "No gas," he said. "Push the high button."

"*Push the high button?*" said Bernie. "Oh wow, I been lookin for this stove all my life, ha ha ha, have to buy myself one. Then when the water boils, see, you got to turn it down and steam it real slow, this thing got a downer button on it?"

Rasmussen measured coffee into the basket of the little drip pot, and punched the high button for the kettle to boil. Rice, for Christ's sake! Well, it was only to be expected that in all these years Bernie would have come up with fifty-seven varieties of new craziness. And if he didn't drink coffee, it might mean he'd go off to sleep that much quicker. For Rasmussen there was no hope of sleep.

Bernie had fallen into silent contemplation of the saucepan, as if to help cook the rice by the force of his brain radiations. Rasmussen was glad enough to go along. If he had thought it would work more than once, he would cheerfully have kept a pot of dirty rice going on the stove throughout Bernie's stay. But his brother had always tired of things quickly.

When the coffee had dripped, Bernie only shook his head disapprovingly, and Rasmussen got through his first cup and his first Camel in the dining room alone. But the re-apparition of that cartoon-made-flesh, now bearing almost sacramentally a soup plate heaped with grimy particles, came as a momentary echo of the first visual shock. "Christ, Bern . . ." he said.

Bernie sat down and regarded the rice with a sweet little smile.

"Wonder the cops don't pick you up wearing that damn-fool outfit." Rasmussen had to say it.

"Peace, baby," said Bernie. "It's just clothes. Don't be

gettin spooked by some pieces of cloth." From one of his undergarments he took out a small beaded pouch and extracted a pinch of white, which he sprinkled on the mound. "Sea salt," he said. "None of this iodized shit." From somewhere else he produced what looked to Rasmussen like an ordinary yellow oilcloth tobacco pouch, unzipped it, and shook a thin even layer of some greenish-brown herb, oregano or thyme perhaps, over the lot. "Iodine's a poison, you know that."

Rasmussen was reminded of Jerry Durham's crazy wife, who'd read some book, and believed insecticides in the air were slowly poisoning her. Jerry would come to work at Ace Liquors many a morning swollen with mosquito bites, and dab them with anesthetic lotion until his fingers got so numb he'd keep dropping bottles, and even small change. Rasmussen had finally had to let him go.

"So tell me what's been happening?" said Bernie. "Been a long time, hey, baby?"

"Same old thing," said Rasmussen. "Store's still doin pretty good, you know. More competition now . . ."

"You still lushin away like the old days?" said Bernie, without breaking the rhythm of his thorough, patient chewing. And what the hell was he bringing that up for? Rasmussen would have liked to know. One thing about Bernie: he had never shown any favoritism among the various liquids, vapors, vegetables, pills, or powders that would get him out of his mind. The only questions had been those of availability, quantity, and leisure to consume. One morning twenty years ago, coming around on black coffee after x days and nights on cream sherry, goofballs, and marijuana, Bernie had dropped an accordion-pleated filler from a Benzedrine inhaler into his cup, and told him, "Don't worry, Jack, I'll never be a junkie. I move around too fast." So what was he getting so nosy about now?

"Few beers," said Rasmussen. "Why, you quit drinkin?"

The spoon paused before the black gap in the beard. "Me? Aw sure, baby, I put that shit down a long time ago. Alcohol is a poison."

Rasmussen took a closer look at the peaceful hairy masticator across the table.

"You put like a plant in alcohol," said Bernie. "It's dead in seconds! Say lemme take a good look at you." He whipped off his blue spectacles, creating an odd impression of baby-pink nakedness around the small glassy blue eyes which now squinted diagnostically at Rasmussen. "That's a bad lot of white you got under the iris, baby," he said. "And your old lady, she's a lot worse."

"Well, none of us are gettin any younger," observed Rasmussen. "And that's a plain fact."

"I sure don't feel any older," said Bernie. "I feel *great,* and I'm your brother, I wouldn't lie to you."

Younger, older: they had always meant something else to Bernie anyway. Look at *his* eyes, thought Rasmussen. They must have changed in ten years. Cushioned in their soft pink folds, Bernie's eyes looked right back at him, as clear and blue and innocent as . . . when? It gave him a bad moment, the piercing of the idea that they had looked exactly the same for thirty years or more. *I've got your number,* they said. *Do whatever you're going to do, say whatever you're going to say. Go ahead. It's got nothing to do with me. I even thought of it already, and you're wrong. Maybe I'll tell you about it, maybe I won't, but I've got your number.*

"Come on, baby," said Bernie. "I could always stare you down. Anyway, shit, you ain't competin with *me.*"

But something was gone out of them, too, Rasmussen thought. Some little fire-point of baby rage had disappeared, or been driven further back into his head, out of sight. And the hard clear transparent coating on the eyeballs, like water glass: that had got thicker, the eyeballs themselves seemed preserved behind it now. Rasmussen saw this, and drew no conclusions. You couldn't read Bernie. He'd quit trying years ago. He'd been right the first time, back in Santa Fe. All you could do was keep the maximum distance away from him.

Rasmussen filled his cup. "So what you figure on doin down here, Bern?" It seemed as good a time as any to ask.

"Figure? I don't figure anything, baby. I mean, one thing at a time. There's no hurry about *any*thing, you know that?" Bernie looked reflectively at the table as if considering a cosmological expansion of his last words. "It's like . . ." he began. "Aw it's a hang talkin about it, you know?"

"Just thought if you're lookin for a place I could take off part of the day and run you around while you looked." Around, around. Say to Santa Monica or Santa Barbara or Long Beach or the Mexican border.

Bernie chewed and nodded. "That's groovy," he said reasonably. "But like I just got here about ten minutes ago, so lemme finish my rice first, hey?"

"Just thought . . ." said Rasmussen, and was rescued from further thinking by a *thunk* against the front door. He sprang up and out through the living room. When he came back slowly, scanning the front page—TANKS QUELL OAKLAND FIRE MOB, HIGHER SE ASIA TROOP LEVELS URGED—he hardly heard Bernie say, "Got to get your fix, hey, baby?"

As Rasmussen settled back into his chair and turned to face an account of yesterday's double disaster at Chavez Ravine—DODGER HURLERS SHELLED FOR RECORD 41 HITS—Bernie scraped the last of his rice together, thumbing three recalcitrant grains into his spoon. "You waste one it's a sin. Millions of people starving every day."

Houston, for Christ's sake! If they couldn't beat Houston

once in three games, what hope was there? Immersed in contemplation of the Dodgers' low estate, Rasmussen hardly noticed when Bernie stood up and scratched his belly. And starting tomorrow, five games with the Cards!

"Well, peace," said Bernie. He came around the table and clumsily hugged Rasmussen's head against one padded hip. "Man, it's great to see you, Charley," he said. "Just don't worry about a thing now." With that he jingled off to the living room, awakening in Rasmussen the hope that if he just fell asleep for a couple of hours, escape to Ace Liquors would be possible, leaving them to cope. . . .

And indeed, the next hour and a half were a gift of pure bliss, broken only by one stealthy trip to the toilet, where Rasmussen chose to antagonize Ann by not flushing rather than break the delicate web of silence. When Bernie slept, there was no waking him: this boded well for his immediate project.

And, miraculously, when Ann came in at seven-fifteen, she seemed not in the worst temper. Her I-saw-him-there look, answered by his nod at the living room, created the illusion that they were on the same side: without trusting it, Rasmussen had to be grateful for it, and for Margie's uninstructed silence as the three of them started on their frozen orange juice and cereal.

Was it some kind of trap? Rasmussen didn't ask. He ate his breakfast, shaved, put on a clean shirt, his cap and coat sweater, and came out hissing orders: "When he wakes up tell him to come by the store and I'll drive him round to look for a place." Ann gave a short nod.

Passing noiselessly over the wall-to-wall carpet, Rasmussen made out the shape of his brother, supine on the couch, arms folded. His black Stetson lay on the floor, and his boots.

Opening the front door, he saw the entering sun gleam on Bernie's pale, defenseless bald spot, and the weedy beginnings of all that hair. Bernie was no kid after all. Rasmussen got into his Pontiac and drove off to work feeling great.

Not so rubber-gloved Ann. Having convoyed Margie through the zone of infection, out the door, and off to school, she gave her brother-in-law's form one long glare of unmixed loathing and went back to decontaminating his segregated soup plate, spoon, and saucepan.

As she mixed detergent and disinfectant under a maximal blast of hot water, Bernie's image went on staining her thoughts: lying there in state, arms folded, like some diseased emperor, his blue glasses still in place, his filthy boots dirtying the carpet. . . .

Insulting as a dirty word scrawled on the spotless white wall, the plastic bag of brown rice caught her eye. She snatched it up, carried it at arm's length into the living room, and dropped it onto the floor beside him.

Having thus quarantined the physical evidence of his presence within a more manageable area, she went back into her kitchen thinking about autoclaves, like the one in Dr. Kastenduyk's examination room. The normal breakfast dishes—Rasmussen's, Margie's, her own—she stacked in the washer, to be joined there by David's, if and when he got out of bed, the lazy bum.

Or if he were only sick . . . Ann herself was never sick; she loved it when David or Margie was. One of the best weeks she could remember was the time both of them, and Rasmussen, too, were flat on their backs with Asian flu. That week she went around humming.

So if David could be kept in bed for a couple of days, until Bernie left . . . Although she customarily thought her son immune to any sort of influence whatsoever, Bernie would prove the exception if anyone could, give the devil his due. And what form could this influence possibly take but dirt and dope and sex practices?

David came into the kitchen and said, "Where's Uncle Bernie?"

"Sleeping," she said. "What do you want for breakfast?"

"I don't care. Cereal. Where is he, in the living room?"

"Let him alone if you don't mind."

All right then. All right then. Bernie must be dealt with. Otherwise he would sleep all day, fail to look for a place to stay, and spend all night doing God only knew what, although Ann could guess. Wake him up, then. Deliver Charley's message. Let him get on his little scooter and go find his loving brother.

But clattering the dishes as she set David's place was the cowardly way; besides, he could sleep through the Bomb. And David was in there already. So she swept into the living room, yanked the drapes full open, turned on the home-theater television full blast, and yelled down at him through cupped hands: *"Bernie get up!"* Perhaps she should have shaken him, too, but she had taken off her rubber gloves. David watched her, smiling. *"Bernie, get up I say!"*

She needn't have taken so much trouble: Bernie was awake. Since Rasmussen had gone off to Ace Liquors, he had lain at peace, slowly slowly ascending to an invulnerable height in a glass balloon full of liquid crystal, where the sounds of the house reached him like coded bulletins from a far-off land; he could decipher them any time he liked, but preferred not to.

Get up I say! The tape-delay mechanism played it back in his head, along with the patterns his eyelashes made, just now manifested by the flood of light through the blue glass windows of the balloon. A sweet smile of total understanding stirred his beard. A poem, one of thousands he had composed privately over the years, took shape:

> *Ann—*
> *ti—*
> *septic*

A haiku. A mini-haiku.

> *Ann—*
> *ti—*
> *septic*
> *Ann—*
> *ti*
> *Ann*

Forgotten at once, it enriched the space it left behind. You beat Time that way.

I thought you wanted to let him sleep.

Please go and eat your breakfast.

The television set boomed at his balloon from over there somewhere, *washday miracle tender as a kiss to your hands,* and Beautiful, thought Bernie. Should he kiss her hand? Of course. Had she gone away? She had gone away. Later, then . . .

"Coffee or milk?" said Ann, back in the dining room.

"Milk," said David.

"*Bernie?*" she called at the living room. If only David were not so certain to hang around the house at least until the mail came. . . . Ann was perfectly resigned to the Army taking him, but not to the morbid way he sat around waiting for his notice. He should be out in the fresh air, having some terminal fun with his friends. He should then reappear, made healthy and straight by his new uniform, and tell her how much good the Army was doing him. Finally he should write letters full of interesting variations on this theme, from Camp So-and-so, in Colorado, or Wisconsin, enclosing snapshots of himself grinning with a clean-cut buddy, their arms around one another's shoulders after winning the division Ping-Pong championship. . . .

But the prospects were not good: David had no close friends, only that awful-looking one called Hart, who must be 4-F in every possible way. And now the first thing he did when he got up was go looking for Bernie. . . .

She poured David's milk. If he didn't obey this time, she would call Charley at the store and tell him to do something. *"Bernie get up!"*

A languid groan rewarded this latest effort: "Aw shit. Wow, look at that." Then he began giggling to himself. What was he up to now?

From the doorway she saw: Bernie, on hands and knees, pinching at the beige carpet, collecting, grain by grain, the rice he had kicked flying when he sat up, the clumsy ox. Each retrieved grain he would blow free of fluff before putting it in his cupped left hand.

"What's he doing?" said David over her shoulder.

"The vacuum cleaner will get it up," she said.

"Out of your mind, man," said Bernie, without looking up. "This is what I eat, and it's a sin if you . . ." He went on tweezing, blue glasses close to the carpet, whose color made the grains hard to distinguish.

"After it's been on the *floor?"* Ann was divided between her own sincere horror and satisfaction at the proof of her own eyes: Bernie *was* nothing but a degenerate animal who ate filth. "David," she said, "don't you *touch* that stuff if he tries to give you any. Don't touch *anything* he gives you! Come and eat your breakfast," and she was gone into the kitchen.

What *was* he doing? David asked him, and Bernie's blue eyes rolled up at him, uncharacteristically avuncular above the metal rims. "Harvesting, baby," he said. "Like in those rice paddies, hey? Makes you realize . . ."

He went on harvesting, leaving David to think, not anew of rice paddies, which he did already every day, but of how genuinely *weird* his uncle was. For once they'd been telling the truth, The Cap and Mrs. Clean.

Look at that coat, look at that hair, listen to him jingle. David had seen hippies aplenty, but never such an ancient model as this one. He had the faint unfamiliar sense of being in the presence of something historical, like a 1942 Chevrolet. "There's some under your knee," he said.

Mrs. Clean reappeared beside him. "Bernie, Charley said come by the store and he'll drive you around."

"Groovy," said Bernie. "Which knee?"

"I'll take you right now, I've got to go shopping."

"Yeah, well, that's OK," said Bernie. "I'll make it in a while."

"David?"

"I think I'll wait around for the mail."

Mrs. Clean released her soundless sigh, one of her specialties. "Remember what I told you," she said, and left with a noiseless slam of the front door. In her wake, audience laughter foamed up like detergent from the television. A man wearing a basketball uniform and pushing a shopping cart full of groceries had just fallen and skidded into a display of canned soup. He sat up and grinned abashedly into the camera.

"Liable to die of cancer," said Bernie.

David assumed correctly that the prognosis referred to Mrs. Clean rather than to the fallen athlete in the supermarket, but wasn't sufficiently impressed to ask for further details. He got them anyway.

"It's a proven fact," said Bernie. "You live uptight all those years, all that frustration turns into this little crab, just chews your insides out." He rolled one more uncle-look upward, missing David by a yard. "That's what cancer *means* is crab, you know. In astrology."

"You ought to tell her," said David. Would Mrs. Clean subdue her hatred of Bernie long enough to boast of all her negative smears and last year's triumphant biopsy?

"Go against Nature, baby, and you find out." Bernie transferred another little collection of grains to the plastic bag and arched backward to stretch, reminding David of a double amputee: he'd really be something to see on one of those little roller-skate platforms. "And the bad part is," Bernie went on, "the sins of the parents visit the children, they really do."

Tell me about it, thought David.

"Hey, you want to turn on?" said Bernie.

"Not right now," said David. "I'm waiting for the mail." In truth, he would have liked very much to be high when the mail came, just in case it brought his Notice to Report. But he had fused the two ideas inseparably, by thinking of them together for too many mornings: so now it seemed that if he *was* high, the Notice *would* come, and conversely . . . But this was nothing he would tell anyone, not even Bernie, the only member of his family likely to sympathize.

And Bernie, whose last good mail had been a Scotch-taped paper bag full of peyote buttons from Texas in 1958, was not about to ask him what he was waiting for. "You change your mind," he said, "all you got to do is ask." Now he got his heels under him and sprang to his feet, arms flung wide: "SHAZAM!" he cried. "You dig Captain Marvel, baby? In the funny books, you know?"

"Sure," David lied. "Captain Marvel." He was trying to identify the thing his uncle had in common with his father, aside from not being a genius.

"Yeah, Captain Marvel," said Bernie. "I was into all that shit years ago, when I was your age, baby, before all the anthropologists dug it. Like it's our *mythology*, Captain Marvel, and the Shadow, the Green Hornet, all like that." He sat down on the couch, spreading his red wings expansively. "Yeah, first time I met Kerouac he asked me, 'What was Captain Marvel's real name?' I told him, 'Billy Batson, Crippled Newsboy.' The Shadow was Lamont Cranston, and the Hornet was really Britt Reid." He reached for his boots.

Then David saw: the permanent red marks at the cheekbones, as on a boxer whose face has been jabbed steadily for several rounds. Bernie and The Cap both had them, though Bernie's blue shades half hid his.

"And like the inner meaning of all that mythology, see, is the possibility of *transformation*, like they stop being all kind of square losers and liberate all this fantastic energy inside."

Under all that beard, David wondered, did fainter splotches also spread down the jaw and neck, disappearing under the collar? He consigned it to Unsolved Mysteries, somewhere in the shadow of such favorite Giant Riddles as: Did The Cap and Mrs. Clean actually make me fucking, or did they get me with Blue Chip stamps?

He noticed Bernie scrutinizing him with a curious knowing concern, and went to look out the front door for the mailman. Yessirree, up at the end of the block . . .

"Thing is," said Bernie, "I really used to go round with Charley and your old lady about this transformation shit. Yeah. Fact is, I think I still scare the shit out of em both."

David hardly heard him.

"You're up pretty tight yourself, baby," said Bernie. "Or what is it, maybe you're just an inside cat. I mean, I'm not exactly a guru yet, but I got a feeling for some people, you know?"

David closed the door. He always let the mailman push it through the slot.

"Take for instance: fun. I mean, just bein who you are. Your father and mother never have got into fun much, you know? So where's that leavin you, baby?"

Fun. Half of David's mind thought, with perfectly concealed disgust, of Barbara La Motta and Laurie Dunn. "I guess I get my share," he said.

"Your share? What's your share? You got no business even thinkin about shares, baby! You ain't cuttin up no pie, you know. Whole world's your pie! Your share is all you can experience! And *more makes more!*"

David was spared inventing a response to this burst of evangelism by the arrival of the mail through the slot. He picked it up. A red-white-and-blue message from Procter & Gamble, and, "Oh, *yeah?*" he said.

There.

"What's the matter with you, baby?" said Bernie. "What you got there?"

"Shit," said David. He should have turned on.

FIVE

Rasmussen sagged in his swivel chair in the back room of Ace Liquors and tried to get his mental breath back. Christ, she could have phoned! But not her. No, she had stuck her head in the street door and said, "Give me ten minutes to get home. I want to *be* there. Then you call up and tell him to get over here. He's making messes all over the living-room rug." Rasmussen would have asked what kind of messes, but having delivered her crisis bulletin, she had leaped back into the blue Volkswagen idling across two Customer Parking spaces and buzzed furiously off.

Messes?

Well, he had no business being surprised, and indeed he wasn't; merely curious. Surprised at messes? No, not when the puddles of Bernie's vomit stretched back like a chain of lakes across the years, all the way to 1946. That first puddle, he could see it still, in their first, little house in Norwalk, just outside the bathroom door. He even remembered thinking, It used to be peeing his pants, but he's a big boy now.

Ann had cleaned up that one. The first time and the last, she had said, and kept her word.

And all the other messes: the fat hairy Armenian girl he had screwed in the locked back bedroom, David's now. "Criminal rape," Ann had said. "Didn't you *hear* her?" Rasmussen had not only heard her, he'd bleached the sheets. A virgin, for Christ's sake!

Ann had wanted the inside lock removed then, but Rasmussen had hesitated one day too long. Bernie got "inspired," locked himself in, and painted the whole works flat black, windows and all. Those little gold splotches on the walls and ceiling were stars, he said, when he finally staggered out, black himself and punchy with fumes. That and a lot of other horse puckey about Art and Nature. It cost Rasmussen three hundred dollars before that room looked halfway decent again, and to this day a sort of five-o'clock shadow lingered beneath its pale-yellow paint. Talk about messes.

Hell, what was Bernie himself but one single contagious mess composed of a hundred small ones? Or not so small: the last one had covered the whole house, *and* the garage, *and* the Oldsmobile. But he hadn't vomited last time; maybe it was the beginning of a trend.

Now he gazed around him at the walls and pillars of cartons: Jim Beam, Old Crow, Bourbon De Luxe, Gordon's, Smirnoff, Gallo and Roma, Hamm's and Burgie and Falstaff, half pints, pints, and fifths, screw-top quarts, half-quart fliptop six-packs, money in the bank, water under the bridge. Rasmussen had to pee; coffee did that to him.

"Ten minutes to get home." He still had three minutes to go, and broke open a fresh pack of Camels en route to the toilet, which Don hadn't cleaned, of course; he never did. Rasmussen secretly approved. At home, ten minutes away, you could safely have made soup in the toilet bowls; that is, if you didn't mind the flavor of perfumed disinfectant. He had once accused Ann of exactly this. "You bet your life you could make soup in them," she had snapped proudly. "But it takes your filthy mind to think of something like that." After a while Rasmussen had even ceased to get any pleasure from the fantasy of peeing in Ann's soup. The best of things get old.

Ah, he knew that well enough. Only the worst of things seemed to keep their flavor, and he'd had little enough of the best. But something was better than nothing, by God! Drained of philosophy for the moment, he flushed it all away.

The Camel still unlit in the trap of his mouth—it was how he kept under forty a day—he phoned home. "It's me," he said.

Ann's metal voice tingled with fresh crisis: "David's Notice came and Bernie burned it. Now you talk to him."

Talk to Bernie? Talk to David? While Rasmussen waited to find out, he reflected that burning the Notice didn't matter all that much. Your actual draft card was something else, a ten-thousand-dollar fine and five years in jail, wasn't it? And they had it coming to them, if you asked Rasmussen. Having fought one war himself, he expected every man and boy to do no less. Otherwise, what the hell had he been doing over there?

"Charley, I think your old lady's freaked clear out, baby!" Bernie's voice came loud, sudden, muffled with emotion. "Like she really wants to hand him over to the fuckin Army, man. . . ."

"Aw, God damn it now, Bern, just hold on there," said Rasmussen. "Just hold on a minute. . . ."

Incredibly, Bernie did so.

"Ah . . ." said Rasmussen.

"Now don't go tellin me you don't give a shit, either,"
said Bernie.

"Well, it's a family matter. . . ."

"Goin in the *Army?*"

"God damn it, Bern, you're stirrin up trouble again!"

"Peace," said Bernie. "*Peace!* Control your anger."

His strenuously softened tone spurred Rasmussen to executive action: "OK. Now why don't you get on over here?
I'll call up my relief man, and we'll go find you a place."

"Wow, a *family* matter . . ."

"And you tell him I said to keep his draft card in his wallet, hear?" said Rasmussen, and hung up hard to show he
meant business. He set his Camel aflame with a jet of gas
and stalked out front, feeling a step ahead of the game. A
dark-skinned man in sunglasses and a green beret passed his
display window, looked in, and kept going. A girl closely
resembling his daughter went by with her eyes on the pave-
ment as if looking for significant cracks.

Wondering if the man had been a real Green Beret, Rasmussen didn't notice Margie—for in fact it was she—any
more than she, in passing, noticed the source of her family's
material blessings.

Margie always stopped for red lights, and had some weak-
eyed degenerate approached her with intent to molest, she
would have known what to do: on these two counts she
had been more than adequately programmed for years. Otherwise, she was happily adrift on the stream of her consciousness, heading home on automatic pilot more than three
hours early.

She had no trouble concentrating, because she never
tried. Things happened, feelings came, one after another in
an endless chain, stretching normally from Just-now to In-a-
second, connecting her to nothing, binding her not at all.
That most *things* happened outside her pink skin and all

feelings inside it was a distinction she had yet to make. Teachers and TV panelists spoke of the Difficult Years, but, broken up into minutes and seconds, these Years as yet gave Margie no difficulty. By the same token, she was denied the leverage of the Difficult Years, which, skillfully applied, might have pried loose all manner of indulgence and loot, even unto motels and kittens. But perhaps a serviceable awareness of this game and how to play it still slept inside her like that sleek, brown, full-breasted, bikinied girl, whose white smile, the image of her mother's, no hideous orthodontics obscured.

What Prince Charming would kiss that Sleeping Beauty awake? A good question. For the time being, however, Margie existed comfortably enough, as much protected as imprisoned, within the conviction of her present total unacceptability; that it might conceivably last forever was unthinkable, and she never thought of it. Things happened, feelings came, more things happened.

Uncle Bernie, for example, arriving in the middle of the night, one dream interrupting another. At breakfast she'd still had them all mixed up: Uncle Bernie like something in a funny book, kittens tumbled together all furry and warm, a great motel lit by sunny blue water. . . .

Thus things happened. But the particular Thing Uncle Bernie might do which would drive her mother to a motel —this defied Margie's imagination. She could only hope for some transcendent naughtiness like making wee-wee on the living-room rug, and this hope had faded as she ate her cereal.

But faded only to ambush her two hours later as she malingered in a quiet corner of a volleyball game: *What if Uncle Bernie did his Thing while she wasn't there?* Could she trust her mother to act on it? Margie didn't think so, and when Miss Glenn's voice whipcracked around her ears

—Rasmussen, you're goofing off!—she had declared herself sick and said she wanted to go home.

The nice hot shower she had—all by herself!—washed away her thoughts of Uncle Bernie and the motel, so it shook her up now when she walked in and heard the noise, then saw his actual dream figure standing in the dining room, shouting full blast at the open kitchen door. Dirty words, too. Perhaps she was just in time.

"—like tryin to talk to some fuckin automatic *robot*, man!" Bernie was saying. "All your sympathetic centers frozen up solid behind that shit!" Then, as if he had picked up her silent presence on radar, he swerved in full cry and bore down smiling upon his glum squat fascinated pink niece, pressed his right forefinger to his lips and shooed her back into the living room, where in another voice he said, "Say there, baby, how you doin? You dig what they're tryin to do to your brother?"

"Who's that? Are you talking to yourself now?" At her mother's cry from the kitchen, Margie retreated a step, and Bernie whispered, "Hey, baby, don't run away. What you got in your magic bag there?" He hunted through her red plastic purse, found her transistor—"Hey, does this thing work?"—turned it on and started dancing before Ann got there.

"What are you doing home? Don't you touch her! Margie you get in your room!"

But Margie was transfixed. *All you need is love,* sang the Beatles in Bernie's hand as he writhed and stomped, hearing another drummer than Ringo. "All you need is love," he sang-along. "Man who's touchin her? We're just dancin, you blind or what?" He tilted his head back, gave a couple of convulsive ecstatic backstrokes, and yelled, "Dancin! New invention called dancin!"

"If you did that out in the street they'd lock you up,"

said Ann. She took spellbound Margie into rigid custody and marched her out, followed closely by Bernie, whipping and thrashing and twisting, chanting "All you need is love" in ragged unison with John and Paul.

Ann executed a smart about-face in the kitchen doorway and leveled off at him point-blank: "Will . . . you . . . please . . . stop that obscene *thing* you're doing and give us one moment's peace?"

This must be it, thought Margie.

"Obscene? Oh wow! What's obscene is you talkin about peace! Man if you had one minute's peace it would kill you, you're a walkin war all by yourself! We start dancin, you start shootin! Talk about fuckin *over*kill!"

"Margie does not care to dance with you right now."

"That's the Pentagon talkin, baby. She does all the talkin for the troops. . . ."

"And one more thing," said Ann. "If you refuse to leave, will you please try to keep your filthy mouth shut while you're here?" With Margie well in tow, she stepped back into the kitchen, as if through the looking glass, and swung the door closed in Bernie's face.

"Fuck that shit," he said.

These magic words made the door open again at once.

"Are you deliberately trying to start a fight?" said Ann. "With me?"

"I don't fight," said Bernie. "I *love*, baby. And you still believe in word magic, that's how superstitious you are, man. Like they're just words! Now tell me *shit* ain't natural —for most people anyway. And *fuck* is the most beautiful thing in the world."

"*Will . . . you . . . stop it?*"

Bernie whipped out his prayer bell and waved it in front of her face, naughty-naughty. "Peace, peace, peace, peace," he intoned. "Fuck, fuck, fuck, fuck. Try that for your mantra, baby. Hundred thousand times a day might save your life."

Ann shut the door again.

Margie, who had had *fuck* carefully explained to her by Patricia Nunez, twice, and still couldn't quite believe it, felt sure that *that* must have been the Thing. "Are we going to the motel now?" she said.

"We are not," said her mother. "And what are you doing home from school at this hour?"

Bernie went off bopping and shuffling, jingling to the bland rhythmic tickle in his hand, down the hall with Simon and Garfunkel to the door of David's bedroom.

Half high but still nowhere, David lay on his bed registering the approach of dehydrated transistor music. His uncle, a Navajo Wolf Man in blue shades, appeared in the doorway then, and said, "How's every thing, honey? Gettin better all the time, hey?"

"Uh-huh," said David, not looking for an argument.

"I got a message for you," said Wolf Man. "Your old man said to keep your draft card in your wallet. Like we got him worried, baby."

"Thanks."

"You know the one thing everybody round here is good at?" said Wolf Man. "Givin other people orders: like 'Take a bath,' 'Get in here,' 'Stop that dancin,' 'Don't say shit'—I mean, it's *totalitarian!* Like you're in the Army already and you don't even know it."

A smile thin as a wrinkle moved across David's face.

"I'm glad you're smilin, honey," said Wolf Man. "But if you let em ship your ass off to that evil fuckin Army, means they already sucked your mind out, you know that?"

David opened his mouth moronically, and said, "Du-hhh . . ."

"Man, I shouldn't have turned you on after all," said Wolf

Man. "This is the time when you've got to *confront,* like I told you. I mean, *I don't want you to go.* Say, look here. . . ." He tapped the bunched fingertips of his right hand on his forehead below the black brim. "That means I recognize you as a sentient being, baby, know what that is? Another being that's got *sense,* it means. Now you're supposed to act like one."

"They put you in jail," said David.

"Baby if those nuns and monks can set theirself on fire, it's the least you can do. . . ."

"Set myself on fire?"

"Set your draft card on fire, asshole!"

Then David made another connection between The Cap and Wolf Man: they both wanted you either to be like them, or to fake it. "Can't see going to jail," he said.

"So split to Canada! Or like Sweden! What are you layin there *smilin* about?"

"I can't talk Swedish," said David. "I'm just an average American."

"Average average average *shit!* Nobody's average! Everybody's holy! But you really are somethin else. . . ." The slack, haggard boy on the bed made Bernie think vaguely of hospital wards and defeated young junkies with TB. No, he said to those thoughts. "Peace. Listen to me, baby: you are the first cat I've met sounds like he's droppin out *into* the Army! Now you got to concentrate your mind on it! Now! What you want to do? What do you *want* to do?"

The trouble with pot, thought David, was, ah, well . . . two things. (*What do you want to do?* echoed a corner of his mind. *Oh, man . . .*) Thing One was the transparent wall it made between you and you, heart beating loud on one side, brain hearing heart from the other. Thing Two was that it changed nothing, really. It got you temporarily away from where you were. But nothing changed.

"Aw, what the fuck are you smilin about?"

Why, about the swift muffled approach of Mrs. Clean, swooping down on Wolf Man from behind to say: "Still at it. Well, it just happens to be a crime to burn your draft card, and also a crime to encourage somebody to do it, and if you don't get out of this house before I count ten I am personally going to call the FBI and report you."

Bernie turned and met her assault with soft grave dignity. "Peace," he said, massaging the air between them with one calming stroke. "The war's in you. Deep breath, let the evil spirits out." He demonstrated with one long whooshing exhalation.

"I've got the number memorized," said Ann tautly, not about to waste all that valuable internal pressure in a sigh. "They're very interested in people who go around stirring up boys against their country. And you," she told her only witness. "You don't have to just lie around listening to him, either."

A new installment of David's high came crawling up the back of his skull. Wolf Man had pretty good stuff.

"What a real fuckin shame this all is, man," said Bernie. "You're holy, too, you know that?" He shook his head slowly. "Even you, evil as you are."

"Charley's waiting for you, and he hasn't got all day." She stood aside, offering him the door.

Watching Wolf Man shamble mournfully out, David added it up: one brother was the same as another to Mrs. Clean; she was just too much for them. He would like to see the person who could zap her and make it stick.

"You look terrible," she said to him now. "Are you sick? Maybe you should stay in bed."

"No, I feel great," said David.

Bernie was out of the driveway in the Volkswagen, off and away, before Ann knew what was going on. David lay suspended in a humming golden high. It really was two-stage stuff, all right. Only his brain smiled when he heard Mrs. Clean barking into the phone:

"I *said*, I want to report a stolen car!"

SIX

The generous pinch of *Cannabis sativa* from his uncle's yellow pouch, sandwiched between the pried-apart chocolate wafers of a Nabisco Oreo cookie, munched up and washed down with cold milk, went on spreading its modest blessings through the system of David Rasmussen the Last. Say he was not at his best? Perhaps, but not at his worst, either. Somewhere in between, then, and certainly in his most characteristic posture, that of recumbent inertia.

Did it matter in the least? Almost certainly not, for—as David the Last would have been the first to agree—his best was not that good, nor his worst that bad. Neither was he that different from his "normal" self when "under the influence" of America's second most popular weed. A time-and-motion study would have revealed that he was no more prone—or supine—to inertia after eating marijuana (he did not smoke) than before. No more and no less.

His inertia was in fact no mere posture; it was the quintessential expression of—to use the phrase of parents and teachers—his *attitude to life*. Thus, although perhaps only

David himself could see it, the inertia had its positive aspect, saying, without the waste motion and distortion of language, all he had to say to the world.

Early on in the Difficult Years, unassisted by *Cannabis* or divine visitations, he had seen the way things were, the way they were going to go on being: nothing worked but power, nothing was free, nothing lived up to the ads, and nothing you did mattered much.

That settled it; the rest was proofs and corollaries, connective tissue binding together the Four Nothings, the Everlasting Gospel. And David the Last was no evangelist.

All the big power had been distributed by the time he came on the scene. Beautiful, dangerous, special, the people who had it gave off an unmistakable light: David knew once and for all that he was of another, lesser race. On the occasion of John F. Kennedy's inauguration, his father told him, straight-faced, that he, too, could grow up to be President. David laughed out loud in his face for the first time, and caught a full-arm smack alongside the head, which dazzled his brains for a few moments, as if he had touched the President himself.

The big power was out of the question, and that left all sorts of little power, such as the power to whack your kids around with impunity. But looking at his father—hardly the picture of fulfillment and satisfaction—inspired in David no lust after such measly power. Nothing lived up to the ads.

And nothing was going to change. Or, to put it more precisely, he, David the Last, was never going to change anything. This perception might have warped or crippled him more seriously had there been more things he wanted to change; but, by and large, the world seemed OK to him, and even if it hadn't there was no chance of swapping it for another world, so why get uptight?

David the Last had never heard of the Absurd by name,

but he lived with an all-inclusive daily sense of it which should, according to some of the best minds of the age, have brought him either to suicide or to existential commitment. His IQ was officially 112; perhaps he wasn't bright enough to see the virtue of killing himself. Or perhaps he was just too young.

His mother cherished like a guilty secret the hope that he might yet prove a "late developer," like the son of an acquaintance and fellow member of the erstwhile Westpark Interfaith Youth Council, Mrs. William O. Silver.

Eddy Ray Silver had slept through adolescence, clocking an average of 16.7 hours a day in bed until he flunked out of high school, whereupon he boosted the figure up to around 18.5. This phenomenon contributed to his rejection by the Army, and, just as Mrs. Silver was about to begin feeding him intravenously, Eddy Ray underwent a miraculous change: he finished high school at night in a matter of weeks, whizzed straight into UCLA, where he was discovered to be a mathematical genius, no less. Now, at twenty-three, he was a PhD earning tens of thousands per annum, with a house in Pacific Palisades, a Jaguar 420G, two Weimaraners, a wife, and a child.

Using Eddy Ray's timetable as a norm, there was still time for David; a month or two anyway. David himself had one maddeningly invariable response to any mention of Eddy Ray: he smiled. Undeterred, his mother had inquired among his teachers, hoping for some hint of encouragement.

But, with a single exception, his teachers—those who noticed him at all—thought David merely quiet and even-tempered, an adequate student who never earned an A and never failed. One gym teacher, an ex-paratrooper, had described him as "the kind of kid you can't run an army without." He meant it as a compliment.

Only Mr. Perry, David's eleventh-grade history teacher,

had his doubts, based upon a dream in which David, the unsuspected model of obedient mediocrity, had gone ape and slaughtered Mr. Perry's mother, mother-in-law, two daughters, and wife, sexually assaulting post mortem all but the last of these. Mr. Perry always looked twice at David Rasmussen after that, but of course said nothing of his dream to Mrs. Rasmussen.

This would have made David the Last smile, too. He rarely laughed, but he did smile a lot, somehow without showing the perfect white teeth inherited from his mother.

A partial list of things which dependably made him smile would include: Advances in nuclear weaponry, Advertisements, Athletes, Be-ins, Boy Scouts, Cancer, Christmas, Computers, Date bureaus, Extermination camps, Father's Day, Girlie magazines, Go-go dancers, Green Berets, Hiroshima, Insane asylums, Love-ins, Man in space, Mother's Day, New medical discoveries, Old people's homes, Political figures, Protest marches, Radio sermons, Reducing diets, Scientists, Television commentators, Thanksgiving, The population explosion, and Youth programs.

Many words and phrases produced the same effect, among them "progress," "competition," "will power," "self-confidence," "expanded consciousness," "human relationship," "individual responsibility," and "national unity."

There were a few questions, too: "How do you (*really*) feel?" and "what do you (*really*) mean?" and, most of all, "What do you (*really*) want (*out of life*)?"

A smile was the response of David the Last, but his answer was inertia. Did the best theories insist that there must be a private warhead of life-giving sex and violence cached somewhere below his belt? He would have smiled at that, too.

He'd had Barbara La Motta, a chinless but otherwise pretty girl with an obsessive dread of being out of it. He'd had Laurie Dunn, a freckled captive in a tent of red hair now seeking her freedom as a flower child somewhere in West Hollywood. Barbara twenty-five or thirty times, Laurie only twice. He wouldn't say it hadn't been worth it; the first time with Barbara had taken a great load off his mind. But the truth was that Barbara was as graceful and well-sprung as a jeep on a dirt road, and, what's more, she gave off a disagreeably brackish air attributable to compulsive multiple coats of spray deodorant. Laurie had been better, despite being given to hoarse glossolalia from the moment of intromission; but she had been already bound for satori, answering personals in the Free Press, and David could never have kept up the psychic overhead on their relationship. In the course of things, he supposed, there would be others, roughly in the same class as Barbara and Laurie. But someone as beautiful and dangerous as Rosanne Larkin, he knew, was never going to be more to him than a bothersome handful of spasm in the morning. And he doubted that even she would live up to the ads. Nothing did.

As for violence, David the Last knew even more surely where he fit into the scheme of things: somewhere below the twenty-fifth percentile, *not* counting spades, Mexicans, Vietcong, and Red Guards. His record in the three unavoidable fights of his earlier teens read: 2 lost by TKO, 1 No Decision thanks to the intervention of a coach. He once knocked Pig Bird around briefly, and even if The Cap hadn't creamed his brains directly afterward, David would have had to say that even successful violence didn't live up to the ads.

But as his mother said, very privately, to herself, he was still young. And perhaps "experience," in which his father's last hopes for him lay, would yet reveal in him the latent primal components of manliness. For the time being, however, inertia was his magic armor for a battle he refused to fight, his ace in the hole for a game he refused to play, the very jewel in his crown with no salvation in question. Let Judgment Day come: it would find David the Last lying down, smiling, a bit wasted as usual but not uptight. Let it come. Nothing lived up to the ads.

SEVEN

Crisis Bulletin Number Two from the home front had jangled and buzzed in Rasmussen's right ear while his mouth was heavily impacted with Big Mac burger. *He's stolen my car and I reported it just now but he won't come over there of course God knows where he's gone but if he does* you get those keys away from him!

He had swallowed with a clunk like a man double-clutching a truck. "Don't be such a God damn fool; he's got to come back for his motorcycle and if you get him picked up you'll have to go all the way to hell and back to find the Volks. . . ." Not bad on short notice.

If he's got my car what does he need with the motorcycle? Anyway, it's my *car, registered in* my *name, and he stole it from* me!

"Bought and paid for with *my* money, and *I* was cosigner. . . ." Rasmussen had hesitated, needing one more first-person pronoun to match her. "And he's *my* brother!"

Oh yes indeedy. He is your brother. Then the dial tone. Was she giving him this round?

Rasmussen didn't ask. He called the cops, explained to three or four of them that a friend had borrowed the Volks, and secured a promise to have it taken off the hot sheet. He was doing pretty damn good on the phone today, he had to admit it.

Now the electric eye in the street door beeped him to attention, belching, and he went out front to greet his customer—a Green Beret, by God, the same one who had passed earlier!

"What can I do you for?" said Rasmussen.

The Green Beret scanned the shelves through contour dark glasses. A nigger or a Mexican; with the beret you couldn't see his hair. But Ace Liquors wasn't honored with the presence of the Special Forces every day in the week. "Lemme have a fifth of that Chivas Regal there, Ace," said the Green Beret. "Hard to get where I been."

Rasmussen took it from the shelf, thinking what a sloppy uniform they went round in. But then, hell, they didn't pay these guys to look pretty on parade. This one still had the .45 slung low on his hip like a cowboy; must be just off the boat. "How's about two for the price of two?" he said. He had lots of patter like that; it made the customer feel at home.

The Green Beret smacked his thick lips: "Mmm-*mm!* Yas-*suh,* Cap'n! Say, look here, Ace, you got a glass handy so's I can take me one little taste? Sholy would preciate that."

Rasmussen dismissed the State Board of Equalization and decided to live dangerously. He ducked into the back room thinking about the dangers *this* guy had come through, the ambushes by Cong in black pajamas. Another warning beep made him pause, glass in hand. Hell, he would just wait on this new one fast and then pour the hero his shot. He wished

David were here to have a look at a real man, even if he was a nigger probably.

But what was he doing at the street door? Christ, it was another Green Beret, taping something inside the glass, and . . . *son of a bitch!* Rasmussen's heart swelled up big and melted down somewhere behind his liver, for there was the first one at the end of the counter to his right, spotlighting him with a big white smile just in case he might miss at three yards with the .45 in his hand.

The reassuring thoughts were right there (*I'm insured, I been stuck up plenty of times before*) but Rasmussen couldn't reach them any more easily than he could grab the .32 on the shelf under the register.

"Sign there say you out to lunch," said the second Green Beret. Rasmussen watched him softly heel-and-toe up to the counter: no Mexican was that black, and this one had a carbine slung over one khaki shoulder. "Yeah, you fuckin VC really gettin soft, takin lunch breaks an all."

"An drinkin Chivas Regal, Sarge," said the first one. "Looka there."

The black one shook his head, *tsk-tsk-tsk.* "*Ain't* that somethin," he said. "But you know it's liable to be some kinda booby trap in it, they tricky motherfuckers."

"Well, I say zap him then, don't take no chances."

"Right," and the carbine came as if magnetized into the black hands and slid along a groove in the air above the counter until its muzzle rested on top of Rasmussen's belly. The first one was next to him then, the .45 punching the register open, NO SALE. A brown paper shopping bag was thrust at him—"*Scoop,* motherfucker!"—and slowly, carefully, he had to set down the glass he still clutched before cleaning out the cash register. "No fuckin silver, neither!" said the carbine muzzle in his solar plexus. Which one of them was whistling? Rasmussen fumbled under the tray for the tens and twenties.

"Sarge," said the first one. "I believe this squinty cocksucker holdin out on us. We gonna look mighty damn silly gettin in the heelicopter with this bag of old chicken-shit. . . ."

"Safe's in back," said Rasmussen, and that sprang his thoughts loose—*I'm insured, I been stuck up before*—as the .45 fell like a girder on his right shoulder and he went to his knees.

"G'on an duck-waddle your ass on back there an open it up then," said the one with the carbine. Rasmussen did as he was told, to the whistled slow march behind him, mournfully jaunty, terribly familiar. What was it?

Never mind. I'm insured, I been stuck up before. Hold that thought. Rasmussen dialed the combination to the weekend's receipts.

Sunlight filled the room, the back door was open.

"Right there in the sack," said the first one, and the whistling became song.

Sure. What else? "The Ballad of the Green—" and "*Zap!*" went the lyrics as the Colt barrel sank into his neck. Rasmussen was out before he could feel glad it was no worse.

Ann's first thought when she saw the squad car pull into the driveway was that they had caught Bernie before Rasmussen could stop them. But where was her car? Then she saw that it was not Bernie but Charley who climbed stiffly out of the screened back seat. Ann treated herself to an audible sigh.

When he came in and tramped speechless into the bathroom, she followed. When he had gulped three aspirin, washed them down with water, and defiantly peed, just as if she were not standing there two feet behind him, he said, "Stickup. They took the Pontiac."

That sounded reasonable enough to Ann, even familiar. After all, it was the fifth—no, sixth—time. And the insurance covered everything. But she could make no sense of the details: Green Berets, sign on the door, whistling, singing, niggers (he *would* keep on using that word!). He sounded as crazy as his thieving brother.

Rasmussen said he felt like somebody had dropped a safe on him. All he wanted was to sit down and have a cold beer in peace, if she didn't mind.

Ann didn't mind in the least. "What about my car?" she said, and left him to ponder that with his beer. She started the vacuum cleaner. No car at all now. She considered pointing this out to Rasmussen, but, being not utterly pure of mercy, pursued instead the muted avenging thunder of the vacuum down the hall.

Margie was employing her afternoon's holiday in cutting things out of magazines. She didn't look up when her mother zoomed in on her. Now that she had traded in her blunt play scissors on a grown-up pair, she did rather fine work, specializing in the windblown hair of models.

"Daddy got robbed again!"

Margie accepted this stoically. While her mother stood on one edge of the blue chenille rug and ground away at it with the vacuum, she lifted her bunny-slippered feet out of the way and hunted for a new head of hair.

"They stole the Pontiac, too!"

This strident news undercut Margie's pleasure at finding a blonde in a green minijumper hanging upside down from an aerial ladder. "Well, how are me an Jody gonna get to the show, then?" she said.

"I can't hear you!" sang her mother in a piercing happy

voice, but Margie didn't ask again; shouting always gave her a sore throat. She tore out the upside-down girl and went to work. If she couldn't go to the show, then she would make fudge, rich chocolatey fudge with nuts in it, *mmm.*

David, alerted by the undulant drone of the Clean Machine on its daily round, lay where he was in the back bedroom. When Mrs. C. got there he would leave, but not before. Like mealtimes, the afternoon visits of the Clean Machine provided him with dependable stimuli to movement, for who could be sure she wouldn't vacuum him along with everything else? No agency on earth could keep her from carrying out her mission. Not the Pentagon, not the CIA or FBI, not even the Hearn Security Service.

But last year, when Bert Hearn, Jr., had accused the Westpark High PTA of sheltering Red agents who poisoned young minds with closed-circuit television, David dreamed a masterly plan: an anonymous letter would inform Bert Hearn, Jr., that the PTA conspirators got their orders from Peking over a transistorized intercontinental short-wave receiver, disguised as a vacuum cleaner and belonging to a "Mrs. Rasmussen." The letter would suggest that Bert Hearn, Jr., pretend to represent a company which manufactured a revolutionary new model vacuum cleaner. . . .

At that point, however, David's mind had boggled, and inertia had taken over. He was, in fact, too deeply convinced that nothing imaginable could separate Mrs. C. from her Clean Machine. They were in the hall now, and coming closer. Hart wouldn't be home from work yet, but David knew where he left his key, and Hart didn't care. Not about anything but his soprano saxophone. That was why David liked Hart.

He timed it perfectly. Just as Mrs. C. came wheeling in, David was off the bed and out, ahead of the lecture about lying around all day. *"Did you hear?"* Mrs. C. called after him. No; whatever it was, David didn't hear. He was out the back door and gone.

Meanwhile, back in the living room, Rasmussen debated whether or not to go for another beer. The massive ache in the upper right quadrant of his body seemed to be subsiding a bit as the sound of the vacuum cleaner receded. But when the phone rang, he croaked, "Somebody get that," and, amazingly, somebody did.

Margie thought it might be Jody, about going to the show, but it was Uncle Bernie, who wanted Daddy. "Are you gonna bring Mama's car back?" she dared to say. Uncle Bernie said that was what he was calling about.

So Margie hovered nearby as her father dragged himself out of his chair and took the phone. He listened for a few seconds and said, "Yeah, and they took the Pontiac, too." Then he listened for what seemed to Margie a very long time before he finally said, "Ah, for Christ's sake, Bern. How the hell can I? I told you they took . . . *No!* God damn right you better; you think I'm gonna walk over there and carry you?"

Margie heard the vacuum cleaner sigh and be quiet. "OK, OK, for Christ's sake," said her father. "Where is it?" Wincing, he pinned the receiver between head and shoulder, and wrote something in jabbing pencil strokes on the message pad, tearing off the sheet at once and stuffing it into the pocket of his coat sweater. "*If* they find it," he said, looking at Margie, witnessing, taking it all down to report. "Yeah yeah yeah yeah," he said, and hung up hard. It was a wonder Ann hadn't come running out already.

Indeed, only a distraction of some magnitude could have prevented this, and in fact Ann had just discovered in the yellow-tiled shower stall of the rear bathroom three enormous silverfish. She reacted like lightning, twisting the Hot handle, ducking back without getting wet, and stood to watch the filthy little invaders washed boiling and wriggling back down the dark drain.

But something was wrong! The holes in the drain now seemed too small for them to pass, as if they had already grown too large to go back. Ann had a bad moment with the thought of how monstrous big they might become if . . . She saw them now stuck fast against the drain, their disgusting little bug bodies sending up infection with the steam. Without a thought for her own safety, she spun out a long garland of toilet paper, wadded it loosely, and flung herself, breath suspended, at the drain, drenching her own head and arm as she pinched up the sickening vermin and in the next instant hurled the sopping handful plop into the toilet, and flushed.

"Ugh!" she said passionately to the echoing tile vault of the bathroom, and took a panting breath of temporary relief. That proved it. Disinfectant wasn't enough. You needed poison, something concentrated, to purify the dank subterranean passages all the way to their source. The nest. You had to kill them in the nest.

Rasmussen badly wanted time to think; worse, he wanted time not to have to think. He sank back into his chair and the thinking went on unbidden. Without the Pontiac he couldn't possibly go find Bernie, who said he no longer had the Volkswagen but knew where to find it. Without the Pontiac nothing was possible, right? He looked at the dead television screen as if to absorb its soothing blankness.

But here she came. Rasmussen could hear the wrath in her muffled tread, and let his eyelids fall, hiding their telltale flutter with one cupped hand and trying to keep his breathing natural as he felt her there, glaring.

"*Where's the poison!*"

He stirred, blinking, and saw her, hair all wet snakes, an escape from a nightmare.

"The what?"

"I *said,* Where . . . is . . . the . . . poison? There was almost a whole new bottle in the kitchen and it's gone."

"Aw, how the hell do I know? It's *your* poison."

"They're coming up out of the drains now!"

Now virtually convinced he really had been asleep, Rasmussen rubbed his eyes, and when he opened them she wasn't there. Maybe he would still get a breather after all.

No. A car in the driveway, feet on the porch, the door chimes. Rasmussen got there first, apparently by default, opened and saw the cops, different ones. He didn't know whether to be glad they'd found the Pontiac or not. "They beat it up much?" he said.

"Beg pardon?" said the cop in front.

"Where'd you find it?"

"What?" said the cop. He glanced at a black notebook. "Are you Charles A. Rasmussen?"

"Yeah, I got stuck up and . . ."

"Bernard . . . Bern-hard J. Rasmussen your brother?"

Rasmussen stepped outside and shut the door behind him. "Yeah," he said. "Why?" Three was a crowd on the little concrete platform. The silent cop moved off onto the lawn, and looked at the house as if checking for exits.

"Seen him the last couple days?" said the cop doing the talking.

"What's the trouble?" said Rasmussen. "He don't live here."

"We got a call from the San Francisco police. Seems your brother, ah, Bern-hard, took out a Honda motorcycle last, ah, Saturday. For a test ride, just for a half hour supposed to be. The home address he gave, they never heard of him. No accidents reported. . . ."

Rasmussen waited. He could have written the rest himself.

"And the, ah, Golden Gate Speed Shop wants their motorcycle back. He gave your name as a reference. Property owner. You got a liquor store, right?"

"Got stuck up today. Stole my car, too. Thought you found it."

"So you haven't seen your brother, eh?"

"Not just lately. Damn-fool trick letting somebody have a motorcycle with no local reference."

"Trying to make a sale, I guess." The cop slapped his notebook shut. "So you give us a ring if he shows up, or you hear from him, right?"

"He'd have to be nuts to show up here after giving this address, wouldn't you figure?" Rasmussen wanted to hear another opinion on that one; he had his own already.

"Never know," said the cop. "Only lead we got."

Ann was waiting inside the door. If Rasmussen had felt strong enough to open the door hard he would have caught her with it where she stood clutching the poison bottle, eyes glazed with satisfaction. "Now you're just as guilty as he is," she said.

Rasmussen went back to his chair, and let himself down.

"Why didn't you tell me he called? Where is he? I suppose he wrecked my car. . . ."

Right through his extra skin, Rasmussen felt her voice reverberate, a livelier pain lighting up the dark ache from head to waist. "*Listen,*" he said, and that hurt, too. "I had about all I want for today. All we can do is wait, and I want it quiet while I wait."

"You want, you want. . . ." But she left him. With clinical precision she poured the entire contents of the poison bottle down the shower drain in the rear bath. But the house was quiet.

And it remained quiet, wordlessly quiet even through a

punctual six-o'clock supper of creamed tuna, rice, and frozen peas. David hadn't come home, but Ann said nothing.

Rasmussen hadn't even heard her go out, but at a quarter to seven she presented him with a fait accompli. "I borrowed Bunches' car," she said. "You've got to drop Vi at night school, leave Margie and Jody at the show, and then go find Bernie. They might never find the Pontiac, and I want my car back tonight."

"What?" said Rasmussen, but much too feebly.

"You've got about three hours, and Vi's late already."

"Where am I supposed to find Bernie?"

"Margie saw you write it down."

"Well, if you're gonna get your water hot," said Rasmussen, "why don't you just take her to a motel? Go on, take a cab, I'll pay for it."

Ann didn't even bother to field that one. "Or I will call the police and tell them about my car. *And* the motorcycle."

Rasmussen's body pushed itself out of its chair. She wouldn't actually call the cops, he tried telling himself. She was just bluffing, hitting him when he was down. He pulled the Dodgers cap a notch tighter on his head. It hurt.

"*Margie!*" said Ann, and to him: "Vi's waiting on you."

Ten minutes later a desk man at the Seventy-seventh Street Station in Los Angeles dialed Rasmussen's number. He wanted to tell him the Pontiac had been found abandoned on Avalon Boulevard. But he got no answer.

EIGHT

Strange to say, Rasmussen was a new man as soon as he backed Howard Bunch's racing-green Mustang out of the next-door driveway. Robbed and beaten unconscious, betrayed into felonious complicity, humiliatingly dispatched like an errand boy on a probably impossible mission—all within the last six hours—still he felt his spirits lift and his aches fall away as he muscled the unfamiliar floor shift through the tight, racy gears. What's more, this astounding transformation seemed so natural that he didn't give it a thought.

Vi's warm and not-quite-motherly solicitude did him no harm, either. "You poor man," she said, not once but three times, and began a story of her own no-good cousin Virgil, who took dope *and* robbed stores, as if this supernatural coincidence somehow explained Rasmussen's own complex of woes. Bathing his misery in her company, he put off his resentment at learning how many family secrets Ann had revealed, and, warmly pressed for details by Vi, even withheld the fact that his assailants had been niggers.

It stopped too soon. When mouse-faced Jody climbed in back beside Margie, Vi turned to ask them what show they were going to, and then they were at night school, where she got out daintily for such a well-rounded woman, telling Rasmussen not to worry if he was a little late: she would be having coffee right *there*—see?—at the Pizza Palazzo. He had been meaning to ask her what she was learning at the night school, but now it was too late.

Three minutes later he left the girls in the open maw of the Park Theater and turned for the freeway, a little drunk already on the throaty muffled roar of the Mustang, a richer echo of all the Ford V-8's he had lusted after hopelessly back in the 30's. Once headed northwest on the broad concrete course, he settled into the bucket seat and tramped down on the accelerator. A grim fatal aggressive 100+ octane joy fueled his arteries. He felt immortal.

Which would have inspired no joy at all in Howard Bunch, worrying hard already about having let someone else drive his new car for the first time.

As if Howard didn't have enough to worry about. He had only said yes to Vi's complicated and heartfelt plea through the bathroom door because he didn't want to be interrupted in the delicate application of an expensive, transparent, water-soluble salve to all the stubborn little plague spots of itch, rash, dermatitis which had been tormenting him for weeks.

And then, as the beloved velvety rumble of the Mustang's exhaust had faded, there *she* was, knocking on the *front* door, moaning and carrying on about how impossible her life was, and wanting a repeat performance of her Sunday treatment. What was Howard going to say, no? After answering the door wearing nothing but his imported foam-green raw-silk Japanese robe?

He only wanted to get back to his ointment, and to worrying in solitary peace about his Mustang. He put on his best mature insurance man's frown of concern, and said, "Isn't it a bit risky?" But he already knew the riskiness was half the good of it for her, and probably about 90 percent of it this time. "I don't care," she said. "They're all gone. We've got hours, darling."

Those last two words rang in his head like one hollow gong of despair kicked twice. "Well, I'm expecting a client to call by here in a little while."

"We won't answer," she said.

OK, then, into the Baby's Room, cool and faintly dusty, where the wall switch lit up the specially chosen wallpaper: bunny rabbits and teddy bears and baby elephants, integrated topsy-turvy in cream and yellow and pink and brown.

Trouble was, if you hadn't driven the Mustang before, you were liable to underestimate its power. Oh, he was insured, all right. But the very thought of trying to get a claim of his own through Liebermann or any of those adjusters . . . She was wriggling out of her clothes like a snake. Well, she sure didn't need a girdle. And it did stop the itching for a little while.

But afterward he would *have* to take a shower, and that *was* the trouble. Callaghan, that little red Irishman, best dermatologist in Southern California, had laid it on the line: "Call it unspecific dermatitis all they want, it's caused by too much soap and water, I see it all the time. So just stop bathing, my friend, and this stuff"—scribbling the $17.50 prescription—"three times a day, sparingly."

Nervous, shivering, ready to start vibrating like an electric rack, she clutched at him. "I'm dying," she chattered into the arm of his robe.

Don't do it here, thought Howard.

"You don't have a thing," she said.

"Ah hell," said Howard. "Wait a minute." In his briefcase. She wasn't the only one he treated. No, indeed.

While Rasmussen, passing a smoking rattletrap Falcon full of Mexicans on the right, congratulated himself on the fact that the Dodgers were in St. Louis, as if he had drawn up the National League schedule himself. Otherwise the traffic jam approaching Chavez Ravine would have cost him half an hour at least. He swept beneath the Santa Monica Freeway and curved north. Feeling too free to think of where he was going, he estimated that he would be there—wherever it was—in fifteen minutes, maybe ten.

Wrapping her thin arms around herself, Ann thought Howard would take forever. Rather than think of herself waiting there naked, she glanced around, at the yellow bassinet, the fenced crib of paler yellow, and the junior-size single bed spread with shiny plastic. As if they had bought stubbornly for the child who'd never come, as if having a place for it at every age would *make* it come . . . "Guess what?" said Howard. "They're in my briefcase, and it's in the car."

Standing there safe inside his robe, he looked almost pleased. And she would be forty-three tomorrow. "Oh come on anyway," she said. "I'm dying."

"Isn't it a bit risky?"

Ann felt herself shaking to pieces. To stop her teeth chattering she grinned them hard. Through the white rictus she said, "Come *on!*"

"Smart bastard!" said Rasmussen in the same clenched fashion to the Alfa Romeo humming past him. But he was just 0.8 miles from the Silver Lake turnoff, said the sign. Grudgingly he eased up on the gas. Probably couldn't have caught him anyway.

With the loss of speed, he was reminded of his mission,

but the fifteen-mile spin along the freeway had keyed him for it: he felt ready for anything. At the corner of Sunset Boulevard he gunned the engine and growled the address at a passing youth with more hair than Bernie.

"That way, man," came the mild answer, with a prophetic wave in a vague northerly direction. Three more gruff queries to passersby brought him to exactly the top-heavy, side-slipped, dry-rotting wreck of a dark-brown three-story house he always envisioned when reading about slum clearance in the Times. Five or ten tons of matchwood on the hoof.

Rasmussen slid to the curb behind a bronze 1950 Hudson sedan like a tomb from some bygone civilization. He switched off the ignition and looked again. Was that music the place was leaking, or the contented whine of feeding insects? Rats would starve there, he thought.

But his revived sense of mission took him across a trackless lawn of devil grass and ice plant, up onto the eroded planks of a front porch soft beneath his soles but supporting him at least long enough for him to push the doorbell.

Inside he heard something like three radios going at once. No one would hear the doorbell over such a racket. He thought for an instant of kicking the door open and spraying the inside with slugs. Instead, he pounded five times with his fist, and felt each one in head, neck, and shoulder. That nigger had zapped him good.

Still no answer. This kind of place you probably just walked into, he decided, and did so, feeling and seeing his hand come away from the knob stained with grease or tar or paint and wiping it on the seat of his pants as he took one tentative step into the ugliest, messiest rat's nest he had ever seen in all his born days.

Mattresses, packing crates, and what the inhabitants probably called paintings. A giant hanging thing like two warped airplane propellers, past which he saw two black hairy kids

—boys probably, twins maybe—playing with a caseless table radio, a phonograph, and a tape recorder, *all going at once, for Christ's sake!*

MOVIE TONITE, said a handmade sign pinned to one propeller. The radio gave out electronic rock in slow waves, the phonograph Bach's Brandenburg Concerto Number 2 (33 rpm at 45), and the tape machine a prepared mixture of Ravi Shankar and gusty audience laughter: into this sound of hell Rasmussen tried saying, *"I'm looking for a guy called Bernie!"* One kid looked over his shoulder and took no notice at all. Yelling further at them would surely be a waste of time, and might rev up his headache again, if the noise didn't.

But it already had. Between throbs, Rasmussen picked his way across the room as if it were mined and, watching his step among the mattresses, got clipped hard on the ear by a propeller tip, but kept his feet, shying away from an unbanistered staircase, choosing instead an open doorway.

At the other end of a long room walled with more "paintings," Rasmussen saw a crowd of hairy, motley folk seated on more packing cases around a kind of table. Close by stood Bernie, like a proctor or a house man in a casino, surveying them as they fed. "Yeah, Charley," he said, and seeing neither mattresses to stumble over nor hanging objects to put people's eyes out, Rasmussen ventured closer.

Christ Almighty, what a collection! A chalk-white girl all in black with jet-black glasses; a twisty little Jew in an orange fright wig (or was that his real hair?); a girl as big as a hippo wearing fatigues; a tall specter in a Levi jacket like a tintype cowboy, with mad colorless eyes and a straggly yellow Fu Manchu moustache; a smaller, hairier model of the two black house apes in the front room, and . . .

"Marco, this is Charley my brother," said Bernie to the

least outlandish of the six feeders, a cheery red-cheeked man whose prophetic black beard filled the neck of an unpressed blue work shirt.

"Hi, Charley," said Marco, pushing back his crate. "Sit down and have some beans before the next wave."

"No, thanks," said Rasmussen, rolling an eye at the terra-cotta slop in the lopsided bowls, which looked as if they'd been made on the premises, most likely by a spastic wood-carver. "Don't mean to interrupt your . . ."

A woman—unmistakably—came in through beaded danglers from an adjoining room carrying another of these bowls, and offered it to Bernie. "Here you go," she said, looking up at Rasmussen out of one large blue eye, swimming in peace behind round steel-rimmed spectacles. The other eye was aimed outward at a vast rectangle of scarlet and lime-green splashes on the wall to Rasmussen's right. "Hi," she said. "That's a groovy hat."

A fat, squatty little thing she was, somewhere between twenty-five and forty, with a lot of cobwebby hair unsuccessfully collected into a motherly bun. Was she pregnant? The faded paisley pup tent she had on made it hard to tell.

"Louise, this is Charley my brother," said Bernie, and to Rasmussen: "I left mine in the car so she cooked me some." He sat down in the corner nearest the table and began spooning up brown rice.

Rasmussen crouched next to him. "Listen, I had to borrow a car and I gotta get it back in a hour or two, so where the hell is hers?"

Bernie gave up on an attempt to gather his legs into the lotus position. "Ridin the bike kind of fucks up your leg muscles," he said.

"That's another thing," said Rasmussen. "You never told me that God damn thing was stolen!"

"Peace," said Bernie. "Control your anger. Nothin is gonna happen to that short. Cat's gonna bring it right back here tonight."

The ghostly girl in black stood up, said, *"Je dois pipi,"* and ran out. Rasmussen gaped after her, and Marco told him, "She had a bad trip at the Brain Drain, see, and now all she talks is French."

"Doesn't he want any beans?" said the walleyed woman.

"See, all you got to do is wait, baby," said Bernie. "You ever notice how nobody's got any patience anymore?"

Ann was waiting, too, for Howard to finish his shower, so she could take hers. Of course she felt better; she always did, somewhat. Yet now it seemed that while she had lain horizontal for those few minutes the nest of packed irritation and furious dissatisfaction in her breast had only been tilted elsewhere, relocated now in the worst place of all, damped but unplaced by those viscous, dangerous, most unwelcome juices which she tried unsuccessfully not to feel. Was he going to stay in there the whole night?

"Howard?" she called, and was surprised to hear how out of breath she sounded. But, rewarded by the silencing of the shower, she sat up, the clammy plastic clinging to her bony moist back. She felt forty-three-tomorrow, every day of it.

Howard was far from finished in the bathroom, however. Sure enough, Callaghan was right, the soap and water had aggravated his spots: they were clearly visible now, and itched individually like separate fiery stigmata. He patted himself dry and set once more to applying his salve, vowing that he would get out of next Sunday while knowing good and well that six days would find him dispensing the usual Sunday treatment to her on the red Naugahyde couch of the lounge where neither they nor any other members of the

Interfaith Youth Council had held a Sunday luncheon meeting for going on two years now.

So engrossed was he in the clinical precision of his dabbing that he didn't hear her until she rapped once with one tense knuckle and walked in, clothes in her arms, to catch him balanced on the edge of the bathtub watching himself in the medicine-cabinet mirror while he got at a particularly awkward set of itches on his hindquarters.

"What are you *doing?*" Ann was instantly reminded of Charley's eczema. "What have you *got?*"

Howard looked down at her and cleared his throat. "A little allergy," he said. "Nothing contagious."

She didn't know whether to believe him or not, but now she had to get under the shower without another second's delay. And he was still up there like some kind of posing statue. "Would you *mind* letting me in there?" she said.

Howard stepped down from the edge of the tub with a deliberate dignity that made her want to kill him. "Go right ahead," he said, and swallowed. "Don't mind me."

But when Ann had got into the tub and drawn the plastic curtain closed, careful to touch it only with thumb and finger, she heard him go out. Plastic curtains were much harder to clean and thus less sanitary than steel-and-glass doors. This one, green-and-white floral, *looked* clean enough, but you couldn't be sure. In these reflections she took shelter until the hot water began to punish her. Then it seemed that the romance of her secret liaison with Howard was being washed away, second by second, in the purifying streams. Mustn't get her hair wet; her neck ached from the effort. And the more serious washing would have to be done at home. It was all too sickeningly intimate and domestic, walking in on him just now. He could at least have put off his disgusting hygiene until she'd left.

Back in the Baby's Room, Howard was wishing he had done just that. No one would ever know what that cool aplomb had cost him: to be caught up in the air greasing your butt, by the lady next door! Well, not *greasing*—the stuff was water soluble. Howard couldn't stand anything greasy on his skin. But the principle was the same.

His insides had turned to water the moment she walked in, as if they would run out his feet and down the bathtub drain. But his knees hadn't quivered, and the dryness of his throat hadn't stolen his voice. "A little allergy"; it was even the truth. Only the allergen was his secret.

His therapy completed for now, he put his robe on once more, went out, switching the light off, came back in, switching it on again, and tried to see the room with his wife's eyes. No evidence he could see, nothing out of place. She hardly ever came in here anyway. And he wouldn't overlook the extra wet towel, either.

OK, then. If Vi came home tonight steamed up by something her child psychology teacher had said (it didn't take much to get her in the mood), he would think of an excuse. Because he was not going to take another shower tonight.

But Ann was, the minute she got home. For now she dried herself carefully, got dressed, and, by unbreakable habit, bent to check the drain plug in the tub. Yes, a little swirl of accumulated hair. Fighting down a shudder, she lifted out the plug with two fingers, emptied it on a tripled square of toilet paper, and made the mistake of looking at it closely: there, mixed with her own, were wetly matted little black curlicues kinked like pigs' tails, or spirochetes! Nigger hair! Animal hair!

She had to get home before she threw up, and dashed without a good-bye out the back door, through Bunches' back yard, clamping one hand over her mouth as she made for the hole in the hedge behind Bunches' garage, making it through the hole but no farther before her gorge rose and she stumbled and fell to her knees, retching on the bald grass beneath David's bedroom window.

That was how David, just home from Hart's, found her. And when he saw her, he smiled.

Rasmussen had nothing to smile at. Not one damn thing. To begin with, he had foolishly accepted a bowl of beans. Damn good, too, with peppers and garlic and salt pork and ham bone—strictly forbidden by Ann because of their disgusting aftereffects. But they had left him, predictably, with a raging heartburn, and he had been rushed from home without his customary supply of Magnalum.

Then Bernie's explanation of the missing Volkswagen had been worse than none at all, a garbled mess about a broken movie projector which someone called Richard had rushed out to replace. Of course it turned out Bernie had no idea at all where this "Richard" had gone to.

And now a second wave of freaks and kooks and nuts had gathered around the table—this must be the mess hall for half the weirdies in Southern California. *Mess* hall was right! And more were arriving all the time. There was Marco, who turned out to be a clubfoot, telling a kid with a fur hat and a chestful of fake medals that when Richard got back the show would go on.

"Yeah, but *when?*" said Rasmussen, compelled to keep the question in Bernie's ears lest he try to slip away from it, and from Rasmussen's watchdog presence, into the growing crowd. He failed, painfully, to belch away the red-hot bubble which seemed lodged forever behind his breastbone. He wanted a glass of water, but didn't dare trust Bernie alone.

Now a ragged cheer arose in the front of the house, just as the guard was changing and half a dozen fresh oddballs sitting down to give themselves heartburn. Back came the jumbo girl in fatigues, and the little orange Jew, cackling through a mouth like a split melon. Between them they convoyed an obvious queer in a rainbow shirt and skin-tight brick-red pants. You name it, thought Rasmussen, and they've got it here.

"You got it?" yelled Marco. "I've been afraid we'd like have to give out rain checks."

Was this queer Richard? The one Bernie had lent the VW to? As Rasmussen turned to find out, Bernie nodded reassurance, and said, "Say, Richard, glad to see you, man."

Man, thought Rasmussen. That was a good one.

But Richard had occupied the last empty packing crate and was craning his bird's neck to see what was in the pot. "Well, baby, I *didn't* get it," he told Marco. "I ran into fantastic complications. . . ."

"Get the keys, for Christ's sake," said Rasmussen. But Richard was telling Marco, and all hands, about his complications, and Bernie seemed loath to interrupt him.

"How did *I* know that little light meant I was out of gas? I was lucky it stopped dead about a block from Pepe's, this guy I met in the joint, right by the park there, where Dondi got busted that time? So I go up to Pepe's, and what a *scene!* There's this sailor, and like he's a spade, and Pepe has this fantastic love-hate thing for spades, and anyway this guy is tearing the place *up*, like he claims Pepe *robbed* him while he's been sleeping, also he's got to get back to San Pedro. . . ."

"Just get the keys," said Rasmussen.

"Louise, these beans are out of sight!" said Richard. "So Pepe says he'll get the car going if we can run this crazy spade back to San Pedro. So what choice did I have?"

As he paused to take a spoonful of beans, Rasmussen broke through Marco's running accompaniment of laughter and said, "*Where's the car?*"

"What I'm *telling* you," said Richard. "So anyway, they

get some gas, and we get on the Harbor Freeway and go zooming down to San Pedro, this sailor had some shit from Hong Kong or somewhere, baby I'm *still* stoned, seemed like we got there in about a minute and a half!"

By now everyone seemed hysterical except Rasmussen.

"So . . ." Richard commanded patience with an uplifted spoon. "We get there, and this sailor remembers his money, and starts calling Pepe a thieving little *faggot*, you know, and starts choking him, right there on the dock?

"Well, Pepe went *wild*, man, I knew he would, he's got this terrific ambivalence about spades, and besides he's got karate that won't quit! So he gets out and starts chopping this poor cat *up! Kicks* him, and *knees* him, and sticks *fingers* in his eyes! Then here come these two monsters in peacoats, so we jump in the car and split. I mean, like I never got out in the *first* place! And the last we see of this cat he's *crawling*, on his hands and *knees*, up to these two monsters, and leaving I swear this trail of *blood*, man, like a samurai movie!"

"So where's the car at?" said Rasmussen. "It belongs to me."

"Anyway, back we come *swoosh!* to Hollywood, but by then the place is closed, for the bulb, I mean. And Pepe is late for work, and I see what time it is and I'm afraid I'd miss dinner, and we're right by the bus stop, so I just grabbed a Sunset bus and came on out. . . ." As if sensing the anticlimax of the ending, Richard applied himself with new energy to the beans. Marco was still laughing, the fat girl wiped eyes and chin with one olive-drab arm, and the orange Jew gasped strangling for air.

"So you don't have the car here," said Rasmussen.

"I just told you," said Richard. "Pepe's got it at work. In Malibu."

"Where in Malibu?" Rasmussen wanted to be very sure of

everything. He was already sure that if he didn't control himself his skull would explode.

"The restaurant where he works," said Richard. "I haven't seen him in months, am I supposed to be supernatural or something?"

"I WANT THE GOD DAMN THING BACK RIGHT NOW!" The echo of his cry swelled pulsing in Rasmussen's head. "RIGHT NOW!" he roared, as if to drive the pain away by sheer volume.

Richard looked around for witness to his innocence in the face of this mad hostility. "When he gets off," he said gently. "He'll bring it back. Right back here."

"When's that?"

"Two o'clock."

"Control your anger, baby," said Bernie. "What does she want it in the middle of the night for, anyway?"

"Hey, what's happening?" said a new arrival, whose head —or maybe it was just his hair—came to a sharp point. "What time's the show?" said a little blonde next to him.

"You just missed it," said Marco.

"Aw shit," said the blonde. "It's my birthday."

"Listen here . . ." began Rasmussen. Birthday. But what was the use? He was boxed. He would have to take the Mustang back. He would have to trust Bernie—that was a laugh!—to stay here and bring the Volkswagen back, if this Pepe didn't lend it to some other queer or freak in the meantime. Birthday?

"What day is it?" he asked the room at large.

"Monday," said someone.

"*I mean the date, for Christ's sake!*"

"Peace, baby," said Bernie. "Nothin bad is gonna happen."

"The fourteenth," said walleyed Louise. "Saturn is ascending."

That settled it. All Rasmussen would have needed was to

forget tomorrow. "I'm goin," he told Bernie. "You just better bring that car back is all. You fuck up this time and we all go to jail, and I mean . . . *jail!*"

"Drive carefully," said Bernie, and in the front room the multiple musics doubled in volume.

But where, at this hour? "Where can I get some flowers around here?" Rasmussen wanted an answer from anybody.

"Some what?" said Bernie.

"FLOWERS! FLOWERS! FLOWERS!"

"Wow," said a girl standing nearby. She handed Rasmussen a wilted nasturtium. He looked at it uncomprehendingly for a moment, then jammed it in the pocket of his coat sweater and made for the first door, against whose frame the girl in black, minus her black glasses, stood propped, eyes closed, her face at first sight as ghastly smooth and featureless as an egg. Rasmussen recoiled, saw in place of her eyebrows the two delicate and barely visible curves of surgical stitches, and slipped gingerly past her into the hellish racket of the front room, stumbling on mattresses, caroming off a boy printing NO above MOVIE TONITE and leaving the two propellers a-spin as he plunged holding his breath out into the fresh air, on which he choked, and still ran coughing, dying of heartburn, to the racing-green Mustang, which miraculously no one had stolen yet.

Pulling furiously away from the curb, he heard and felt the right front fender of the Mustang catch grinding against the old bronze Hudson, but—"Fuck it!"—he floored the accelerator and ripped loose and away into the night in search of Magnalum and roses.

NINE

Ann lay on her bed and let David fix his own supper: that was how bad she felt. It was all coming down on her now. Some core of strength to fight it all seemed gone, as if she'd thrown it up with the creamed tuna and horribly recognizable green peas. In the hollowness it left there burned a bright bitter eye which appreciated how it all had to happen when she was a few hours away from forty-three. Didn't she like things to come out even?

The past spewed up its condensed hatefulness into her emptiness, but where and when had her life turned, like curdling milk, irreversibly for the worse? Ann didn't care enough to ask.

You think you're making a profit, trading four men for one? Aunt Judith said that a day or two before Ann had caught that filthy train for Georgia. *Well, you've got a thing or two to learn, dearie.*

Ann kept her mouth shut and thought, *Well, then I'll learn them.* Because Rasmussen looked like a bargain from where she sat, though she did precious little sitting in her father's house. Running was her specialty: running to fetch water, to get meals ready on time; running upstairs twenty times a day whenever Petey hollered, running to answer, "What is it?" whenever one of the others called her name. And when she wasn't running, she was wearing out her knuckles on the washboard, or was down on the floor scrubbing away their dirt. Cinderella was her favorite story well into adolescence.

You could iron standing in one spot, and darn socks sitting down, so Aunt Judith did those things. Ann got to run their clothes back and forth to Aunt Judith. But it preserved her "girlish figure," all that running: so said the family joker, Brother John, the eldest. Her father noticed her only in negative comparisons with a dead martyr called "Your Poor Mother." Otherwise Ann might have suspected she was doing a fair country job of tending three grown men and one blubbering secret upstairs monster which had to be fed by hand as if he weren't two years older than she, had to have his hair combed and his nose wiped, the flies brushed off his fat cheeks and the fleas from his cat picked off him and his pot emptied and washed if he hadn't missed it, which half the time he did.

This day-and-night blessing was known as "Your Brother Petey," and Ann would have put a pillow over his wet red face and sat on it if she hadn't been so dead sure she'd be the only one accused; because her father and Brother John and Brother Albert, who never went near him, all loved him.

So that when her Prince came, and said the magic words, *Get out of Santa Fe,* she would have married him if he'd been a harelipped hunchbacked two-headed nigger. You bet your life.

Let Aunt Judith sit there in the light of the fringed lamp and prognosticate all she wanted, with her lap full of the last holey stockings Ann would ever deliver. A widow with one child, Cousin Bob, a failure even at cutting brush with the CCC: what did *she* know?

She had even used the wrong word, for it wasn't a matter of making a profit, but of cutting losses. Men made the money in the world, Ann would grant them that. At least some of them did. But what God (a Man himself) had really put men on earth for was unceasingly to make dirt. Whether they made money or not, they all made dirt.

Three times a day they dirtied their cups and plates and silver. They dirtied towels and napkins at a touch, and clean clothes the minute they put them on. Wherever they walked or sat they left dirt; merely standing they made dirt: outdoors they spat, indoors they made stinks, and laughed—*Pa, John's lettin them super-dupers tonight!*

They pretended to worship the cleanliness which they demanded that women maintain, but secretly they loved their dirt, perhaps because it was their purpose on earth. The proof was in how little trouble they took keeping even their own bodies clean: Ann washed their underwear. And even when they went through the motions of bathing, and in clean nightshirts went to sleep between clean sheets, even then, often as not, they would leave mysterious stains behind them.

Ann hadn't finished high school, but there was nothing the matter with her arithmetic: even if one of them hadn't been a nonstop prodigy of fluids, slimes, and filths, four men were bound to manufacture more dirt than one man, let him be a veritable giant of dirtiness, a Jesus of dirt sent down to earth by God, that dirty old man. And Rasmussen, in his uniform, looked rather clean. He smelled faintly of Lysol and didn't spit once. So Ann didn't hesitate long.

At that, she had almost lost him, although over the years this had naturally become one of her best-kept secrets from herself. Going to the cabin with him had been a huge gam-

ble. The single common belief of all the girls at the USO
had been that if you let them they'd never marry you,
would give you a baby, go overseas and get killed. "Like
that!" said Sally Oakley, snapping her fingers.

Later she would say of that gamble: "I just lost my head."
Perhaps because she had acted that night like another person. With no tactical instruction whatsoever, she lied viva-
ciously about the difficulty of maintaining her virginity, and
teased him about "ruining an innocent girl." If he was impressed by either gambit, he didn't show it.

Inside the tourist cabin, window open to air out the stale-
ness, thick moonlight sifting in through the dirty screen, she
stood with no clothes on, letting him watch her out of the
darkness. His unseen stare tickled. Stood there with the
moon in one eye, pinching her breasts in her hands, not just
to make them bigger, but to feel what she was gambling.

"Come ahead," she said, teeth chattering, shaking her
voice. Another person spoke the words; she hadn't practiced
them. "Come on, this is what you want, isn't it? Come on
then, you'll have to come and take it." He did that, all right.
I can do my dirt, too, she thought. *It's happening now.* It
hurt in a way she couldn't have imagined, tears and sweat
seemed to pop out all over her at once, but you had to call
it joy. She didn't cry. Men couldn't stand crying women.

Rasmussen didn't say the word *love* to her that night. In
twenty-five years you could count the times he *had* said it
to her on your fingers and have a cat's cradle left over. But
for the little while before she had to go home, they told
each other their troubles, hurrying, hardly listening. He
talked about his grandfather and Bernie; she made one of
the worst mistakes of her life by telling him about Petey.

His sudden silent interest should have told her she was
giving away something of value, but on and on she went,
spinning out a long lyric of disgust, leaving out no detail,

making up new ones. She didn't even know how badly she wanted sympathy, all the sympathy in the world.

"Feebleminded, eh?" said Rasmussen at last.

Ann repeated the family dogma on the subject: "My poor mother fell downstairs when she was carrying him."

They walked back in silence to within a furlong of her house. She hadn't broken the news there yet, except daily in small ways: dry-mopping the floors instead of scrubbing them, soaking their underwear in double Clorox instead of washing them, letting Petey lie in his own mess and whacking him when he howled. A sore reflex of conscience became confused with the soreness between her legs, for she went three more times to the cabin with him, and continued putting off a showdown with her father until Rasmussen vanished without a word, and the curse did not come on time. Then, with no men in earshot, she cried.

Eleven days later they were married by a justice of the peace in Breedlove, Georgia. The best man was a Corporal Oldham, the witnesses a Mrs. Ashberry, the JP's wife, and her sister, a Miss Gill, who doubled at no extra charge as maid of honor. So charged with desperate emotion had been the days between her abandonment and her wedding that Ann could never afterward have described them exactly. Even if she had wanted to, a thousand subsequent reckonings of gain and loss had lacquered them over with a cumulative merciful opacity.

The irrelevant she remembered: cold fried pies and lukewarm coffee in paper cups handed through the windows of the cross-country train; a radiantly drunk soldier who grabbed her behind and yelled out to his buddies' delight that the meat on her wouldn't make a hamburger for a midget; Miss Gill, who smelled of kerosene and lilac water. . . . But even the honeymoon had been spent in a tourist cabin, indistinguishable from the one in which she had staked her bet. The only difference was that she didn't have to go home when he was through with her. That *was* home. It was by no means too soon for regrets, but Petey's pot was fresh enough in mind to keep them in proportion.

She scrubbed the cabin so clean that the proprietor should have given the rent back, but Ann at seventeen was not yet shrewd enough to know her particular talent had a cash value. It was all she knew how to do, so she did it. And she had to concentrate on the cabin itself, because the Army kept Rasmussen good and clean.

If he hadn't gone off to the war so soon, she might conceivably have reviewed her bet, and found a way to hedge it. But the undreamed-of blessings of being Private Charles A. Rasmussen's legal spouse—free, white, seventeen, and married—so immediately showered her that she didn't have a second thought for three years.

A few months after David was born she read an ad for an essay contest in the back pages of a women's magazine: "Describe the Best Years of Your Life" (in less than five thousand words). Like a year-old memory of morning sickness the certainty went through her: they had been the three years he was overseas.

Those three years had even begun well, with the trip back across America on a less crowded train. Was it the wire-thin gold circle on her ring finger? Or a look of *don't touch me?* Or some aura of her fresh-proved knowledge that men could be handled, at least one at a time? If anyone had tried to start a conversation with the skinny, solemn, inward-looking girl, she might simply have shown the papers in her purse: they said who she was. But no one did, and no one grabbed her, all the way to Los Angeles.

There, as if running on rails, she threaded her way through the huge confusion of the war boom to Santa Monica, a room at the YWCA, a job at Douglas Aircraft, and night school. The tiny room was spotless (she cleaned it anyway); the job paid almost a dollar an hour and required no running; the night classes would get her a high-school diploma in a year. For the first time in her life she felt *on her way*. To have asked where to would have seemed not only irrelevant but destructive of the feeling itself, closer to intoxication than she had ever been, or would be again.

Everyone said they were long and lonely, those days. On the assembly line, the portable radio sang of it. If you were a war wife, you were supposed to say how long the days were, and the nights. Ann did so, anxious not to be out of step. But the secret truth was that they went by much too fast: working, studying, sleeping never quite enough, she had no time to spend the riches of pay check and allotment. She made time, though, to clean the big apartment she shared with a girl she met at the Y and two more from the swing shift at Douglas. It wasn't much work; women were so much cleaner than men. Anyway, Delores and Betty Ann were.

Not quite so the glum oxlike girl named Mary Woody who shared a room with Ann. Mary had a perceptible moustache and no perceptible waist. She wasn't married, never went out, ate as much and as messily as Brother John, and within five minutes left any room she was in a shambles. Of course she wasn't dirty like a man, but she chain-smoked, and always brought the smell of the assembly line home with her. Half the time she didn't wash. Except for playing the radio she made no noise, and it was six months before she said anything other than yes or no to Ann.

Then one night she came home from work a little after midnight and said, "Do you know where Firebaugh is? Firebaugh, California?" Ann didn't, and the conversation was over.

One morning Ann woke up to find Mary propped on one elbow and looking at her in the strangest way. "Do you ever think what if they *all* got killed over there?" Mary said. "And none of them came home, ever?" Ann said she didn't see any point in thinking about that.

"Do you really miss him a lot?" said Mary. "You don't act like it."

Ann delivered a short monologue on what a marvelous husband she had, and how terribly she missed him. Mary grunted and turned her back. Several months later, when Mary moved out after a fight with Delores, and Delores explained why, Ann imagined that she'd had a narrow escape. That the dirtiness of men could actually possess a woman like an evil spirit! The sheer horror of it gave her a specialized paranoia, and for weeks she looked closely at her fellow workers, austere in overalls, to see if any of them seemed suspiciously bewitched, or bewarlocked. Some of them did, and she gave them a wide berth.

This unnerving experience had its good effect, however, reinforcing in newly diplomaed Ann a specific curiosity in what made people the way they were. She was scared silly by the world of bars and dances, populated by "Victory girls" and uniforms full of diseased irresponsible lusts. Reading was not only rewarding, but inexpensive and clean. Ann didn't mind being called "the brain" by Delores and Betty Ann and Sue, who had replaced Mary. Privately she came to agree with them, and weren't all the magazines she read since her graduation beginning now to speak of the "unlimited opportunities" which would fill "the postwar world"? When Delores, married to a sailor, got pregnant by a one-armed foreman in Tail Assembly, it only confirmed the superiority of Ann's judgment; but she managed to conceal her mixed delight and disgust as she briskly supervised

Delores' brief post-abortion convalescence. The psychology book she was reading had quite a few things to say about the sources of promiscuity.

Also about the typical consequences to girls of losing their mothers at an early age. It was true—and thrillingly so—that "The female child may push herself to extraordinary, even excessive lengths, in attempting to fill the place of the lost mother within the familial structure." So far, so good, thought Ann, although in her case the question of who pushed whom remained open to question.

But the rest of it made her smile, especially the part about how the death of the mother "leaves the child free of competition for the father's affection, and allows her the satisfaction of becoming symbolically his sexual partner." If it hadn't been so funny, it would have been disgusting.

The beauty of it was that she could have it both ways, recognizing her similarity with "typical" motherless girls, *and* her unique individual differences. Grounds for feeling both normal and superior were right there in black and white.

Rasmussen came home a tech sergeant, ushering in the period of unlimited opportunities. How was Ann to know she had just lived the best years of her life? She met him at the Greyhound bus station in Santa Monica. Luckily he was still wearing his uniform, for the few blurred snapshots they had exchanged had not quite done their most important job. The one of two bleary, doubtless drunk GI's propping each other up before a nameless door in Naples she had come to see as a picture of two soldiers, one of whom was her husband. But the other couples were all embracing, so they did, too. Once more he almost broke her back, quite as if he didn't know he was squeezing not merely a body kept clean and faithful, but the saver of almost $2,300 and the possessor of eleven units of college credit.

To do him justice, however, Rasmussen found immediate use for at least the first two of these: the war apparently hadn't worn him out at all. He said there were two things on his mind, and he applied himself to them energetically, night and day.

The one she had expected, and with the help of several enlightened books had prepared herself for loyally. If at the outset it happened much more often than the books called "normal," still it was itself "normal," and no doubt its very frequency helped her get used to it more quickly. Unhappily for Ann, just when she had got used to it, and even mildly to enjoy it, the frequency fell off sharply, never to increase again.

This coincided with the actual initiation of the other thing he had in mind; "this plan I got," he called it. With her savings, and his mustering-out pay, and a GI loan, he bought a lot and built a liquor store. There'd been lots of time to think overseas, and he'd figured it all out. The plan called for finding "the right place," with no other liquor stores nearby, and a "high growth potential." The days between their first bruising rapid-fire nights he had spent studying maps and hunting sites by bus and thumb over some 750 square miles of greater Los Angeles.

"Why do they call it Westpark?" she asked him, when he pointed out the right place to her on a map. For the yellow area under his finger was east even of Watts, and west of nothing at all. Indeed, the name did not appear on the map, so shrewdly was Rasmussen guessing ahead into the period of unlimited opportunities.

"Because it sounds good," he said. "Westpark. What difference does it make?"

The right place, when she laid eyes on it, looked distinctly more desolate than her worst memories of Santa Fe, N.M., where at least there were trees. She didn't mention the visible lack of anything resembling a park, but did ask him why he wanted to call the store Ace Liquors.

"You never played cards, so you wouldn't know," said Rasmussen, hands-down champion poker loser of his platoon. "But ace is the best you can get, see?"

Well, they'd been there ever since. If you didn't count marrying Ann, Ace Liquors had been the one smart move Rasmussen had made in his entire life. Maybe he realized that, for he had never made another move since, smart or otherwise. With the building of the store, and a couple of years' sweating to secure it, his life had come to a quiet halt. Not to mention Ann's.

For no one who had come through the war without a real buddy would have thought of taking a partner. He couldn't even remember the name of the other soldier in the Naples photo, and his plan specified going it alone. This meant minding the store, seven days a week, twenty hours a day, and paying a relief clerk would have cost them more meals than either cared to miss. Rasmussen opened up at 6 A.M. to serve old Munn and Gomez, the winos, and any other emergency cases; he dozed on a surplus Army cot in the back room for a couple of hours after his noon sandwich while Ann watched the front, then he took over again until 2 A.M. On a quiet week night he might close around 1:30. As far as anyone could tell—Ann certainly included—he liked it.

He even preferred cooking his own breakfast and making his own sandwich for lunch. The Army, Ann told herself, had made him independent. Any decent supper hour conflicted with the best business of the day, so Ann would usually cook something on the double hot plate in the back room, and share it with him there, to the accompaniment of the Los Angeles Angels on the radio. They might as well have lived there, she said finally, and saved the rent on the little house in Norwalk. Rasmussen wouldn't hear of it. "We won't be doin this much longer," he said. "We can't *live* here."

He must mean *she* couldn't, thought Ann. He already did.

Well, that was all right. If she was left the house to herself, and vast expanses of free time, there was the less reason for her not to pursue her own rather vague ends, which coalesced around a vision of herself, in a white laboratory smock, telling people patiently but firmly what was the matter with them. No good reason at all, except that when she enrolled in four morning classes at Compton Junior College, and asked him for book money, Rasmussen hit the roof. In her own chronology of their war, that first engagement was always to keep a certain clarity and importance.

"If you think I'm breaking my ass so you can sit around in *school*, you got another think comin. A grown woman like you!"

Ann explained that it would make absolutely no difference in the services she provided him: she would still spell him after lunch, fetch his supper, and be there at 2 or 2:15 A.M. in the unlikely event that he wanted anything else of her.

"*Kids* go to school," said Rasmussen. "*Men* work. . . ."

And what did women do? Ann should have known the answer to that one before she asked it.

"They keep house. They keep things clean. They . . ." No readier to mention children than she, he seemed to search for the right phrase between a swinging *Strike One* and a *Ball Two, outside,* from the portable radio. Searched, and found: "They take care of the home front!"

She laughed in his face, and had a hard time stopping. There were so many things she could have said back that in the end she said nothing. If that was his game, how could she lose? If that was what he wanted, he would get it. Luke Easter of San Diego hit the ball out of the park and the crowd groaned. "Son of a bitch," said Rasmussen.

Why hadn't she left him then and there? A good question, but it didn't occur to her until too much later. Perhaps she still thought her arithmetic better than Aunt Judith's. Perhaps she still hoped for things to get better, even on his terms. Or perhaps Rasmussen was right when he said, "Trouble is, I spoil you, that's all."

Oh yes, he had done that. The bright new eye inside her could appreciate that now, as forty-three came closer. How could she ever pay him back? Things would never come out even.

But never say die. If she felt like a dying woman, still she wasn't dead. If the hollowness inside made her feel like an imaginary person, *he* was real enough, opening the bedroom door now to say, "What's the matter with you?" No wonder he looked worried; she was never sick.

"Happy birthday," he said.

"You're in a big hurry," said Ann. "It's not my birthday yet." But of course, tomorrow was his bowling night. "Did you get the car?"

"Bernie's bringing it in a while," said Rasmussen. He took three steps forward and placed a white florist's box on the foot of her bed. "Here," he said.

"Thank you," Ann said. "Where is it?"

"He's bringing it. You oughta be glad he's not here now, when you're feeling bad."

"I feel fine," Ann said. "Where is the car?"

"Damned if I'm gonna get in a fight, after the day I had," he said. "On your birthday . . ." He disappeared.

Ann got up, still feeling imaginary but quite strong enough to walk. She went to the kitchen and told Margie to stop eating and go to bed. She switched on the garbage disposal, opened the florist's box, and lifted out the fern-shrouded, long-stemmed red roses, careful of the thorns. She turned on the cold water.

When Rasmussen came out to get a beer a minute later, he saw her carefully feeding the roses, one by one, down into the whirling steel blades, blossom first. He gaped at two long green stems thrashing round and round like the delicate legs of a dying bird.

TEN

For the second time in the past three hours—it must be a record—David conceded an ungrudging measure of admiration to Mrs. Clean. From being discovered on hands and knees puking up her guts in the dirt, she had recovered with undeniable style.

Hey, Mom, what's the matter? The appropriate words had been right there in his mouth, his hand on her arm to help her up. Gargling, spitting, out of breath, she had groaned that she was dying. But at once, *No, I'm all right.*

No explanation at all—David gave her points for that— until after she had spent twenty minutes in the bathroom, and then only a terse official statement: the press officer for Mrs. Charles A. Rasmussen, pale and serious, blamed recent losses on "coffee and cake over at Bunches." The dispatch included references to all the excitement David had missed, along with his supper, and concluded, *I'm going to lie down for a while.* Over and out.

And then just now, the roses. True, only The Cap would have brought roses home in the first place. But he could never have thought of anything as good as stuffing them down the Waste King. If anyone had any brains in the family—David smiled—it was Mrs. Clean.

They were at it again now, the best pitched battle since before the Cease-fire. Where did they get the energy? The Cap had been robbed and slugged, Mrs. Clean had left her supper in the back yard and lain in a coma for three hours: you would think they'd be ready to call it a night. Or at least get a new routine.

But they only had one: saying how bad everything was, blaming each other for it, and then saying, "How could you?" If they didn't know the right answer by now, they never would. The right answer was, "How *could* I? I just *did*, that's all. So go get fucked." If either of them had ever said so, David might actually have had a favorite parent.

No chance. That left nothing to hope for except the rare touch of originality which could raise their brainless sniping briefly to the level of a spectator sport. But you couldn't exactly sit enjoying that all night. Nor were Culp and Cosby funny, so when The Cap yelled, *"Enough is enough, God damn it!"* David agreed, shut off the TV, and headed for his room.

But they knew how to keep it just loud enough so you couldn't sleep, and passing Pig Bird's door he stuck his head in, on a whim neither sadistic nor merciful. "How d'you like the show?" he said.

Margie heard him through a set of filters contrived to let through only her father's dirty words: these she tabulated, as if they had some intrinsic value, to be discovered at some later date perhaps; much as she had once, until dissuaded by her mother, collected little boxes of pebbles and feathers and peach pits. Now she heard David, but understandably thought he had said, "How'd you like the show?" meaning the movie she had just seen. *The Surf Soldiers* it was called.

"I loved it," she said.

"Oh, *yeah?*" David said.

Nothing but the pleasure of recapitulating a good movie or television drama could spur Margie to a narrative effort of more than one sentence. So, with an ear still cocked for dirty words, she put aside her reflexive distrust of David's smiling interest, and began to tell him.

About these two boys who were the best surfers and surfing was their whole life, it was all they did, with their girls, who were the best girl surfers, and the beginning was about this great surfing party with a contest that these two boys won, of course, and then after, they built this huge bonfire and sat around it and barbecued these steaks with a perfect full moon shining on the water. *That's the* shittiest *trick I've ever seen in my life,* said her father.

Then when they get home they find out they've both got to go in the Army! And they both look real sad because that means no more surfing, and their girls cry. But then all their surfer friends have this big going-away party for them, even greater than the first one, all the surfers from all over the world come, and they have this super surfing contest, and these two boys are happy, but they're sad, too, because they're worrying about going in the Army, so maybe they won't win the contest. *Maybe you need your* fuckin *brains examined.* . . .

But they do win the contest, and after, around the bonfire, they get all these presents for being so great, but they're still sad, although they're happy, too, but they don't show it, and say it's the greatest thing that ever happened to them. *Being a plain* bitch *is one thing.* . . .

Then: they *do* go in the Army, and there they are in uniform a whole lot tanner than everybody else but it doesn't matter because they have to march and run and crawl around in the mud and shoot and learn to fight, all in this real fast blur. And before they go overseas they want to have just one last surfing party, but there isn't time, they have to get on this big ocean liner and go fight. *And you've always been a* bitch. . . .

Then: there they are on this boat, with all the other soldiers, getting ready to land, and they see this big enormous beautiful beach with all these big beautiful waves, and one of them asks this big mean sergeant, "Is *this* where we're going?" and he says, "That's it, soldier," and this one turns to the other one and says, "Do you see what I see?" and they're both real happy now, and the other one says, "Looks like we're going to be *the surf soldiers!" But to pull a* shitty fuckin *trick like that you got to be a super* bitch *and insane, too!* Which was the name of the movie, of course, which was why they called it that.

Having watched Pig Bird's color rising steadily throughout this performance, and her eyes take on an uncharacteristic brightness, David said, "Yeah, well, that's great, Bird." Maybe The Cap was right about feeblemindedness in the family. And here he had always thought Pig Bird was *typical.* Maybe they were both right.

"Can I have your room when you go in the Army?" she said, doubtless reminded by the end of her synopsis.

"Why don't you ask your daddy and your mommy?" David said. "It's not my room, I just sleep there."

"Well, pardon me for living," said Margie. Jody always said that.

"I try and try, but it doesn't work," said David, and left her to puzzle that one out.

Surf Soldiers. Rah rah rah. As if he needed to be reminded. David lay down on his bed with nothing to smile at. *Future* was nine days ending in the Army. *Present* was Pig Bird wanting his room, The Cap and Mrs. Clean out there swapping How-could-you's. As he did often enough to have interested any competent psychiatrist, he let his mind play back his earlier conversation with Hart. Why not? He wasn't queer. Thinking about Hart took nothing out of him, and even put something back in.

"If you don't play an instrument," said Hart, "way I see it, it's all nothing: Army, your folks, burning your draft card. . . ." Nothing pluralistic about Hart. David agreed it was all nothing.

"They don't care, you know," Hart said.

David knew.

"And you *don't* play an instrument." Dr. Hart, pointing out the end of his term to a terminal case.

That was true, too. Independent laboratory tests had proved that David's musical gifts were a minus quantity, and, numbed by the example of Hart himself, who could tell you that a chair squeak was a glissando from E to F sharp, he had never considered bucking the odds.

Hart scrubbed at his hands, stained dark brown by a day in a Standard Oil of California grease pit. "Look, I'm a spade," he said. "No, if it was me . . ." He stopped. David knew Hart hated to be on either end of advice.

"If you were 1-A," David said, "and you didn't play an instrument, what would you do?"

"Blow my brains out," Hart said, and scrubbed harder. "This Boraxo isn't worth a shit."

Far from disheartening him, this intellectual rigor cheered David obscurely, but not in the direction of suicide. He watched Hart change clothes, and pick up his horn case. "I've got a gig," Hart said. "No, not a gig, a rehearsal. Stick around if you want."

But David had already played through Hart's best LP's— Coltrane, Eric Dolphy, and then some New Thing things— and he was getting hungry. So he walked Hart two blocks to the bus stop. "Not a rehearsal, either," Hart amended as he sat down on the bench. "What it is is four other guys who don't know what they want to play. But it's a Monday."

Zero bullshit. That was Hart, the only person David had ever met like that, yet not in any superman heroic way. Heroes were by definition bullshit, and Hart tested zero on that count. And nobody could qualify as a hero anyway who looked like something that had crawled out from under a piece of sidewalk, some kind of insectile freak untouched by sun or air.

Although he didn't eat enough to keep pimples alive, a permanent bumper crop of them fought for space on his mildewed skin, which would change color alarmingly when he blew the soprano saxophone, going from an impure clay yellow to crab pink, and back again the moment he stopped. His hands changed color, too. You noticed because they were grotesquely large, as if they weighed as much as all the rest of him put together.

Then there was his right eye. Behind the thick glasses David had never seen him take off it looked twice the size of his left eye. When he played, it would pop out, huge and yellow and mad, leaving the impression that the other eye was dead, or made of glass. At twenty-one, he was losing his hair.

David remembered the time, before Hart had dropped out of high school in his senior year, when Bantam and Willie Dee, two relatively harmless spades, were giving him a going-over.

"Hart," said Bantam. "We gonna send you to the Ugly Olympics, man. You ugly as a bagful of assholes."

"Naw, man," said Willie Dee. "He a *whole* lot uglier nat. You know, Hart, your mama tellin me the other night— when she got done givin me some head, you know?—say, 'You know how Hart got born?' I say, 'Naw, but it must of been some kind of unnatural disaster.' 'Well,' she say, 'two boxcars bump together, an he dropped out of a hobo's ass!' "

Now the one thing you had to do was make some show of jiving them right back; otherwise they would get on you and right away it wouldn't be funny anymore—they would be hitting on you for dimes and quarters, and bopping you just for fun. So David had waited, with the faint sour smirk of the spectator stuck with the losing side, to see what Hart would say.

He said nothing. Stood there taking in Bantam and Willie Dee with one giant yellow eye, and said nothing. The eye had no contempt in it, no embarrassed retreat. It just glared independently, and his silence silenced them. Hart *really* didn't care, David thought then, and they must know it.

Raymond Taylor didn't know it. A big spade clown who played second-stringer linebacker and trumpet with equal indifference, he grabbed Hart's instrument in the music room one day a few weeks later, and poured a Coke down the bell. When all the Coke had run out, and nobody was laughing anymore, Raymond handed it back to Hart, who stepped in swinging at Raymond's head like a high outside pitch, and didn't miss. It cost Hart twenty-five dollars to have the kink smoothed out of the bell, but he didn't pay for Raymond's six stitches. Hart didn't care.

But he didn't make a big production out of not-caring, either. He had no affectations, saying what little he had to say in plain English unembellished by jive. David came to understand this as part of Hart's complex, troublesome, necessary dealings with spades. Bantam and Willie Dee and even Raymond Taylor had been relatively minor encounters: combat training with blank ammunition, perhaps. Raymond had only accidentally brushed the live wire when he touched Hart's horn, for otherwise Hart would simply have ignored anyone who played the trumpet so badly. (After the scene in the music room, David had said to him, "If you weighed twenty pounds more you'd have killed him." Hart said, "If

I'd hit him in the mouth instead it would've been doing
him a favor.")

Spades had always given Hart trouble. "Naturally," said
Hart. "They invented jazz. They go on inventing it. No
great white players. Not one. Spades get fucked over like
they do, it's natural. But you want to play jazz, you play
with spades. Or it's nothing." That was as much as he ever
said, and he didn't like argument any better than advice.
If Hart had a philosophy, it was: "Shut up and blow."

David's imagination withered at the thought of the ex-
quisitely, infinitely varied and shaded rejections Hart had
survived in five years of trying to play with spades. Perhaps
he had been told to pack up, sent home, frozen out, sneered
at, put down and put on so many times it didn't bother him
anymore, but David couldn't believe so, even if Hart never
complained. "It's natural," was all he would say. And if he
had successes, he never bragged.

Did Hart secretly aspire to becoming the first great white
player? You couldn't tell. He didn't expect much of the future. Jazz, he said, was already 90 percent wiped out by
electronic pop music. He would love to wire them all into
one 220-volt circuit and throw the switch, he said. No, he
didn't believe in mergers. But beneath this vengeful pessi-
mism he still gave off radiations of utter self-sufficiency and
deep private satisfaction. He had his thing and he did it,
and the everything-else he sacrificed to it seemed no sacri-
fice at all.

Sex? "There's this Mexican lady in Compton who lets me
fuck her a couple of times a month." A little later on, as if
that had been too ambiguous, he added, "She's old enough
to be my mother." Zero bullshit. Envying Hart was beside
the point, and so was being his friend. But apparently, even
if you couldn't shut up and blow, you could shut up and
listen. David liked doing that, and since Hart did no more

than merely tolerate himself, there was nothing wounding in being merely tolerated by him.

Thinking about Hart made David feel good. Nothing else did, not in the same way. Once David had thought this might be because Hart had no mother or father, but he speculated no further, because that kind of psychology made him smile.

A quiet had fallen in the front of the house. The television was on again. In default of supper, David had made himself a sandwich; now hunger overcame inertia and drove him toward the kitchen once more. Incredibly, his paper napkin and milk glass were still on the dining-room table. They had quit. He peeked into the living room. Was The Cap sleeping there?

The measured bark of the 11 o'clock news should have told him, because The Cap usually watched Joe Pyne at this hour and saved the news for breakfast, when he could get the fresh worst out of it. But David came all the way round in front of The Cap's chair before he saw the head slipped sideways, and the trap mouth hanging open.

". . . Marines carry out the bodies of their comrades killed in the fierce three-day battle," said the television. And there they were, David saw. Look at those dead Marines. He glanced more closely at The Cap, and on an associative impulse put his ear close enough to the open mouth to hear the faint whistle of breath.

"New replacements," said the television, "carry out their first patrols near the capital. . . ."

Maybe they needed replacements, The Cap and Mrs. Clean. In the old days, before the Cease-fire, they would go on half the night and then be fresh enough to start all over at breakfast. Yes, they needed replacements. Too bad David hadn't inherited any of their energy. That left nobody but Uncle Bernie.

ELEVEN

The fat girl's loyal Marxist parents had named her Pasionaria, after the belle of the Spanish Civil War, but she preferred to be called Happy.

"Sound like one of the Seven Dwarfs, baby," said Bernie, exploring her amplitude on the mattressed planks of what she called the "love room" up on the lightless third floor. "And you got to be the biggest dwarf I ever seen."

"Seven what?" said Happy.

"Dwarfs. Like Snow White and the Seven Dwarfs."

But she had never heard of them—was it a rock band? And Bernie decided against asking her what year she had been born. Who needed complications? Not him.

Not Happy, either, who lived up to her chosen name better than the one on her birth certificate throughout some twenty-five minutes of squashy grappling, punctuated by giggles, belches, farts, and squeaks of "I love you, Bennie." A good time was had by all, and, after a brief smothering nap half under her slack superabundance, Bernie's disengagement was no sign of love lost.

Dressing in pitch darkness took a while. Fortunately Bernie had plenty of time, and when he found that he'd put on Happy's fatigue jacket, he chuckled to himself, and, without considering how well-equipped she was by nature to resist far colder temperatures, spread it tenderly over where he remembered her lying.

Buttoning and jingling his way toward the glow of the staircase, Bernie almost didn't notice the feeble light in a little dormered alcove of a room next door.

Someone was drawing something on the floor in the dirty yellow wash of a flashlight. Wild! Bernie, squinting, made out a girl, thirteen or fourteen, barefoot, her flowered dress bunched high about thin, smudged thighs, kneeling tightly gathered in the fetal position, carefully lettering with a green felt pen.

He ducked into the little cell, saying, "Yeah, baby," and bent to read what she'd written:

> I WANT TO DIE
> I WANT TO DIE
> I WANT TO D

At the sight or sense of him looming above her, the girl shrank into the corner of the alcove, thin arms wrapping head against knees, still more tightly cramped into the original coil of the womb.

A bad trip, a real bummer, and she was making it worse by fighting it. Bernie had been there himself, and all his heart went out in loving support of the poor little teenie. The blurred edge of light showed him her dirty toes clenching like paws for some foothold. "Go with it, baby," he said very gently.

But you had to die to all your corpses before the real you could flower. That was how *transformation* really worked.

No one could do it for you, and the younger you were the better. The girl emitted a grinding whine like a jammed machine, and Bernie whispered, "Come on, honey, come on an die." Because *he who loses his life shall find it*—oh yes he believed that.

Withdrawing softly, he kicked something out into the hall, and picked it up. A transistor radio. It gave no noise when he thumbed the knurled switch, and with a last silent blessing he left it inside the alcove where she would find it later.

Then he went on downstairs, stooping on the second-story landing to lace up his boots, looking in his rumpled red coat like some aging young wastrel lord returning to the dicing tables after a random bout with some lusty young serving wench. Truly he felt that way: merrily tousled, soft in the bones, and radiant with an aimless comprehensive bonhomie.

In his absence the crowd had overflowed the front room and dining room into an extra parlor which now housed a dusty collection of Marco's sculpture in clay and papier-mâché. The scheduled showing of films, announced by word of mouth and hand-lettered posters in three bookstores and four coffeehouses, was responsible for the turnout.

Richard's two newest works, *Strobefuck* and *Leather Pleasure*, were to have been shown, as well as a rerun, by popular demand, of his first success, *At the Steam Bath*, which was felt locally to have far outstripped Genêt's *Chant d'Amour*. News of the disabled projector caused keen disappointment.

But such were the loyalty and fellow feeling among the assembled votaries that they not only took the postponement as a normal impediment to art and thus an endearing testimony to its authenticity, but went on lovingly to rejoice in Richard's successively embellished accounts of his after-noon's adventures. All hands agreed that Richard was a fig-ure to conjure with in the world of true cinema.

If anyone was seriously discomfited by the NO MOVIE TO-NITE sign on the mobile, it was a darkly burning youth named Mitchell, who arrived with a film can containing his own complete cinematic works: *Killjoy*, a twenty-minute se-quence of a couple in Greek tragic masks writhing in slow-motion copulation on an American flag, this whole set piece intercut with stock footage of World War II infantry bat-tles, naval cannon, and mushroom clouds, as well as cru-cially placed stills of Auschwitz, Lyndon B. Johnson, bleed-ing Negroes, Richard M. Nixon, Sheriff Rainey and Deputy Price of Neshoba County, and an emaciated Biafran child. But even Mitchell did not walk out, so irresistible was the atmosphere of unself-consciously free-swinging polymor-phous camaraderie.

Irresistible certainly to Bernie descending, his own inex-haustible love batteries recharged by what he already re-membered as a liaison as sweet and free as it had been brief and spontaneous. What a beautiful scene it was! His people! Surely identifiable by their wild, imaginative motley un-kemptness, and the emanations of ecstasy they gave off in a perfume of marijuana smoke, flowers, and beautiful natural good-time sweat.

Next to the mobile, Richard was enchanting a cluster of nodding appreciators. ". . . And, baby, I thought, *Why* didn't I bring my camera, because there he was leaving this *trail of blood,* I mean, like *Kurosawa!*"

Bernie was not about to interrupt him. Something soft under one boot made him look down. A piece of mattress? A hand or a foot? No, a fat little animal, with a curly tail. A dog, its smooth hairless body painted red and black and yellow in a design of interlocking scrolls and plumes. Bernie dropped to one knee to look closer. Wild! What a beautiful thing! The design went all the way around the body, covering belly and haunches. "Hey there, baby," said Bernie. "How's every thing?" The dog didn't look up. But when he began scratching a yellow spot on top of its head, between the red-pointed ears, its sleepy eyes opened round, two luminous soft brown eyes, ecstatically unfocused. The dog was stoned.

"Pure vegetable dye," said a voice from a couple of yards away, and past four or six legs Bernie saw stretched on a mattress someone with long black hair around a face and bare upper body painted to match the dog. Not a girl. "Everything I am is in her, and she's in me, too. It's *extensions*. . . ."

"Too much!" said Bernie. "What's her name?"

"Whatever you call her. I don't tell anybody her real name. Or she'll die. It's *tribal*."

Bernie nodded. They were really into some weird deep shit, these two.

"Everyone can have all they want," said the dog's partner. "Names. All you make up is you."

"Yeah," said Bernie. "Yeah." It had the mad wild ring of truth. Why *should* anybody be hung up with just one name? He traced out one yellow scroll-and-plume along the dog's flank, thoughtfully, and stood up.

"Two things wrong with your film," Richard was telling Mitchell. "One is, it's too *subtle*. The other is, *you left out Che Guevara's corpse!*"

"No, man. No, man," asserted a bushy third party. "Film is just a stage, because everybody *is* a film, twenty-four hours a day, man, if you're conscious enough to dig it *inside and out!*"

Bernie, thinking of names, drifted past all this. Thing was: your name ought to express the real you, but any name you might take was somebody else's, unless you dreamed up something fantastic like Thelonious or Bo Diddly or what did Happy say her real name was? Look how many Johns and Roberts and Williams and Richards there were. And Charleys, and plenty of Bernards, too, though not many Bern*hards*.

"Why shouldn't an American guru give you a mantra in English?" said a girl in a pink brocade jump suit. "I mean, it's ethnocentric. . . ."

"Forget that shit and listen." Her companion hid bony hands in the sleeves of his hooded loden jacket and closed his eyes. *"Hare om namo Sivaye Hare om namo Sivaye,"* he crooned. *"Hare om namo Sivaye . . ."*

Indian names! Something else! Ramakrishna and Krishnamurti and what did they call the Downtown Swami in New York? *Bhaktivedanta!* And Bernie remembered two with special fondness, from a jar of mango chutney in the kitchen of the London curry place where he'd slept three nights, eating cold rice and dal for breakfast: Vencatachellum and Manockjee Poonjiajee! Oh yes.

"Hey, where's De Vaughn?" said a blonde in blue plastic. De Vaughn? *That* name rang a bell. Little De Vaughn the trumpet player? It had been twenty years. Another blonde, maybe the first one's twin, waved at the door of the sculpture room, which happened to be where Bernie was headed. There on two long tables—one-inch planks trestled on sawhorses—stood a collection of vaguely mythic, unmistakably Negroid heads, twice life-size, as if the same rude archetype had sat for them all. They seemed variously to express subjugation, despair, saintly composure, puzzlement, contained anger, and perhaps some nameless but unquenchable spirit. They all looked a lot alike. The only noncranial piece in sight was a disembodied papier-mâché fist, clenched in some semblance of a Marxist salute. It stood alone and apart on its own base, as if unsure of which head it belonged to.

But the action was elsewhere, around the far end of one table, where half a dozen people watched a chess game between Julius, the crack-smiled kid with orange hair, and a trim, freckled coppery little Negro with wide athlete's shoulders in a faded Malcolm X sweatshirt. The same De Vaughn! He was talking up at the kibitzers, fast and bright-eyed, in a hard jivey hustler's patter. Bernie remembered the voice, too.

"Yeah, the universe is expanding, baby. Law of nature. Everything getting further an further apart from everything else, stretch your mind around that. Exploding energy, everything takin up more space all the time *just bein itself*. Constellations and galaxies, stars and people all the same. No marriagedivorce out in space, no, you got spiral nebulae! And you standin there talkin about *politics!* Mean about as much as who wins the National League!"

"De Vaughn," said Julius, without taking his head out of his hands. "De Vaughn, you gonna move, man?" Bernie, edging closer, saw De Vaughn glance at the board and move a castle. "Check," he said. "An don't move your bishop there or it's mate in two. Listen here: what's a man? Male energy. What's a woman? Female energy. That's basic. Now that energy wants to expand. Yeah. Yeah. But what's in the way? Marriagedivorce. Nonstop brainwash from the cradle to the grave. Left over from the caveman. *Vestigial,* you call it. Man, we ain't got no monkey tails no more, but we got marriagedivorce."

"Say, De Vaughn," said Bernie. "How you doin, baby?"

De Vaughn measured him in a glance, said, "Doin fine," and went on with his spiel: "What the whole country's based on, man. The whole economy an the so-called culture. Cap-

italism, socialism, any ism you got, that's just the tail of the
dog. Marriage! Home! Family! Motherhood an monogamy!
Read the books, read the ads, open your eyes an look around
you! Marriage *is* divorce. Marriagedivorce. That's why I got
my Freedom School." He moved a knight and said, "Check."

Well, twenty years was a long time, and Bernie knew he
must look different, even if De Vaughn looked the same, except for the new muscles. He must have got off junk somehow, and concentrated on girls, which used to be his num-
ber-two habit back in those days, when his number one
allowed it. "Say, De Vaughn," he said. "You remember Ca-
margo's, man? You remember the Fall Inn?"

"What you want to go draggin up the past for?" said De
Vaughn cheerily. "I been off probation for *years*, man." Bernie swept off hat and glasses, and thrust his face forward for
inspection. "*Bernie,*" he said. "I used to, you know, *sing* and
hang around, remember?"

Then De Vaughn began laughing, at what he remembered, or what he saw, or both. "Bernie . . . aw, man, *Bernie?* Are you Bernie? Cut it out. . . ." When his laughter
let him, he told Orange Julius: "Listen, *this* cat used to
come on like he was the white Babs Gonzales, know who
that was? Actually he sounded more like a kinda bebop Car-
men Lombardo. Bernie? They *after* you or something? Man,
I thought you was General Cornwallis or somebody like
that. . . ."

"Yeah, man," said Bernie. "Well, *you* lookin good. You
still blow?"

"Aw, man, I never could play the damn trumpet—you had
ears you'd known that back then. Want to go again, Julius?
Set em up. I'm black again, ha ha ha."

"Yeah, well, I didn't make it, either," said Bernie.

"You tellin me," said De Vaughn. He laughed, coughed,
and in a quavering falsetto began to sing: "Oobleeah dlee-

oodleeoobah blee-*bleeee* bleeoobleeoobop—should have heard this cat Bernie wail back in the forties, man."

"So what you doin now, baby?" asked Bernie. Whatever it was, it agreed with him.

"Playin chess, man. Fact is, I'm beatin old Julius' brains out right this minute."

"So how big a faculty you got now, De Vaughn?" said the pale-eyed cowboy with the yellow moustache.

De Vaughn came up off his packing crate fast, flexing his grin, his right hand flying automatically up to guard his chin while his left hooked the questioner harmlessly in the ribs. "Float like a butterfly, sting like a bee, *with both hands*," he said. "What you *mean* is: 'How many girls you got turning tricks for you, De Vaughn?' Right? But you dead wrong, baby. My Freedom School is strictly nonprofit." He sat down again, shaking his head.

"Cat thinks I'm a damn pimp, you know? Thinks he got the revolution down *cold*, in his damn little red book. Ha! Tell you something, Mitchell—*get your hands out of your pockets*, just leave it alone, it'll grow—it's the age of revolution, all right, but everybody makes his own. *Each according to his ability*—ha! didn't think I knew that, did you?"

"De Vaughn," said Mitchell, "you are a romantic autodidact, you know that?"

"There he goes callin me names just because I don't love Chairman Mao, ain't that something? Naw, man, I say *fuck* Chairman Mao, an all them damn tractor heads. I wouldn't have Chairman Mao in my school, man. One reason, he's too old. Second reason, he's a fool."

"Aw, just a minute ago you were callin it a Fool School," said Mitchell. "How do you—"

"Some of these kids, like, you know, Rudi the Red, an Danny the Rouge, maybe they into something, talk about the revolution of the *orgasm*—I hate that word, man, *or-*

gasm, sound like some kind of disease, why don't they just say *come?* But anyway, what I mean is some of those kids are *thereabouts,* know what I mean? But they try that shit in China they'd be dead. In two minutes, man, and why? Tell you why: because they know free fuckin means anarchy, man, an you know they ain't havin none of that! Old Mao's a fool, but he's not that big a fool. He know you can't keep all them ants in the hive puddlin steel an makin machine tools an all that shit if they out fuckin everybody else's old lady!

"But why I wouldn't have him in my school is he's a *half* fool an they the worst kind. Naw, you give me a complete fool, hundred-percent fool, white Catholic or Protestant fool, don't matter which. You give me a tract-house tax-payin registered-votin installment-buyin TV-watchin fool with high blood pressure an a ulcer an a old lady like a skeleton in Saran Wrap: *that's* the kind of fool I want in my Freedom School! I can *work* with that fool, man!"

"Wow, you really blowin, baby!" said Bernie. Talk about transformations! De Vaughn had become something else! Describing poor old Charley and Anti Ann just now like he had a pure vision. "Don't quit now," he said.

"Thing is, guy like you, Mitchell, you got no feelin for the middle class. An in this country that's where it's at. You concentrate on all them complete fools in the middle, man. Unlock *that* energy, an the pieces gonna be comin down for fifty years!" De Vaughn swept a white bishop off the board. "Come on, Julius," he said. "Lemme see you smile, baby."

TWELVE

David dreamed of a vaporous gray jungle, one encircling monochromatic silhouette of fronds and vines and overhanging trees, where he stood guard in a hollow tree trunk sheared off at eye level so that just the unhelmeted crown of his head stuck out. He was armed with Hart's soprano saxophone, which he could neither shoot nor play, and from off in the gray undergrowth he could hear invisible presences coming closer.

He knew he should stay alert, but had to keep fighting off sleep. Hart was due to relieve him, and give David back his rifle in exchange for the saxophone, but somehow David knew he was not coming. Awkwardly he tried to dig between his bare feet with the mouthpiece end of the saxophone, to make a little more space in which to hide himself, but his hands were boneless and without strength, and he was afraid he would ruin the horn, so he did the best thing left: aimed it like a blunderbuss out at the oncoming presences, much closer now. But he knew it wouldn't fool them. . . .

Margie dreamed she was flying low over Westpark, but losing altitude because her head was so heavy from all the metal in her mouth, and when she flew over the playground at General Patton Junior High School, all the kids looked up and pointed, calling, "There's Margie! Hi, Margie!" but she couldn't answer because her jaws were sealed shut with wire and solder and she couldn't even get her lips all the way closed to hide it, and some boys threw apple cores and rocks up at her and one hit her right on the mouth and made it bleed. But she flew away from there, only to feel herself sinking right toward the Medico-Dental Building, where her mother and Dr. Lasky were waiting for her, calling, "Come down, Margie," and she didn't want to because when she did Dr. Lasky was going to put more metal in her mouth. But flying had made her wings tired, and her head felt heavier and heavier, big as a watermelon pulling her down. "Come down, Margie," they called, and she did. . . .

Ann lay frozen in a sheet of glass between sleep and waking. Thoughts came to her there, but they had no weight or substance. She had thought: *I'm forty-three now.* It seemed meaningless. She had thought: *I'm having a nervous breakdown.* It neither frightened nor comforted her.

Above, consciousness waited, full of one certainty: she couldn't go on, she was done, through, finished. Below lay an unattainable sleep she neither feared nor craved. Pressed between the two in her brittle glass sheet, she felt no pressure. If she didn't move, she wouldn't break.

But it had taken her several hours to achieve this numb equipoise. She had fought Rasmussen without reserves, hiding that exhaustion from him, finally breaking off a phrase unfinished because she couldn't remember what she had been saying, and, when she groped for it, felt as if a plug had been silently pulled, cutting off the current that drove thoughts into words. She had walked into the master bedroom, closed the door, and lain down on her bed without undressing or even brushing her teeth.

He hadn't followed her. Maybe he thought he had won. Let him think so; she hadn't the insides left to care. Or maybe he was running short of power, too; Ann had no pity to spare: the sense of being used up pressed down too heavily on her emptiness.

And not just that, but the sense that it all added up to zero, as if she had spent forty years' savings at the supermarket and come home to find the soup cans full of rusty water, the cereal boxes full of sand, nothing but ice in the frozen-food packages. Not even zero, but minus, because the careful shopping and carrying-home had left her without the strength to complain; forty years' worth of worthlessness surrounded her, a positive liability. It was she herself who felt transparent and zero-empty, no longer imaginary but not worth imagining, like an eviscerated plastic bag.

But sleep would not come, and some diehard reflex set her mind to search for some redeemable memory out of all that vast bad debt of frustration and failure and disgust. She hadn't had much practice at it.

Memory entered her: a night when they had gone, innocently, to a party in someone's garage only a few blocks away. What was their name? They had divorced and moved away. Harris. Roy and Ethel Harris.

"That's it back there." A man sitting in a bed of zinnias pointed down the dark driveway. People stood around in the dark, drinking out of paper cups. No one they knew, though Ace Liquors must have provided some of what they drank. "Right this way," said a man with a bottle. By the garage door, slid open a foot or two, they hesitated, looking for a light inside, then somebody grabbed Ann's arm and pulled her into the dark stuffy car-smelling place, where the floor was soft and she stumbled and fell, a man's voice said,

"Hi, neighbor," and flopped on top of her pushing his stinking whiskey mouth all over her face, sticking his hand between her legs and she screamed "Charley!" twisting away and hearing a radio in the dark playing slow dance music before Charley came in cursing and fell right next to her and was fighting everybody in the dark, punching a woman who called him a son of a bitch until a dirty light bulb went on in a bird cage and Ann stood up seeing Charley and another man wrestling and cursing on their knees, mattresses all over the floor, a woman with nothing on but a floppy brassiere trying to sit up and pull up her panties at the same time, and still staring back at the woman Ann broke out through the door and half a minute later Charley came flying out and the last thing they heard walking away fast was a man saying, "Who invited *them*, for Christ's sake?" and the man looked up from the zinnia bed and said, "That was a quickie, who are you, Peter Rabbit?" and Charley kicked at him, missed, and almost fell down himself.

But walking home, while Charley cursed and said he was going to call the cops the minute they got back, Ann had been on fire from it all: that woman naked with people all around, doing it to each other blind in the dark worse than pigs, and Charley rushing in crazy to save her, no place for her excitement to go but toward him, and more than ever before in her life Ann wanted him to do it to her the second they got home, hard and raw and furious in the dark.

He didn't call the cops, saying as they went in the front door that it was probably better not to get involved, they'd all wind up in jail, bad for business, too. "But that's the last party we ever go to around here," he swore.

Ann hardly heard him, seeing the baby-sitter she had forgotten about, realizing that Charley must drive her home. He would come right back, he said. It would just take a minute. "Hurry," she whispered in his ear, and waited for him, keeping her fever up by replaying what she had seen in Harris' garage.

But when he got back, after what seemed half an hour at least, the whiskey he had drunk to nerve himself for the party caught up with him, helped along by the shots she heard him pouring, and he climbed into his own bed saying he felt "all shot."

"Charley for God's sake!" she hissed. "Come over here, I'm dying! Please!" He had obeyed, groaning, and afterward, as she lay feeling even more cheated than usual, Ann had thought: That's all you get out of it. The bigger the buildup, the bigger the letdown.

She might have felt even worse had she known that Rasmussen had only been able to perform at all by thinking back to Harris' garage himself. He had seen that woman pulling up her panties, too. What's more, *that* wasn't all she got out of it. She got Margie.

Well, wasn't there, good God, something to remember with the children? The vacation she'd insisted they take, when Margie was five and David twelve, even without Rasmussen. Especially without Rasmussen: who was the vacation from if not him?

And it had been beautiful there by the lake, with all the pine trees, and no smog, so you could actually see the stars. The first night she sat out on the porch of their little cabin wrapped in an Indian blanket until very late, feeling the kinks in her mind relax, and repeating a litany of promise: *We* will *do this every year*. If Rasmussen swore they couldn't afford it, *hooray!* Next year she would find someplace twice as expensive; next year they would stay two weeks, a whole month: *that* would keep him "slaving away," as he called it, at Ace Liquors, although she knew he never did a lick of real work there. She went to bed at two-thirty and slept the sleep of the just.

But what had happened? Margie woke up covered with mosquito bites, and caught cold. David almost drowned in the lake, and the man who pulled him out, a fat red pig who smoked cigars, hung around the cabin as if he expected God knows what from Ann as a reward. Then after lying there on his cot reading comic books for two solid days, David found the strength to walk up to the hotel, where he was promptly picked up by a man who showed him dirty pictures, took him for a walk in the pines, and tried to play with him.

Ann didn't even get the satisfaction of seeing the man taken away and locked up, because by the time the Sheriff's Office had sent up that hick in the jeep, who actually wore a tin star, the man had fled, although they found more dirty pictures in his room, and enough candy wrappers to constitute a fire hazard.

After that they stayed in the cabin, David reading his comic books, Ann reading old Time magazines, Margie scratching and coughing and crying. She wouldn't let either of them out of her sight, and luckily did not suspect that as David sat staring at Wonder Woman he was yearning for bedtime so that he could practice the trick the man had shown him out in the woods. (If the man hadn't tried to do it for him, David would never have squealed.) Ann was, in fact, preoccupied with her own secret, a severe case of diarrhea. They didn't come back the next summer.

So the search had been in vain for a memory of profit amid all that dead loss. But at least it had stabilized her within the negative perfection of glassy equilibrium where now she lay. Feeling nothing, expending no energy at all, she could lie here forever, in a kind of immortality. If she didn't move, she wouldn't break.

In his chair facing the television set, Rasmussen moved, and felt as if he'd already been broken; after long resistance broken and then badly set, his skull, spine, ribs, and right arm fused into a single aching bone warped sideways. . . .

"Hey, Abbott!" yelled the television set.

Rasmussen was only sufficiently awake to know where he was, that he must not move again, and that if he didn't have to pee he could get back to sleep.

He had to.

But not too badly.

"*Hey, Abbaa-aatt!*" bawled the television, waking Rasmussen by just the one degree necessary to recognize Lou Costello as a 1942 buck private. Along a well-worn brain track, he free-associated instantaneously to how she had trapped him, that bitch from hell, with that lie about being knocked up. But instead of anger he seemed only capable of feeling the pain of his broken body, stiff in the chair.

Well, then, he would pee. But in the back toilet. One more word from her and . . . Remembering the roses now, Rasmussen felt he would not be responsible for what he might do. Not that he could hurt her much, the shape he was in. If he raised his right arm it would break off like a dead branch. Just getting up out of the chair was going to be tough enough. . . .

"Costello," said Abbott. "You're a first-class idiot."

Jesus Christ. Abbott and Costello. Nineteen forty-three. Breedlove, Georgia. That son of a bitch of a JP called it "the chapel," and it was nothing but his front parlor, with those lace things on the chairs. And then wanted the money *in an envelope!* Oldham came running out and said, "You got a envelope, Charley? I tried to give him the money and he backed off like it was a forty-five. Says it's got to be in a envelope."

Rasmussen hadn't known fate was giving him one last chance to get out of it by not paying. That would have canceled it for sure; the JP would have torn up the certificate

—that Genuine Imitation Parchment was just ordinary paper. But no, he got an envelope, all right. JP's wife had one right there ready for him. *That's ten cents, please.* He should have stuck the envelope and the dime right up her ass and walked out. How many times he'd thought that!

Antimacassars, they called them.

A top sergeant with a face like a mad bull roared at Costello, who pulled his fatigue hat down over his ears and cried like a baby for Abbott. Rasmussen never *had* thought they were funny.

All right, then, he would pee. Turn off the TV, go pee, come back, and stretch out on the couch. But first he had to get out of the chair. Better have a smoke. Mouth tasted like the Chinese Army just marched through it. All he had to do was fish a Camel out of his left shirt pocket.

When he tried, awkwardly, with his left hand, Costello screamed bloody murder, as if he were the one who was hurting, and Rasmussen heard a car stop in front, sounded like a VW. His untrained left-hand fingers fumbled the Camels out of his pocket and spilled them into his lap.

That would be a first, all right. Bernie actually keeping a promise. But if it was Bernie he wasn't alone. Rasmussen froze, listening to the voices come across the lawn. VW or no VW, he resolved not to answer the door. The chimes gonged, he held his breath. "FALL IN!" bellowed the mad bull sergeant, and Costello fell into a mud puddle. They were bound to hear the TV. But maybe not. The chimes again, and flat-handed pounding on the door. But outside, the conversation stopped; Rasmussen, sitting tight, felt a pang of hope; the door opened, and somebody walked in.

Rasmussen leaned his whole upper body forward in one piece, peered stiffly around the edge of the chair back, and saw Bernie. And somebody wearing a steel German Army helmet, and somebody else, who looked like a professional halfback with shoulder pads under his jersey . . .

And more people: girls: a couple of blondes like twins in shiny jackets, and that big fat cow in fatigues . . .

"Charley," said Bernie. "Hi, baby. I see you there peepin an hidin. You'll ruin your eyes watchin that shit." His right hand came up as if to demand attention, or make a benediction, or halt the troops behind him. "Charley, quit blinkin that way. This is a love invasion, man."

But the troops kept coming: one of the black hairy twins; the tintype cowboy with the yellow moustache; another girl, straggly hair to the waist. How many more were there?

Rasmussen didn't want to know. He sagged back in his chair. Bernie was flying high on something or other, he could tell. All of them were, probably. Now was the time to clear them out, but he felt as hopelessly outnumbered as Costello there. He shut his eyes. "Jesus H. Christ," he said, and groped in his lap for a Camel.

But Bernie was on top of him, yanking off his Dodgers cap, kissing the top of his head, saying, "Aw, quit playin with yourself, baby, get yourself together. This is good news, open your eyes!"

No, by Christ. Let them do whatever they wanted, as long as they left him out of it. If he could just make it to the back toilet . . .

"Wake the living dead," came Bernie's voice, and Rasmussen was crushed breathless beneath a falling mass of flesh, soft and giggling, as the loudspeakers convulsed with distorted thunder and the floor seemed to buck under his chair. Blind, suffocating, Rasmussen twisted his face free from whatever part of her comprehensive softness the fat girl had pressed upon it, and gasped, "Get offa me, for Christ's sake," but couldn't hear himself in the sound of a nigger as big as God singing "I'M A HOOCHIE COOCHIE MAN."

He sucked in as much air as he could and fought back: "PEOPLE ARE SLEEPIN AROUND HERE!"

Bernie shrunk the singer's volume down to mountain size, and said, *That's just the trouble, baby.*

Trapped in his lap by the avalanche, Rasmussen's hand squeezed feebly whatever it was full of. "Eeee," said the fat girl. "Do that some more." She began slowly to grind him into the chair.

"Do what you—DO WHAT YOU WANT!" cried Rasmussen. "BUT GET OFFA ME!"

"Yeah, man," came the voice of a stranger—was it the pro halfback? "You don't want to be puttin the man clear out of action." And with a last grinding shove, the fat girl pushed away clear, and turned to offer first aid, a grimy handful of newspaper. "Have a piece of fudge," she said. Rasmussen only sighed. He'd had it.

So had Ann, of course. Bernie and some more people had come: she registered that much in her glassy immobility. It even seemed natural. The noise didn't touch her. Nothing in her moved but the thought: If anyone comes through that door I'll shoot him. That seemed natural, too. And she knew right where the gun was.

THIRTEEN

Assured his bladder had not burst, Rasmussen made the su-
preme effort, stood up, and set out for the dining-room
door, regarding the invaders sidelong. "Just make yourself
at home," he said. Were they all observing him too closely
to notice his irony? Only the one in the German helmet
brought together the heels of his Faust boots and gave
the short-arm Hitler salute. *"Jawohl, mein Kapitän!"* In the
shadow of the square steel pot, Rasmussen recognized the
twisty little Jew by his split-melon grin. He must think that
was funny.

Perhaps it was the helmet that brought back a morning in
Italy, Rasmussen trudging along a baked mud road printed
deeply with the treads of heavy tanks, and seeing in the
ditch to his right the upper half of a German soldier in
dusty green. *Kraut forgot his pants,* said the man beside
him, and Rasmussen vomited all over his boots. Since that
day, he hadn't thrown up once that he could remember, but
he felt like one of the walking wounded as he hiked along
the spotless hall to the rear bathroom.

In that sanctuary he tried to take stock. Maybe there weren't any choices. Christ, it was five minutes past four! Well, they wouldn't leave. Call the cops? The reason not to slipped his mind at the moment. Didn't they get tired like ordinary people? Maybe the night was their day. The stolen motorcycle, that was why he couldn't call the cops. The main thing was that they didn't wreck the place. If he just went along, then, offered them coffee or a drink, mightn't they just melt away at sunup like night spooks? He flushed, and the decisive crash of seven gallons of water falling seemed to affirm this hope. What else was there?

"Hey, Dad!" Surprisingly, Rasmussen had enough reflexes left to jump at David's voice in the hall. "What's happening?" There in those damn-fool Jockey shorts he wore instead of real underpants.

"Get your clothes on an see for yourself," said Rasmussen, unwilling to ask outright for reinforcements. "Couple of good-lookin blondes out there."

"They get your cap?" said David.

Rasmussen ignored the little smart-ass and made his way to the kitchen, where he fueled up with four fingers of Yellowstone in a water glass. The emergency called for it. Then, glass in hand, as debonairly as he could with a bare head, he reentered the living room, and saw Bernie at the door of the master bedroom: *"Hey Annie can ya come out an play?"*

"Wouldn't do that if I were you," said Rasmussen into the boom of the speakers. He picked up his cap from the floor next to his TV chair, and authoritatively lowered the volume to a hoarse whisper. "Besides, it's her birthday," he said. Christ, if all this racket didn't bring her out fighting, she really *was* sick. "My wife," he explained to the room at large, and fit the Dodgers cap back in place.

"How old is she?" said one of the blonde twins from the floor. *Where the hell was her skirt?*

"Forty-three," Rasmussen said softly. "I think. You know how women get about their age."

"Oh wow," said the fat girl. "Have some fudge."

"Happy birthday, baby," sang Bernie.

"I warned you," said Rasmussen. It looked as if most of them weren't used to normal people's furniture. The other blonde twin and the guy with the football shoulders, a freckle-faced nigger, were sprawled at opposite ends of the couch, but all the others were on the floor, hugging their knees, like a bunch of raggedy-ass birds. But they looked fewer, sitting down there.

"Anybody like a drink?" said Rasmussen. Counting Bernie there were nine of them. Ought to go challenge the Dodgers. Probably beat them. "Cup of coffee? Beer?" And what the hell: "Got whiskey if you want it."

Little smirkings and headshakings rippled among them. The cowboy with the yellow moustache said, "No, thanks, we don't most of us drink," and the rest seemed to approve, as if he had skillfully represented their group interests in the first stage of some difficult negotiation. Hell, they were mostly just kids, Rasmussen saw, his belly warming. He turned the TV chair more sociably into the room and sat down.

"Sweetmeat I'm comin in to get you," said Bernie.

"Nice place you got here, brother," said the nigger with the shoulders. "Everything a man could want."

"Yeah, we like it," said Rasmussen, and the blonde on the couch caught him looking up her skirt, what there was of it. Jesus, she didn't even seem to care! He tilted his glass and peeked sideways at the blonde on the floor. Christ, she seemed to be aiming it right at him, too, and staring back

cool as a cucumber! One-eyed beavers zeroing in on him
every way he looked! Maybe they were whores. Did girls
still wear pants? You couldn't prove it by Rasmussen. Almost spry now, he went for another drink and got back too
late to stop Bernie: *"Here I come ready or not!"*

"Old Bernie there really loves a party, don't he?" said the
nigger. "He really is a *mess,* man!"

Before Rasmussen had time to agree, Bernie was back,
the broken red feather on his hat turning like a weather-
cock. "She is *stoned,* baby," he said. "Or dead, either one.
Lyin there with her eyes open like *in the morgue,* man."

"Shut the door, Bern," said Rasmussen, a little disappointed that nothing had happened. But if Ann really was
out cold, it helped his chances of getting rid of them inside
an hour or two with no damage done. Then he would lie
down on that couch and sleep, sleep, sleep. Meanwhile he
took a full five-second look down the barrel of the blonde
there. It took that long to be sure she had camouflaged her
weapon in shadow. She watched him, and smiled! *Must* be
a whore. A good thing Ann was crapped out in there . . .

Unmoved, unbroken, she lay as Bernie had found her,
looking up out of the glass sheet at nothing. She hadn't got
the gun when Bernie walked in. No *because:* she just hadn't.
The noise in the living room didn't matter. His walking in
didn't matter. If she shot him or not, it didn't matter. He
wasn't the one.

Once in a cold wind her Brother John had told her, "Turn
sideways; you're so skinny the wind'll go right past you."
Now it was as if the huge animal sound of the music from
the living room went right past her. She registered it untouched, and with it Rasmussen's shout: *"I said, pleased to
meet you!"*

Considering the company, Rasmussen meant it, as he
matched grips—and lost—with the big-shouldered nigger.

Who now said, "*Damn,* Bernie, you tryin to blow every-body's mind or what?" Expressing Rasmussen's feelings exactly, and—what do you know?—getting results. Black, white, or purple, Rasmussen wanted all the help he could get. At least this guy looked clear-eyed, close-cropped, and clean-shaven; athletic in his sweatshirt: even if he hadn't been a nigger, all that would have singled him out from the rest of these freaks. Rasmussen always trusted a man who looked athletic, even if he hadn't caught his name just now when Bernie started fiddling with the volume control.

Only when he made out what the letters said across the faded sweatshirt did he have second thoughts. Jesus! And he'd thought they said UCLA or STATE, or, for a stupid second, MALCOLM U, one of these small colleges but still a lot of pros came out of them. . . .

"Take it easy, brother," said the nigger. "This belonged to my little brother, used to be kind of a fan of old Malcolm, you know? Me, I'm the last of the integrationists. Might even say I'm in the integration *business.*"

But Rasmussen was already back in his TV chair, think-ing of Green Berets and of what a God damn sucker he'd already been once today. Yesterday. What was Bernie doing down on the floor?

"More important integratin to be done nowadays than just *race,*" said the nigger. " 'Bring together into a whole,' that's what integration *means.* 'Into a whole,' see? Main thing is to integrate people one by one, what I say."

Watching that silly bastard do push-ups, Rasmussen lis-tened in spite of himself. The *one by one* part sounded OK. Individual initiative: everything he had he owed to it. The country was based on it. When they started *organizing* was when you had to crack down hard, like the Black Pan-thers, for example. . . .

"That means plain ordinary guys like you an me," the nigger was saying. "Not just all these *minorities* you always readin about in the paper. Why, seems to me like nowadays the ordinary everyday people almost a minority themself, an who's lookin out for *their* rights?"

By God, Rasmussen had thought the exact same thing a thousand times himself, but this football player here had really said it. "I wouldn't mind knowin the answer to that one myself," he nodded. "What are you drinkin?"

"Thanks, never touch it."

You might have expected it from an athlete. Normally Rasmussen didn't trust people who didn't drink, but this guy was an exception, and when he made a sit-down gesture at the vacancy on the couch, between himself and the blonde, Rasmussen accepted gratefully. This way, at least, he wouldn't be looking down either blonde's barrel. But the one on the floor shifted, keeping him in her sights, the tricky bitch, and when he glanced down she had the drop on him: *out of the shadow, by God!* If those were her pants they winked and sparkled like gold. He went on nodding.

From the dining-room doorway, David watched the blue bill of the Dodgers cap going up and down like a bird pecking grain, as its occupant—glass in hand; must be loaded—agreed with a muscular little spade in a Malcolm X shirt. There were the two good-looking blondes, too, and Uncle Wolf Man doing push-ups, softly cheered on by a sprawl of unemployed demonstrator types, to the accompaniment of Otis Redding wanting Satisfaction. David, in jeans and a clean shirt, kept his smile crimped under control as he took in this fantastic tableau.

Was The Cap pretending he wasn't aware of the blonde beside him? Maybe, maybe not. The Cap's sex life, if any, had always been a riddle. The blonde was out of David's class, that was for sure; she proved it by dismissing him with a glance and one swivel of her head. Malcolm X saw it and looked his way, and The Cap said, "That's my boy David," and sneaked a peek at the blonde.

"You're cheating, man," said somebody on the floor, and Wolf Man was, of course: pushing up from his knees instead of his toes. Now old dead Otis *really* wanted Satisfaction. David speculated on the shape of an orgy among the assembled parties, and his smile got away from him.

Wolf Man, slowing down on his push-ups and probably looking for an out, saw him sideways and croaked, "Hey, baby, just in time . . ." Sure, thought David, but for what? He sat down in The Cap's TV chair and heard Malcolm X say, in what had to be a put-on voice: "But what does freedom *mean,* say, to a guy like you, already got everything a man could want?" And look at The Cap soak it up!

From beyond the collapsed shape of Wolf Man, a hideous balloon in Army clothes was offering him fudge (fudge?) and David was smiling no when he noticed Pig Bird, in her ice-cream-pink party dress, peeking in from the dining room. Within the same ten seconds, he waved bye-bye at her, Wolf Man yelled, "Hey Margie commere!" and The Cap ordered her back to her room. She disappeared.

"Thing is," said Malcolm X, "there's lots of ordinary guys *seem* like they're free, but they *feel* like they're all locked up inside themself, know what I mean?" The Cap almost nodded his cap off: yessirree, he knew what Malcolm meant, and brushed off Wolf Man's panting charge of being a *love hater* and a *child killer* by saying, "Aw shut up, Bern."

Wolf Man scrambled to his feet, "SHAZAM!" and went after Pig Bird.

She had retreated to her room, where Bernie found her at the mirror, reexamining her hurriedly and experimentally windblown hair. At the sight of her disheveled head escaping like a large bird from the cage of her chest, Bernie's heart spilled over. Look at that dress, sleeveless and low-necked, hinting at her little childy titties! Did she want love? Written all over her! "Hey, baby," he said. "You look *beautiful,* man! Better watch out somebody don't gobble you up!"

Being gobbled up was one of Margie's most persistent horror fantasies, and if she was sure of anything in the world it was that she was not, now, beautiful. But when Uncle Bernie smiled—and right away, that was important—when he took off his blue glasses and looked at her, just as if there were nothing the matter with her, she set this certainty aside, without of course, risking even a flirtation with its opposite. And since there was nobody else around but Uncle Bernie, who was crazy, she chanced a smile, though not big enough to show metal.

Before she could back away, he grabbed her in this big hug and kissed her hard, right on the mouth, so hard her orthodontics cut into her lips and she hardly noticed how wet and tickly it was with all that hair. Her eyes rolled up, she saw his black hatbrim, heard him jingling, and just when she wondered when he was going to let go of her he did, and stepped back, leaving a smell of something that had been in the closet a long time. "Yeah, baby," he said. "You nothin but a little sweetmeat!"

Since Margie could remember, nobody had kissed her at all, except her mother once in a long while, and her mother didn't count, although she usually smelled good, of toothpaste. Now she felt so giddy and windblown she almost turned to look in the mirror. Instead she ran her tongue very carefully over the lacerations inside her upper lip.

Bernie was still full of pleasure, remembering being kissed awake on somebody's couch in Cambridge, Massachusetts, by somebody's little girl, a real lovey little chick about eight years old, tasting of strawberry jam. Beautiful!

"Beaut-i-*full!*" he said. "Look at you gettin pink! Aw, baby, you ready *any* time!" And before Margie could do anything he was dragging her toward the living room. On instinct she planted her feet and said, "No!"

"Come on in an play, baby! It's just a party, whole lot of groovy people. . . ."

Margie opened her mouth, and out it came, from nowhere, pure spontaneous generosity disguised as a delaying tactic, or perhaps vice versa: "I made fudge!"

"Great! Go get it!"

So Margie got her fudge from where it was setting on the back porch, sure to be too hard, as always, and looking like not enough for all those people. . . .

"Come on, baby!" said Bernie, doing a little dance of irresistible anticipation, and carried her off into the living room, like the wind.

Sunk in the TV chair like a referee, David was considering two questions at once: (1) Who would be his partner in the unlikely event of an actual orgy? and (2) What was Malcolm X selling The Cap?

(1) was easy, a process of elimination: neither blonde twin, nor the olive-drab balloon, but the *other* one, with the yard of frayed brown hair and the eyes like cracked milk-blue marbles, a fairly standard flower child on the order of Laurie Dunn, but worse for wear. Just his speed.

(2) was tougher: all the talk about freedom sounded like old-time acid propaganda, but Malcolm X didn't quite look the type. . . .

Whoosh! Enter Wolf Man, jingling, with his red arm around Pig Bird, who had combed her hair with the electric fan and was blushing as pink as her ice-cream dress. *A plate of fudge?*

"Hey, this is Margie!" explained her sponsor. "Margie brought some fudge she made. For the party, man!"

"Fudge?" The balloon grinned horribly. "Wha kinda fudge?"

"With walnuts," said Pig Bird.

The balloon hauled out her wad of newspaper. "I got fudge, too, how's if we put it all together?" She emptied a dozen or so gray-brown chunks on top of Pig Bird's fudge. The demonstrator in the German helmet reached an arm up and took one. What did the letters say across the front of the helmet?

"I used Nestlé's Quik," confided Pig Bird. "It's quicker." Which set the balloon to quivering: "Mine . . . mine . . . mine is slow fudge," she got out finally. "But it lasts an lasts."

So it was like that. For once David spoke out as he thought: "Mix em up," he said. "Like Russian roulette." This got the attention of all the demonstrators except for the shaggy black Beatle in the corner.

"Yeah!" said Wolf Man. "Baby, give your brother a piece of fudge for that." And when Pig Bird dutifully offered David the plate, he added, "Slow on top, quick on the bottom." David took a dusty chunk from on top and dropped it in his shirt pocket. Wait and see. He didn't want to miss a thing.

"You like to fly kites, man?" said the helmeted one. He meant David, who saw that the yellow letters only spelled something out in front, then turned into a design around the back: alternate swastikas and six-pointed stars. He smiled at that.

"So do I," said the helmet. "Man, I *love* kites. Bet you got a lot of space to fly em out here, huh?"

But David was watching the little hostess offering fudge to the threesome on the couch. The blonde took a tiny piece. Malcolm shook his head. So did The Cap. That was too bad. . . .

Margie thought so, too. That big fat girl's fudge had covered hers up completely: nobody had even tasted it yet.

And now Daddy wouldn't even take any. Boldly she mixed the pieces up and pushed the plate at him again.

This time Rasmussen took a piece, just to get rid of her. Although she did look clean and decent and well-behaved, going around offering people candy off a plate. It didn't hurt to show a bunch like this a few ordinary good manners. He guessed De Vaughn here would probably agree with him, even if he hadn't exactly been following everything De Vaughn was saying. What he really needed was another drink.

"My idea," De Vaughn said, "is integrate the ordinary guy by liberating all his locked-up energy, you follow me?"

For some reason this left Rasmussen feeling depressed.

Like Margie. For even Daddy had taken a piece of the fat girl's fudge right out from between two rich, dark chocolatey squares of her own. She hoped it was terrible and made him sick: it would serve him right.

David watched her set the plate sulkily on the coffee table. Which kind had The Cap taken, slow or fast? Time would toll, time would tell. Now Wolf Man dragged Pig Bird over to the sleeping black Beatle in the corner, saying, "You gotta meet this cat over here. . . ."

"British kites are the greatest, man," said the helmet. "I wish I had my British kite here."

Wolf Man woke the Beatle; at least his eyes opened. "Say, baby, this is Margie I told you about," he said. What a sight to wake up to! "Margie, this is Monk."

"No, man," yawned the Beatle. "I'm Diz." It sounded like Wolf Man was running a date bureau. David took another look at the *other* girl, but her hair concealed her tits.

"*Objects trip,* man, you know that?" said the helmet. "Like a kite. Gets way up high above the board and sees all the moves."

"No, man, I'm Diz," said Pig Bird's date. "Monk is my

brother." He didn't look exactly overjoyed. At least he closed his eyes and didn't answer when Pig Bird asked him, politely, what school he went to.

"I *totaled* one kite, man," said the helmet. *"Like a broken bird."* He seemed to reflect on that image for several seconds. "Or you can make one. You ever make one?"

There went The Cap! Toilet, refrigerator, or combination? You could run a nice little gambling game off The Cap's exits.

And there went the blonde! After The Cap? Impossible!

So would Rasmussen have thought, even if she was a whore, but it was true. Just as he cocked the Yellowstone bottle above his glass, in she walked. Rasmussen still had the fudge in his left hand. He wouldn't have to talk with his mouth full, so . . .

"I'm Sandra," said the blonde, with an up-and-down look that seemed to leave no meat on his bones, or bones in his meat, or both. Rasmussen nodded Pleased-to-meet-you, and gestured with the bottle.

Sandra didn't even notice. "I teach in De Vaughn's school," she said.

Christ, they ought to keep girls like this locked up! Rasmussen chewed his fudge ostentatiously to cover his silence. That little zipper pull just hanging there like the brass ring on the merry-go-round! And Jesus Christ! Another brass ring on her little bitty skirt: one jerk and she'd be bare-ass naked! Or did she have a golden winkie under there like the one on the floor?

"You just pull," she said. "It comes right off."

Rasmussen swallowed hard. "It's my wife's birthday," he said, and plunged past her out the door, but not fast enough to miss hearing her say, "That's just perfect."

David saw him come zooming back in as if Mrs. Clean

were after him with the Clean Machine. And where *was* Mrs. Clean while all her favorite nightmares were coming true? Too bad if she missed it.

The couch twin came back, in no hurry, and sat down where she'd been before.

The Cap gulped down half of a whole glass of whiskey.

Pig Bird offered her date some fudge.

Wolf Man took up the lotus position with his back up against one of the loudspeakers.

Pig Bird's date yawned and said he was fine for now.

The Cap gawked around at the blonde behind him as if she couldn't be true, and turned back to face Malcolm with the tip of his tongue sticking out one corner of his mouth. Meant he was *thinking hard.*

"Never, man," said the demonstrator with the yellow moustache. "Those people in Watts got no revolutionary consciousness; they'll just get slaughtered again."

David saw he had competition for his orgy partner, who screwed her forefinger slowly into her fist and stared at the carpet.

"What they really want," continued the moustache, "is like . . . *this.*" His eyes went around the room. "You can't make a fucking revolution with people that want to live in tract houses and watch television!"

The helmet rose slowly in the air, supported by the hands of its occupant, who said, "Gettin too *tight.* Around my *mind.*" A cloud of kinky orange hair expanded slowly into its natural air space.

"I just don't get it," said The Cap.

Malcolm X laughed.

"Hey, can I see your helmet?" said David.

"You can think some heavy shit in that hat, man," said the orange hair, and rolled it across the carpet to David.

The real thing. It weighed plenty. *Amor Vincit Omnia,*
said the yellow letters across the front. "What does it mean?"
said David.

"Love . . ." said the orange hair, "is a winner!"

Fit over David's head, the helmet darkly framed his view
of the room.

The orange hair sank out of sight behind the balloon. Pig
Bird carried the fudge plate into the dining room with great
dignity. The Cap sneaked a couple of his aluminum pills
into his mouth. "In my own house?" he said. "That's going
pretty far!" The orange hair rose from the floor slowly:
"Rice paper, man. And bamboo strips." It went down again.
The couch blonde had her hand on the collar of The Cap's
coat sweater: *What was happening?* The Cap's tongue had
disappeared. "Nothin to lose but your chains, brother," said
Malcolm. The yellow moustache whipped around and glared
at the couch. "Did you ever make it with a chick?" said the
balloon, but the blonde twin beside her didn't answer. She
was watching the couch, too. The Cap looked around, foggy,
defensive, his whiskey glass empty. "Man, I love everybody
here," said Wolf Man out of his Buddha squat. The Cap
stood up unsteadily and cleared his throat. Like an after-
dinner speech. "I had a tough day," he said. "Gonna go get
a little shut-eye." Holding himself stiffly upright, he took
one step after another to the dining-room door, looked over
his shoulder, said, "Make yourself at home," and vanished.
Malcolm X fell back chuckling into his corner of the couch.
"Tough case," he said. "Gonna go down fightin." The couch
blonde, still in no hurry, went out. After The Cap. David's
head felt light, held down by the weight of the helmet. The
twin on the floor got up and followed her sister out, smoothing wrinkles out of her blue plastic ass. *Both of them? For
The Cap?* David looked at Wolf Man, who did a slow Buddha nod and said, "I was tellin you about transformations,

baby." The Cap with both those blondes? It was past smiling at. David lifted off the helmet, and blinked.

"Hey, O.J.," called Malcolm X. "Got your board with you? This may take a while."

The orange hair came up off the floor again. "And impact glue!" it said. "So it don't come apart in the air."

FOURTEEN

Margie saw Daddy coming, and automatically stopped pushing fudge into her mouth. But he just emptied the whiskey bottle into his glass and went out. So eating fudge was all right because her mother said it gave him whiskey fits. The fat girl's fudge was terrible: dry and crumbly and tasting like all those spices smelled in the rack Daddy gave her mother one Christmas and she never used. Margie had spit it right out into the sink, *Phoo!* and washed it away, and started eating her own, which was delicious.

One of the beautiful blondes came in, looked straight at Margie's mouth, and said, "Where'd your papa go, honey?" Margie shook her head I-don't-know and pointed out the door. The beautiful blonde went away. He was cute, the boy Uncle Bernie had introduced her to, with a big nose like Ringo, and Diz was a cute name, but his eyes looked funny, but he hadn't stared at her mouth, but he was probably just sleepy and no wonder, Margie had never been up so late, but she felt wide wide awake.

The beautiful blonde came back and said, "Where'd he

go, ah, your father?" Margie shook her head and pointed again, no, it must be the other beautiful blonde, there were two of them. At her school they wouldn't let the boys wear their hair so long, Kenneth Mims got sent home, Diz had cute hair, he could have a shampoo if he wanted.

Surrounded by the fat girl's ugly gray chunks, one neat little square of Margie's looked lonely, so she ate it, and felt very full, the insides of her orthodontics were all gummed up so she went back to the bathroom to wash her mouth, and over the sound of running water she heard a funny noise in David's room, like Daddy's voice but not words, it must be the whiskey. Her hair in the mirror really looked windblown.

When she got all the fudge washed out, Margie mixed Listerine with two parts water, a Listerine highball Daddy called it and her mother said, "Stop putting ideas in children's heads." Next door Daddy's whiskey fit sounded worse. The Listerine stung the inside of her lip where Uncle Bernie had kissed her and she spit it right out, *Phoo!* and peeled up her lip and saw just one tiny little red place, but it really hurt. Anyway, now she wouldn't offend Diz or anybody inside the Breath Zone. He didn't have a tickly beard, either, but he wasn't tan, either, so he wasn't a surfer and Margie was glad because surfers all had perfect white teeth. Margie hated people with perfect white teeth. It sounded like Daddy was running up and down David's bed out of breath. Margie had never seen a whiskey fit, and might have peeked except when she went into her room there was Uncle Bernie. *And Diz!* And her bed was a mess!

"Hey, baby," said Uncle Bernie. "You know the dog ate up all Diz's pigeons?"

"*Tired* behind all this shit," said Diz.

"Say how's about if Diz crashes out on your bed awhile?" said Bernie. "Room for both of you." He saw behind Margie's thick blush to her secret love dream thoughts. Past a cupped hand he whispered at her. "You're beautiful!" and left them there together. Give people half a chance and the love would just come pouring out. He detoured into the kitchen and put the kettle on for tea, even knowing that Anti Ann wouldn't have any real macrobiotic bancha. *Because you go with what you got.* What a sweet, ready little chick Margie was! Who cared if she was ugly? Didn't the ugly people have just as much natural right to love as anybody?

"Hey, Bernie?" said De Vaughn. "You play chess?"

"Baby I play *everything!*"

"Well, look in old O.J.'s pockets there and see if he's got his little set on him."

Diz stood with one hand on the bedpost and his knees against the footboard, as if waiting for instructions. All Margie could think of were dogs eating little fluffy pigeons, then Diz crumpled forward sideways over the foot of her bed and lay where he fell, with his feet hanging over the end in heavy leather sandals with soles like old pieces of rubber tire; they would get the spread filthy dirty. But when Margie tried to unbuckle one Diz tried to pull his feet up so she had to wrestle them both until he lay still and she got both sandals off *clunk clunk* onto the floor.

In the pale light from the hall his sockless feet looked filthy as the sandals, and now Margie's hands were filthy, and there was a big filthy smudge on her pink dress, in the most terrible place. She had to wash herself, and change her dress, but how could she with him lying right there? Just wait till her mother caught her. . . .

Bernie sat on the couch facing De Vaughn above the tiny chessboard, his black Stetson weightless upon his head, his various shirts and jackets light across his shoulders: they fit him very well. So did the couch: neither too tight nor too loose. He could feel the pattern of the fabric through the seat of his coveralls. His wristbones moved smoothly as he reached for one of the little white pieces.

"Man you can't move that pawn *sideways*," De Vaughn said. "What's the matter with you?"

"OK, OK, baby," Bernie said. "Everything's OK."

"An a rook don't go diagonal!"

"I'm just experimentin, OK?"

"You said you could play. You don't even know the game, man."

"I said I play *anything*. I didn't say I was gonna try an *win!*"

"I guarantee you ain't gonna *win*, but you can't even *lose* right if you don't know the rules, man."

"Fuck the rules, baby. That's what play *is!*"

"Aw, put the thing away."

"No, I am not gonna put the thing away. Look here, De Vaughn, how do you know we ain't gonna make up some new game hundred times better than chess while we just playin? Think of the possibilities, man! All those little pieces an squares there, like there's infinite possibilities!"

"Go on an play with yourself, then."

"I'm surprised, man, I really am surprised. Cat like you sees through the whole other mess, how rules fuckin everybody up. . . ."

"Hey, brother," said De Vaughn. "You play chess?"

David shifted in his referee's chair and shook his head, slowed by the helmet. He had got his smile back by trying to imagine The Cap's transformation at the hands of the blonde twins. The key question was: would they take his cap off or leave it on?

"He stoned or something?" said Malcolm X.

"Naw, he ain't stoned," said Wolf Man. "Nobody's stoned. Hey, come on an play with De Vaughn, baby. I'm too wild for him."

Then David had moved on to consider Wolf Man's plot against the black Beatle, which was all you could call pairing him off with Pig Bird. Did Wolf Man intend to get the whole family laid tonight? What about Mrs. Clean? What about David himself? When the *other* girl, his orgy partner, got up and went outside, David smiled at his temptation to follow, and at the ease with which he resisted, even when his competition with the yellow moustache did pursue her.

"He don't look much like his old man," said Malcolm.

"His old man gonna look different after a while," said Wolf Man. "Old Charley gonna get transformed." He went into his Buddha nod. "Transformed double time!"

"Double time an then some," said Malcolm.

In the bathroom Margie heard Daddy shout, "Christ I *can't!*" and washed her hands louder. *"Can't!"* came Daddy's voice again, and as Margie slipped quietly back into her room so she wouldn't wake Diz, she heard a lady's voice, kind of laughing, say, "Yes you can," a lady in there with Daddy and his whiskey fit! Margie's head spun with a roaring that made no sound, and she closed the bathroom door noiselessly behind her. One of the beautiful blondes? It must be, they were looking for him. What were they doing? Could it be *fuck?*

Although Patricia Nunez had explained it to her and Jody *twice*, Margie still had *fuck* all mixed up with wee-wee and worse things. But Patricia said the boy always wanted to do it to the girl and Daddy said *"I can't"* but he wasn't a boy, either, so probably it wasn't *fuck*. But it was something terrible enough to make Margie forget about putting on the yellow-and-white-check dress Bernice Rombach said looked like a tablecloth. Out front the radio was still going, and

Margie thought of just sitting down on the carpet outside her door so nobody would come along and wake up Diz, who said something in his sleep about "fuckin dogs," but she was absolutely forbidden to sit on the floor in good clothes, but her pink dress was filthy anyway.

She wished she were a dog, not the big fierce kind, just a little cute woolly one with a real loud bark, like in the movie where this little white woolly dog saved a whole family from this big huge flood by barking so loud to the boat men they got in their boat and went and saved everybody out the upstairs window, and at the end this other little dog that belonged to the family too climbed up out of the chimney and got in the boat too and licked this first little dog's face to thank him.

Daddy groaned so loud she could hear him all the way in here. Margie put her fingers in her ears.

"Believe me," said De Vaughn. "That Sandra and Wondra is some double-play combination. Team teaching, you know? Lots of new frontiers in this school. We still gettin some of the problems *isolated.*"

"I don't put science down, baby," said Bernie. "Science can be beautiful."

"Like the long-run and the short-cut," said De Vaughn. "That is a *bitch.* Long-run has been on its way out a long time now, but still there's all this propaganda about how it's more *deep* an *satisfying,* all that I-love-you-forever shit."

"Yeah, that old shit," said Bernie. "It's like."

"Your complete fool, see, he spreads it all over the cracks, that lie, an keeps his energy locked up. So the problem is: how do you make the short-cut *deep* an *satisfying?* It's a bitch. That's why I switched to team teachin, see, cause the fool knows he can't make the long-run with two chicks at once an if he *don't* know it I guarantee you Sandra an Wondra gonna make it plain as day! Aw, man, when those girls were still soloin we had marriage proposals a nickel a pound!"

"Baby," said Bernie, "you ought be president!"

"Still the fool is liable to get the wrong message, and think, 'This is just a taste of what I could do, super stud that I am, if I wasn't tied up in that old *deep* an *satisfyin* long-run.' Yeah. So the girls have got to be kind of mean an evil, tear the fool up, so he don't get the idea he's doin them any kind of favor. It's got to be *intense* and *unforgettable*, so you leave the fool no choice but thinkin about the long-run an the short-cut with his own mind. See, now he *knows* how much energy been locked up all those years, because they just proved it to him in a couple of hours!"

"David!" said Bernie. "You diggin all this, baby?"

"If he ain't stoned," said De Vaughn, "he's some stone philosopher."

David had heard it all, and to prove he wasn't stoned, walked to the front door, opened it, and looked out into the dawn's early light, a thick unpromising yellow. Across the lawn he saw a gray Volkswagen bus parked at the curb. The *other* girl was down on hands and knees in the gutter looking underneath it. The yellow moustache was watching her from the curb. David closed the door and went over to the home theater. The Beach Boys were more than he could take. On the Long Beach jazz station he found an old George Shearing Quartet.

"Good move, brother," said Malcolm X alias De Vaughn. But David wasn't disarmed enough to ask him how big a fool you had to be to qualify for his school. After all, The Cap had been first choice. . . . His smile ended in a yawn. All the action was in back. Out here the party was down to De Vaughn running test problems on the little chessboard, Wolf Man zonked out of his mind, the balloon and the orange-haired kite freak laid out like casualties on the floor. David thought about the fudge in his pocket.

"Yeah, man," said Wolf Man with a luminous smile. "We ought to, you know, celebrate some way. . . ."

David wondered what there was to celebrate.

"Charley gettin transformed, man." Wolf Man took off his hat and scratched his head. "Beautiful . . ."

Oh, that. David would require something better to overcome his inertia. Or he could get high.

What ever happened to George Shearing? The door chimes almost got lost among the vibraphone bells from the home theater. Why didn't they just walk in? The chimes rang again. All right, nobody else was going to open the door, so David did.

A popeyed man in brick-red hip huggers stood there, rainbow-colored arms shivering around a portable movie camera. A faggot? "Hi," he said. "Is this the party?" A faggot. Across the lawn behind him another faggot, gangly and redhaired, was dragging a large black suitcase. Mrs. Clean's VW was parked across the street in front of Farnum's. Someone was sitting in it.

Faggot One looked past David into the living room and said, "There you are!"

"Hey, Richard," called Wolf Man. "Come on in, baby!" David stood aside while Faggot One came in, saying, "You wouldn't believe the shit we've been through getting here!" And Faggot Two, who collapsed immediately on top of the black suitcase, and grumpily flipped his red forelock from his brow.

"Do you realize," said Faggot One, "there's truckloads of soldiers out there? With tanks? And all the heat in California? I wouldn't be a spade this morning for a million dollars, nothing personal, De Vaughn. And then Pepe—where is he?—wants to get out at the roadblock and fight the whole Army because they ask us if we've got any weapons! And then Donald—this is Donald—has to say, 'You've got all the weapons, haven't you?' "

"And this like big SS Gestapo sergeant says, 'How'd you like a taste of my weapon, Cutie Pie?' *Cutie Pie*, for Christ's sake!" Faggot Two shivered at the memory, and surveyed the company with a defiant red-lipped pout.

"We never should have left the freeway," said Faggot One. "But we saw this whole convoy ahead, and figure like we better take another way, and then we got lost."

"Long as you didn't get raped," said De Vaughn.

"So where's this fantastic party?" said Faggot One. "I mean, I didn't risk life and limb coming out here to shoot Julius and Happy! Look at em! Julius! Wake *up!* Done his little nutties already—hey, d'you ever see my Mozart one, Happy in the bubble bath with this enormous rubber sea monster? Four and a half minutes is all it runs. *Julius!* Somebody's wearing your hat. Who are you?"

"That's David, he lives here," said Wolf Man.

"How do you like all these bizarre *denizens?*" asked Faggot One. "I mean, invading your scene here?"

David smiled, trusting not to be misunderstood, and didn't mind seeing the *other* girl come in the front door with a big hairy white cat in her arms. She tried to turn it over, it twisted loose with a squall, landed on its feet, and dashed under the couch. The yellow moustache came in looking disgusted. Supple as a dancer, Faggot Two salaamed and at floor level called, "Kitty kitty kitty." His gold harem pants were velvet, David saw, and the turquoise shirt was of some tearaway material.

"I just want to look at his cock," said the *other* girl.

"Oh yeah?" said Faggot Two. "How come?"

But Faggot One drowned her answer, saying, "So where's this john? Where are your flaming creatures? Where's this fabulous party? I mean, if this is your idea of a put-on, getting us all out here in East *Nowhere* with a *war* going on! All that bullshit about audio-visual aids for your school!"

David was more interested in the *other* girl's explanation, but De Vaughn was saying, "*You* the one that volunteered, baby. I said *if* you made some kind of little movie I could use, I'd split the film with you. That's what I said."

"How can I make a movie if I can't see?"

"Go on an don't be getting bitchy now," said De Vaughn. "You know you wet your pants behind the whole idea; just take it easy an see what develops."

"What's Pepe doing out there?" said Faggot One. "Jerking off or what?"

The *other* girl slowly circled the couch as if considering how best to extract the white cat, and when she passed his chair David said, "Why do you want to look at his cock?"

"I read in this book," she said, "where male wildcats have this fishhook thing on their cocks. . . ."

Oh, well. David took this intelligence in stride. It wasn't every day you discovered a brand-new shortcoming.

The *other* girl's milky blue eyes unclouded slightly. "See, the *barbs*," she said, "catch inside an the female can't get loose."

"Uh-huh."

"Here he comes," said Faggot One at the half-open front door, and here he came: a slim, gliding figure all in black, last seen in a bad dream and ready now to kill someone in the first minute of a James Bond movie. What an entrance! David smiled.

"This is Pepe, my latest discovery," said Faggot One. "Where've you been?"

Out killing somebody, thought David. It's obvious. Black leather pants *and* shirt? But his smile dried up when Pepe fixed him for two seconds with close-set black holes reflecting nothing in a face expressive as soap. This spook was real. "Baby I don't see no party," he said.

"Star material!" said Faggot One. "Kenneth Anger will open a *vein!*"

"So where is this fuck party?" said Pepe. Being a Mexican didn't exactly mellow his image, thought David. Or being a faggot, either. For his look had contained that, too: *eat you, screw you, kill you, all the same to me.*

"Oh, De Vaughn's uptight about anybody *seeing* anything," said Faggot One.

"I told you, wait around," said De Vaughn. "Whole flutter of queens bust in in the middle, liable to give the fool a, you know, *trauma.*"

"You boss of this whole thing, man?" said Pepe.

"I'm just boss of what I'm boss of, baby. Don't fuck it up none an you'll be OK."

"I'm always OK. You want to find out how OK I am?"

"Pepe," said Faggot One. "Don't go getting yourself worked up. We all know what a *dangerous psychopathic killer* you are."

"Yeah, man," said Wolf Man. "Peace an love is the whole thing. We're celebrating. I got a groovy idea. . . ."

"To me it's a lot of shit," said Pepe. "Who's holding?"

David would gladly have offered his fudge, but at this point Faggot Two, still in his supplicant crouch, told the *other* girl, "You shoo him out and I'll catch him. I want to see, too."

When the cat emerged at a fugitive lope, however, it was Pepe who snatched it up so fast his hands blurred, and began to stroke it.

"That's no tomcat, baby," said De Vaughn. "I can see her titties from here."

"I think she's pregnant, poor baby," said Faggot Two.

"Aw shit," said the *other* girl.

FIFTEEN

Viola Bunch let the drapes fall back in place and closed her eyes to rest them from the strain of squinting into the smoggy morning. But she went right on worrying. What in the world was going on next door? Radio commenced to booming at quarter of four, like to blew the windows out. Hippies chasing cats under cars. Now those three sissies driving up in Ann Rasmussen's little car to join the party bag and baggage: not like the folks next door at all!

But it took her mind briefly off her own worries, after lying awake all night with them, next to Howard sleeping like a baby. Not exactly her mind, either, if your mind was in your head, for Viola worried in her belly, which Howard called her stomach, although they weren't the same thing: your stomach was where your food went, just one part of your belly, which contained your whole insides, which Howard called intestines, and all that soft machinery for making a baby, if it worked, which Viola's didn't.

That was where she worried. As if she'd eaten rocks, which would tumble round and round down in there all night, grinding away and blunting each other without ever getting smaller. Then the next day she would be dead on her feet at the UN Day Center, and finally have to take a nap on one of the little cots, which one of these days would break down under her if she didn't watch her diet, which she did, and *watching* it didn't help.

Tonight—*last* night; it was sunrise now—Viola worried for her sister Lily on Eighty-ninth Street, and for her mother in Willowbrook, but most for her sister because her mother would not go out of the house after dark, not for Judgment, while Lily had three boys, and at least the eldest, Dwight, the wild one who called himself Odinga now, would be in the street, and Lily was sure he had a gun.

The psychologist said Dwight was "accident-prone" the time he got hit by the bus (Howard, who paid the hospital bill, said maybe so because he sure wasn't "work-prone"). And last night it seemed to Viola that there were at least half a million accident-prone black people in the City and County of Los Angeles, and a whole lot of them were going to have accidents *soon*, and it was no accident. She worried for them all, in the images of her mother, and Lily, and Michael the baby, and Charles the middle boy, and Dwight, who wouldn't answer unless his mother called him Odinga.

She worried about Howard, who didn't want the radio or TV on when war was breaking out all over the place, and didn't—did *not*—want to talk about it, either. "You're emotion-prone and worry-prone," he said. "I've got my own problems to worry about." Viola couldn't blame him. But she could worry about him freely without bothering him any: it *was* a shame that such a self-made success as Howard didn't seem to take more satisfaction in it, that was all. When Lily made Dwight come on his crutches to say thank you, the boy said, "Uncle Howard, Ebony magazine would be proud of you, man," and even if he did say it in his cool mean hateful Odinga way, it was true. Well, almost.

What kept it from being true was having no children. Which was why Viola put up with it when Howard didn't do his duty by her, like last night. Because Ebony magazine wasn't going to be writing up any outstanding young Negro-American insurance salesman with his wife and new car and *integrated* suburban home, no matter how many awards he won, no matter how much time he put in on Interfaith Youth Councils and Community Cooperation Committees and United Crusade collecting and Young Republicans canvassing—not if he didn't have a couple of polished, clean-cut, white-smiling, good-grade-getting kids for the pictures. That was a natural fact. And he wouldn't adopt one, either. "That's what they've got the welfare for," he said. "I've got my own problems."

Being successful was a full-time job, Howard said. You couldn't rest on your laurels, the race was to the swift, the early bird got the worm, and it was every tub on its own bottom. The successful man had more responsibilities than all those *less-fortunate*, as he called them. But at a quarter to four when the radio exploded next door, it had taken Viola straight back to the first place they had lived: second-floor-back apartment in Compton, surrounded on all four sides by less-fortunates. But somebody was always playing the radio all night, next door or upstairs, and dancing and carrying on. But it had the sound of good times back then; coming now from Rasmussen's it sounded unnatural, even Otis Redding, her secret favorite, Howard called him a nigger, and now the poor man was dead. *I can't get no satisfaction,* with Dwight and a thousand other black kids maybe out in the street shooting or throwing bricks at tanks, Good God Almighty, and here next door the radio boomed out in the middle of the night: had the whole world gone crazy by secret agreement?

By daylight it seemed downright sinister. Viola recalled newspaper stories of innocent families invaded by gangs of criminals and held captive for days sometimes. Could it happen to the Rasmussens? Viola felt no special affection for them, but they were better than she had expected when they moved in here, at least. Rasmussens never did anything *bad*. As far as she could tell, they never did much of anything at all. The kids she felt a bit sorry for, especially that little pigeon-breasted Margie, poor little thing, with her braces, and what they called a dull-normal at best. He, Charley Rasmussen, never said boo. Howard thought he was a drinker. But Ann worked herself to skin and bone keeping the house clean, and still found time for the Youth Council.

They were, Viola decided, just the kind of ordinary harmless people who got invaded by gangs who turned up the radio to cover the sounds of torture. No other way to explain the goings-on over there. The last one, all in black: he cinched it. If *he* wasn't out to do evil to somebody, she Viola Bunch was not only blind but crazy.

She didn't wake Howard to ask his opinion. She knew it already. It was "Mind your own business." It was "I've got my own problems." Howard was like those thirty-eight people in New York who watched the girl getting killed, Kitty What's-her-name. And he would be the first volunteer for the Committee on Community Apathy. Viola preferred wiping interracial bottoms at the United Nursery Day Center.

It would be polite to phone first, but those gangs of criminals would make a member of the family answer it and say everything was all right with a gun in their ear. Better just go in person. It was the neighborly thing to do.

Howard slept his clean, snore-free sleep while she dressed

for work and set the electric coffeepot to perk. "Honey?" she said in at him once, thinking that if the gang of criminals caught her it might be the last look she would ever take at him. No more affection-prone in sleep than he was awake, he went right on breathing, and Viola, though her bones were marrowed with loyalty, went out the front door gaily. Fare thee well, Howard.

On Rasmussen's front step it sounded like the whole Count Basie band was inside playing "Hallelujah I Just Love Her So," music from the less-fortunate days. Was she a fool to have stuck a butcher knife in her purse? Viola pushed the button, and waited. Foolish to think a gang of criminals less likely to be torturing the Rasmussens while Joe Williams was singing, but that was what she thought.

> *That's why I kno-ow, oh yes I know*
> *Hallelujah I just love her so. . . .*

Nobody answered. When the record finished, she rang the bell again, and heard the chimes.

The person who opened the door looked less like a criminal than a crime on its way to be committed, Good God, or like the Cowardly Lion in blue glasses and funny-paper clothes, Charley Rasmussen's no-good brother from the middle of night-before-last. The dope addict and car stealer, who yelled, "Yeah, baby, come on in!" as a cat yowled like it was being tortured and shot out the open door, bouncing off Viola's right ankle without losing speed and streaking across the lawn into the morning. *Vivisection,* she thought, and was about to say, *I'm Viola Bunch from next door and I was just wondering,* when the Cowardly Lion grabbed her by the hand and yanked her inside and her purse flew open and spilled onto the floor: glasses case, handkerchief, lipstick, eye liner, Midol, change purse, address book, Doublemint gum, three penny suckers, and stainless-steel butcher

knife. And a roomful of funny-looking strangers watched
it all.

Too mortified to say a word, she let the Cowardly Lion
bow and squat to pick up her things while she glanced
round and saw they were just a bunch of so-called hippies
and freakish homosexuals, probably friends of the no-good
brother. Who shook his Cowardly Lion whiskers up at her
and said, "Baby what you packin a blade like this around
for? We into peace an love over here, know what I mean?"

As if for a character testimonial Viola looked at David
Rasmussen smiling there in a Nazi-type helmet, but support
came from another quarter: "All hell breakin loose like it is,
a lady needs some kind of protection." A *good*-looking freckled brother, very light-complected, said this from the couch,
and Viola relaxed a little. They weren't all hippies and sissies anyway. "Hi there, David," she said. "How are you doing this morning?"

"Hi, Mrs. Bunch," said David.

But the one all in black, stretched out but not relaxed in
an easy chair, was giving her the worst hate stare she had
seen in weeks.

"How's your mother and father, David?" she said. "Everybody OK?"

"You bet your life," said David, with a big smile.

"Say, what kind of pill is this?" The Cowardly Lion had
found the Midol. "They big as cookies, man!"

The freckled man on the couch was watching her.
"Sounded like you were having a party over here," Viola
said. "So I just thought I'd look in."

The no-good brother was reading the back of the Midol
box and giggling. "Baby," he said up at Viola over his blue
glasses. "You don't look like you got any kind of *female
problems* to me!" Nobody had called her "baby" like that

for a long time. It gave her a funny feeling, though *considering the source*, as Howard would have said, it shouldn't have. He looked like he hadn't had a bath in weeks, him or his clothes, and somebody ought to tell him how fakey and ridiculous he sounded trying to talk like a black man.

But where were the other Rasmussens? She asked David, and he said, "They're both lying down." They could hardly be sleeping with the radio going, *All Right, OK, You Win*, good old Joe Williams. If they were, only the Lord knew how. But then everybody had good-for-nothing relations. It was a known fact. And if they happened to bring a lot of their no-good friends by for a party, well, it happened every day.

So when the Cowardly Lion stood up, jingling with little bells, and gave her back her purse, Viola said, "Well, I better go fix breakfast and go to work."

"*Say what?*" said the no-good brother. "Baby you just got here. This is a love celebration, like for my brother Charley. . . ."

"No, thanks, you just go on with your party," said Viola, with the firm-but-cheerful voice she used on babies at the Day Center. "I've got to be going."

"Aw listen, I got a head full of plans!"

Viola smiled and shook her head. She could imagine what kind of plans. Head full of dope was more like it.

"Baby don't you want to be in a movie?" said the frog-eyed sissy in the rainbow shirt. "This is like a Living Theater party."

"Shit," said the bad one in black.

"Believe me, baby," insisted Frog Eye. "Stick around and I'll make you a star."

Viola didn't like being called "baby" by that one, not a bit. But then all of them called everybody *baby* or *man* every other word: jive types ten years behind the times. "No, thanks," she said. "Thank you kindly for the invitation but I'm on my way."

"No!" said the no-good brother, a difficult child getting more difficult. "Beautiful chick like you runnin off with a blade in your purse an all of us gettin into love an good times here, don't make sense!"

"Hey-hey-hey, General," said the good-looking freckled man. "At ease, you know what I mean?" He came and put a calming arm around the no-good brother's shoulders. "General Cornwallis here gets kind of carried away sometimes, you know. Lady says she's got to go fix breakfast an go to work, didn't you hear?" Looking Viola right in the eye all the time. "This lady's a good wife an mother, what you bet? She don't want to hear all that love stuff this hour in the morning."

"I didn't mean to interrupt the party," said Viola, standing her ground. One thing you had to say for these Muslims: they were straight and clean-living, even if Howard did say Malcolm only got what was coming to him, talking about poor Kennedy that way. She smiled at the freckled man, sharing a private amusement with him at this roomful of chumps. "I like to have a good time myself," she said. "But you know how it is. . . ."

"Husband'll be over here in a minute with a Henry Aaron bat," grinned the freckled man. "Right? An you just doin your wifely duty. General Cornwallis here puts all that down, you understand?"

He surely was a good-natured little man for a Muslim. Of course it was Elijah's people that were so gloomy and dressed like undertakers; Malcolm's people were something else. This one looked like he could move a ton with those shoulders, and dressed like a playground instructor.

"Everybody to their own taste," said Viola agreeably.

"And he does get cranky when . . ." When what? Howard was just naturally cranky, never drank but two cups of black coffee in the morning, and would be dead asleep for another hour.

"When you're out carryin on with the neighbors," the freckled man finished for her. "Right? Love, honor, and *obey*."

Exactly then, Viola knew in a hot certain flash what he was up to. Children or no, loyal to the bone or no, she was at least ten years, and maybe the rest of her life, short of *not* knowing what he was up to. He looked right inside you with those eyes. Something melted and quivered in her lining. "Oh I don't know about that *obeying*," she said. "Give an get is how I look at it."

"Right," said the freckled man. "You don't *get* his breakfast on time, he gonna *give* you hell. Cause that's his privilege!"

"Aw, man," said the Cowardly Lion, but he was so far outside the little game of showdown that Viola hardly heard him, or Joe Williams, either. She hadn't played the game in so long she had almost forgotten how. But not quite. And there wasn't much that could happen to her at seven-forty-six in the morning, with the whole Sunday funny papers lying around watching.

"So you get on over there and do your duty," said the freckled man. "We don't want some en-raged husband bustin in here."

"Say you're making some kind of movie?" said Viola. Fifteen minutes wouldn't hurt. And actually nobody in the room looked like they had even five minutes of hell-raising *or* good times in them. Except for the hate-staring one in black, and of course the freckled man, who said, "Now you gonna be late for work, and if you don't mind me sayin so, it's little things like this lead to divorce."

"Go on," said Viola. "Don't be making a big deal out of nothing."

"Lady, I'm a specialist in that field."

"What field is that?"

"Takes a lot of explaining."

"I'm not in that big of a hurry."

"I'm *never* in a hurry."

"Well, they say you live longer that way."

"Longer, an deeper, an better."

"That must be very satisfying."

"Satisfaction," said the freckled man, "is guaranteed. But feelin like I do about husbands an wives, I really do hate *scenes*, an hungry men wavin baseball bats an all. . . ."

"Well, I'm a full-grown woman," said Viola. "And I certainly don't want you getting the wrong idea. And my husband is a very law-abiding citizen."

"They the most dangerous kind."

"And I'm certainly not going to spend the whole day at this party of yours."

"Not my party, lady. I'm just takin care of business."

"What business are you in?"

"I live off women," said the freckled man, and before Viola could think of anything to say to *that*, he had guided her firmly to the front door and opened it. "Go fry your fool his grits now," he smiled. "An don't be callin the police. They all too busy today anyway."

The door closed her out.

SIXTEEN

Spades, thought David. You couldn't beat them, they were in a class all their own. Think of Hart trying to do his thing among people like De Vaughn there!

Nor was he the only one impressed. "Baby you were cold with that bitch," said Faggot One, alias Richard. "I bet you don't leave a girl anything!"

"Yeah, what you have to send her home for?" Uncle Wolf Man sounded disappointed. Had he had eyes for Mrs. Bunch himself?

"Use your brain," said De Vaughn, and sat down on the couch again.

"I bet you're absolutely *insatiable*," said Richard.

"Aw kiss my ass, Richard," said De Vaughn. "Stay in your own camp, man."

David saw the one in black staring hate-kill at the couch. Just let him stay high forever, that one.

"Well, I don't care," said Wolf Man to himself. "But the more people we got for the ritual the better."

"What ritual?" said David.

"You'll see, baby." The Buddha nod once more.

"Where's the bathroom?" said Faggot Two. David waved him toward the back of the house. "In the hall, middle door." *A Boy Scout is courteous.*

Richard silenced Count Basie and tuned in Daffy Duck, minus audio. Orange Julius propped himself upright and said, "You got my helmet."

David said nothing.

"*Jew*," said Orange Julius, and lay down again.

Faggot Two came back. "Locked," he said. "And there's this little girl sitting on the *floor*. And she says, 'He's *sleeping*,' and I say, 'Who?' and she says, 'Diz,' and there's this *boy* . . ."

"One of Marco's kids," said De Vaughn. "So don't be messin. Go piss outside."

"You tell everybody where to piss?" said the one in black. His eyes seemed to grow closer together.

"Peace," said Wolf Man. He pointed at the master bedroom. "One in there."

The silence had penetrated Ann's frozen equilibrium like a signal of something. Her eyes saw the door open. Someone came in. A faceless silhouette. Ann didn't care. She knew where the gun was. If somebody touched her.

"Oh hello," said a voice. "Are you dead?" Black lips in a chalk face. A finger came down, touched Ann's cheek tentatively, and flew away. "*Gaaahd!*" shuddered the voice.

The trance broken, Ann raised her head on the slow stiff hinge of her neck. He ran into the bathroom and shut the door. Ann pushed herself upright, weightless, tasting shriveled metal. I'm dying of thirst. Amazing. A glass of water . . .

She sat on the edge of her bed for half a minute, her body reconsidering its own mobility, then stood up and moved on bird's bones toward the bathroom. No, he was in there. Toward the living room, then. A glass of water . . .

From the doorway she saw them: strangers all over the place, looking at her. On the television screen soldiers with submachine guns walked in a silent line along a water's edge. Near her two bodies lay. Bernie said, "Jesus, baby, you back from the dead!" Was that David inside that steel helmet? Words in which she had no interest formed in her powdery throat and dried out soundlessly. She swallowed pins and needles.

"Where's your father?" she said to the helmet, her voice harsh and faraway.

David looked at her.

"Where's your father?" Having been asked, it must have an answer.

"In my room," David said.

"Gettin *transformed,*" Bernie said.

Ann accepted this information as uncritically as in a dream, neither more nor less meaningful than anything else. Now that she had looked, and spoken, her other senses reported for duty. "Something's burning," she said.

"Yeah," sniffed a man on the couch, perhaps Negro. "Like a motor burning up?"

"Sit down, baby," Bernie said. "Things are going to be happening."

It must be the audio burned out on the television. Making that smell. Two blonde girls dressed like twins came in from the dining room. "Uh-huh," one of them said.

"Oh *yeah?*" Bernie said. "Baby you ought to be thankin these girls here. They just transformed your old man." The one in her bathroom came past Ann into the living room and sat down. "Don't seem to bother her much," said the one on the couch, perhaps Negro.

None of them meant any more to Ann than the man on the television screen, so serious and wise, saying nothing. "You all right, Mom?" said David.

"You must think you look smart in that hat," Ann told him. The smell of burnt metal matched the deadly taste in her mouth. A glass of water . . . She went back into her own bright bathroom, its empty mirror waiting to show her herself, pale but perfectly normal. "The Mummy's *Tomb!*" shrilled a voice behind her.

She filled her glass with water and felt it go all the way down, cold and delicious, into her stomach. She drank a second glassful slowly, tasting it. They were laughing and shouting over each other out there, but she didn't listen. They didn't matter. She felt independent, calm and unconcerned.

"Man, I'm starving," said a girl's voice.

A bunch of wild animals, a separate species.

Ann stood very still before the mirror. The pool of cold water shivered inside her. She felt alive again. Her reflection smiled whitely at her. With fingers light as dry twigs she seized the electric toothbrush and set to work, buffed every chink and surface redundantly white, washed her hands and face in cold water, combed her hair.

There now: moving hadn't broken her, being touched hadn't broken her, she still felt immortal. She could do anything she wanted. Full of a purpose without a name, refreshed, neither tense nor sleepy, she lay down on her bed again to wait.

"Don't forget the cap, baby!"

Bernie? It didn't matter. Their noise was a froth of nonsense. Free of breakfast and the electric clock and the endless task of making clean, Ann felt at perfect liberty to lie waiting for the spirit to move her.

A spirit surely different from those which had visited her husband and left him a carcass drained of everything but a bottomless wonder. Even twelve or fourteen ounces of bourbon and a piece of hashish fudge had not sufficed to blur that wonder, and now, limp as the bed linen which shrouded him, Rasmussen still wondered: *How did all that happen to me?*

A waking cadaver of fatigue, afloat still on the wide wake of his intoxication, buffered both from reflection and from the imagining of consequences, Rasmussen saw himself as a stranger, the leading man in a dream play made flesh. He simply wouldn't have believed it possible. Between the two guttering candles on David's dresser, the joss stick stuck in a hairbrush still sent up its thin twine of aromatic smoke.

Rasmussen gazed through fallen lids at that vaguely sacramental trinity, flame and smoke and flame, paler now as daylight seeped into the room around the curtains.

Three times. He wouldn't have believed it. The last time he had thought would kill him. They wouldn't take no for an answer. Like that impacted wisdom tooth, felt like his brains and whole insides came out with it. But he had got up and walked away from the dentist's office. He wasn't walking anywhere now, not if his bladder burst. *Three times.*

The door opened, one of them came in. Nothing shrinkable was left in him, or it would have shrunk. *No more.* But his throat cleared itself.

"Cool it, Sixty Minute Man," said Sandra or Wondra. "Just tidying up a bit." She went around collecting things, and went out shutting the door behind her as smooth and quiet as a nurse. Rasmussen realized that she had taken away his clothes.

Well, he wasn't going anywhere. The toilet was next door. When he had to pee, if he ever had to pee again, he would make it, he hoped. His eyelids closed. Sleep should have wiped him out instantly, but it didn't. He hadn't in fact been as relaxed in sleep for years as he was now, the filament of wonder still glowing in his consciousness. *How did all that happen to me? Three times!*

Margie watched the beautiful blonde girl go by again, this time carrying Daddy's shoes in her left hand, his trousers, shirt, and coat sweater over her right arm, and taking no notice at all of Margie, still faithfully guarding the slumber of spread-eagled Diz. Since the radio had gone off and the perfumey man had come trying to get into the bathroom, she had been fighting drowsiness herself. The beautiful blondes were no longer in David's room, she was sure of that. But if Daddy was, he had no clothes on: that gave Margie a funny feeling. The mass of fudge shifted uneasily inside her.

Now here came Uncle Bernie again. "Hey, *baby!* What you doin down there?" But he went right past her and into David's room, saying something about school, and Margie didn't want to think about that because it must be almost time to go to school right now.

Uncle Bernie came jingling back with her father's Dodgers cap in his hand, peered in at Diz, and squatted down next to Margie. "Say listen, baby, you ought to go lie down with him in there, you know. Put your arms around him and like kind of love him up real sweet."

"He's sleeping," said Margie.

"Yeah, but lovin is better than sleepin."

Margie shook her head and nodded. Mainly she wanted Uncle Bernie and his old-closet smell to go away. She didn't feel very well.

"Here, wait a minute," he said, standing up and taking out his little bell on a stick. He tinkled it over Margie's head, mumbling something like, "Joy love sweetness thrill pleasure," and pushed his face down at her, "*An you'll feel beautiful!*" and went off, jingle bells, jingle bells, jingle all the way to the front of the house, where he said, "OK, now we got everything we need."

Donald tossed his red forelock and said, "What *I* need is something to eat."

"Me, too," said De Vaughn.

"Yeah, man," said Bernie. "But let's get this ritual figure together an have the feast afterward."

"I love barbaric rituals," said Richard. "Donald don't you want to dance? And can you girls bring your old john back to life?"

Sandra and Wondra were attending upon De Vaughn as he said, "Go scramble me about six eggs, and don't be usin no margarine."

"Richard I'd love to dance, baby, but I've got to eat something before I go to *shreds!*"

"For somebody who's so *anal*," said Richard, "you're fantastically *oral*."

"So we need some sheets an blankets," Bernie said. "Pillows and stuff."

Donald beat Sandra and Wondra out the door into the dining room, and the telephone rang. A piercing scream from the kitchen drowned the second ring, and Donald came cantering back in like a hunchback, bent whimpering over his limp right hand. "*I burned my fucking hand off!*" The phone went on ringing.

Mitchell, sitting nearest to it, crawled a yard and picked up the receiver. Sandra or Wondra came in and said, "He picked up the kettle and it was like red hot."

"What I been smellin all this time," said De Vaughn. "Where's my eggs?"

"Seventy-seventh Street Station?" said Mitchell. "Get fucked, pig." He slammed the receiver back in its cradle, and a smirk escaped his moustache.

"Aw, Mitchell," said De Vaughn. "You got no brains at all?"

Donald held his burned right hand tenderly in his left, and whimpered over it. "Don't be such a baby," said Richard. "Go put some butter on it."

"Crushed ice is the best thing, they say," De Vaughn said. "Have I got to come out an cook those eggs myself?" Sandra or Wondra went back to the kitchen. Donald followed.

"So anyway," said Bernie. "The dummy is a symbol of the old Charley that's dead now."

"You really a stone primitive," said De Vaughn.

"Yeah, but what's primitive?" said Bernie. "Those Indian-African tribes really dig a lot of things in depth, know what I mean? *Objectify* all that inside stuff, get all the poison an violence out. . . ."

"*Look at that cat!*" Richard stabbed a forefinger at the television screen, where a black man on fire had just run out of a dark doorway, flaming arms uplifted, and collapsed in the street. "*Fantastic!*"

Bernie, turning too late, saw on the screen only the bland face of a man sitting behind a desk. "So with the ritual," he said. "You can *see* what's happening, because it's visible, an you're part of it."

"Yeah," said De Vaughn. "Today's a good day to stay off the street."

The phone rang again and this time Mitchell got to it ahead of the second ring. "No it isn't, pig," he said. "But hold on, I want to read you something." He dug a little red book out of his Levi jacket and began to read: " 'We will wipe them out completely. *This is the way things are.*' You listening, pig? 'If they attack and we wipe them out, we will have that satisfaction; wipe out some, some satisfaction; wipe out more, more satisfaction. . . .' "

De Vaughn was coming across the room fast.

" 'Wipe out the whole lot, complete satisfaction. . . .' "
De Vaughn took the receiver out of Mitchell's hand and re-

placed it gently. "Man your brains must be pure fat," he said. "You think they so busy flame-throwin they won't send a car right over here?"

Mitchell tongued one end of his moustache into his mouth and began chewing on it.

"Maybe they got no sheet on you," said De Vaughn. "But they got one on me, an they got one on Richard, an they must have one on old Pee-pee there."

"Maybe it's the Pontiac," said David.

"I'm gonna go move my bus, man," said De Vaughn. He went out.

"Hey, David," said Bernie. "Where do you keep the sheets and blankets round here?"

"Hall closet," said David.

"Aw shit, man," said Bernie as Sandra and Wondra came in with De Vaughn's eggs, and looked around the room. Happy sat up and said she was hungry.

"Where'd De Vaughn go?" said whichever blonde held the plate.

"Bennie, where's the kitchen?" said Happy.

"Man, nobody's got their *mind* on it," said Bernie. "Got to be a spontaneous group thing, but everybody's a slave to their bellies, man. You take like the Vietcong. . . ."

De Vaughn came in and said, "You know there's a cat across the street playin golf on his lawn? One club, man, an no ball!"

"They go all day an night on a handful of rice," said Bernie.

Happy shook Orange Julius. "Wake up an dress, honey."

"I can just see you doin that," said Bernie.

"These eggs are cold, man," said De Vaughn. "They dry, too. Bring me a glass of milk." Sandra and Wondra went out, followed by Bernie, followed by Happy.

Donald came in with his mouth full and a white dish

towel wrapped around his burned hand. "Those two *starlets* wouldn't let me have any butter." He swallowed. "I had to use Wesson Oil, and it *burns.*"

"Told you, man, crushed ice," said De Vaughn.

Sandra and Wondra brought in a half gallon of milk and a pot of coffee and a cluster of cups. Happy followed with a loaf and a half of white bread, sliced bologna, a block of Velveeta, and a jumbo jar of peanut butter. Back came Bernie with an armload of sheets and blankets. "Who wants what?" said Happy. "I'm the mama."

Bernie shook his head censoriously, but everyone else fell to breakfast, except for Pepe, who sat in his chair as if listening with total attention to his own heart beating. Richard nibbled at a slice of bologna while he fussed with his camera, the others got folded makeshift sandwiches bearing the heavy imprint of Happy's thumb. David's contained a chill lump of peanut butter the size of a walnut. Bernie began empirically stuffing one leg of Rasmussen's trousers with a sheet folded lengthwise. A cozy domesticity settled over the room.

"How's that look?" said Bernie. He had managed to fill both trouser legs, which now dangled from the edge of a chair. He arranged Rasmussen's shoes beneath the cuffs. "Body's gonna be the hard part," he said.

Speculating aloud about lighting effects, Richard walked with brisk professional authority to the window and flung the drapes wide, flooding the room with sun. "Wow, look at that old man!" On his front lawn across the street, Mr. Farnum sighted down an imaginary fairway, addressed a point in the grass, and swung his club, an eight- or nine-iron. The swing was picture-perfect, but tensely half-speed.

"Man when the heat comes they won't even have to knock," said De Vaughn. "Richard, shut them things up."

"Fantastic!" Richard snatched up his camera and dashed

out. Through the window he could be seen approaching Mr. Farnum, speaking to him. De Vaughn crossed the room and closed the drapes. "Damn Richard is some kind of exhibitionist," he said. "Or he wants to go back in the joint."

"Yeah, man," said Bernie. "Head's gonna be the hard part." Rasmussen's headless effigy sat facing him, the green-and-gray coat sweater neatly buttoned up, empty sleeves resting on the arms of the chair. "See there, poppin right out like old Charley's gut, you know?"

"Got no hands," said Happy past a semicircular unchewed bite of Velveeta sandwich. "Arms too thin."

"You need a little round cushion for the head," said Donald. He spotted a plump foot-square pink pillow on the couch. "Try this one. . . ."

Richard flew back in, leaking laughter. "I told him I was a roving feature man from CBS! And he *blushed!* Know what he said? 'How you swing is everything'! I told him, 'Keep watching Channel Two because you're going to be famous.' Why is it so dark in here? The whole idea is this sort of horrible natural suburban daylight. . . ."

"Keeps fallin *off*, man!" said Bernie.

"Isn't he going to have a face?" said Donald.

"Leave it blank," said Richard.

"Man he's got to have a face," said Bernie. "Like with plus marks for eyes, or maybe little zeros like Orphan Annie. . . ."

"Hang a weenie out his pants," said Orange Julius.

"Not this Charley," said Bernie. "This is the old one, man. Didn't have a weenie."

Donald produced an eyebrow pencil, and wanted to draw the face. Bernie said he would draw the face. Donald said he knew how to draw perfect mouths, and wasn't it supposed to be a group thing? Bernie agreed glumly, and they collaborated on a face composed of two plus signs radiating surprised eyelashes above and below, two large dots for nostrils, and a lush mouth like a lipstick advertisement. "But old Charley looked worrieder," said Bernie, and added a series of vertical worry lines which combined with the upper lashes to produce a crosshatched effect.

"Thought you told me you used to be an artist," said De Vaughn.

"I was never *representational*, baby," said Bernie. He stepped back to admire. The head fell into its own lap. Bernie took a safety pin from his hat, and secured the completed corpus of Rasmussen's old self. "Now the cap," he said. "Man, that cap is really *him*." A combination of pounding and balancing against the back of the chair finally served to keep it all in place.

"Hold on," said Bernie. "David get up, baby. He's got to be in his TV chair."

David agreeably swapped chairs with Rasmussen's old self, which Bernie carefully transferred and reassembled facing the silent screen, where grim-faced officers of Army and police conferred before a huge wall map of Southern California. "It's him," said Bernie.

The front door chimes rang, E-C-D-G, and silenced the room. G-D-E-C, the chimes answered themselves. The sound of water running in the kitchen was clearly audible. The chimes rang again, reinforced by five measured knocks. After a full two minutes had passed, a foot scraped concrete, and De Vaughn's hand kept everyone still.

Not until a motor started outside, three minutes later, did De Vaughn fly noiseless to the window and squint past the edge of the drapes. "Uh-huh," he said. "There they go. You an your little red book."

Mitchell chewed his moustache.

"I'd love to shoot a bust," said Richard. "But you know they break the camera first thing."

"An then your head, man." De Vaughn poured himself another cupful of milk. "Good thing you didn't have all that natural suburban daylight comin in, right?"

Happy burped. "All that time I was holding it," she said.

"OK," said Richard. "First I'll shoot just him, up close, *one enormous eye. . . .*"

"Hold on, baby," said Bernie.

"Then Donald and the girls dancing around him nude, maybe just Donald and *then* the girls, simple first and then complex it up. . . ."

"Peace, baby," said Bernie. "What you tryin to *organize* everything for? I mean, it's got to be spontaneous or it's nothin. . . ."

"What makes you think a ritual is spontaneous?" said Richard. "You want dancing or don't you?"

"How can I dance anyway with this *thing* on my hand?" said Donald. "Supposed to be a *veil* or something?"

"Well, this silly asshole is out of his mind," said Richard. "He wants dancing, he doesn't want dancing. He wants a group thing with no group. . . ."

"Peace, baby," said Bernie. "Control your anger. Like this is what it is: my brother Charley has got a new life, he's free, and that's what the ritual is celebratin, right? Anybody feels like dancin, they dance. Or don't, man. Dance out the old life, dance in the new. It's a beautiful idea. But if you try to force it, you fuck up the ritual."

Richard had turned away to show Orange Julius how to hold the Sun Gun.

"Well, I tell you," said De Vaughn. "My girls ain't available for dancin."

"Now what are *you* getting so tight-assed about?" At the home theater, Richard changed the news for an ancient Farmer Alfalfa cartoon. "I mean, they're *your* girls, and the film is for *you*. . . ."

"No no no no no!" yelled Bernie. "*Natural,* I told you. Nobody got to do anything they don't *feel* like! If I do it all by myself it'll still count. . . ."

"Well, everybody get out of the way then," said Richard. He shooed half the room clear of nonparticipants, turned Orange Julius and the Sun Gun like a single object, and switched the blazing white glare full on the seated figure of Rasmussen's old self.

Bernie began tinkling his prayer bell and muttering in his beard, as if warming up his motor. Richard, camera whirring, backed away from the dummy, and Bernie, as if on cue, began shuffling slowly around it. "Death of the old, birth of the new!" he said, cleared his throat and said it again, punctuating with shakes of his bell. "Brother Charley is *dead,*" he confirmed.

"Some ritual," said De Vaughn from the darkness.

"Come on, Donald," said Richard.

Bernie marked time, as if waiting for inspiration, glared once into the Sun Gun, flinched away, and began intoning in heavy tetrameter:

> *Charley's dead, Charley's free*
> *Free as you an free as me*
> *Charley's free, Charley's free*
> *Poison hate an vi'lence gone*
> *Joy an pleasure comin in*
> *Ne-ew life about to begin*
> *Round an round, round an round*
> *Put the hate an vi'lence down*
> *Sing an dance, run around*
> *Love an love an love an love . . .*

Joined by an attenuated white body in the spotlight, Bernie paused in his chanting for a series of exorcising shakes of his bell at the Dodgers cap. But when Donald, having discarded his dish towel, and wearing only a filmy gauze bikini bottom, sinuously began a combination of hula and expressionist modern dance, Bernie resumed in a louder, more confident voice, making short medicine-man runs at the closed door of the master bedroom:

Anti Ann, Anti Ann
Charley is a ne-ew man
Try an stop him if you can
Old one dead, new one live
Love an love an love an love
Nuh-nuh-nuh-nuh-nuh-nuh-nuh
Anti Ann, Anti Ann
Anti Ann, he's a man
You can't fuck him up no more
Anti Ann, he'sanew man
Free man free man free man free
He's as free as he can be . . .

Bernie was on a return trip back toward Rasmussen's old self when he vaguely saw Donald scream and disappear in a crouch. From behind him he heard a sound like a cannon going off, and fell on his face.

The spirit had moved Ann at last, and she had come out shooting.

SEVENTEEN

Her right leg asleep from the knee down, Margie fell scrambling into her own room, grabbed for the foot of the bed, and missed. The shooting had stopped, the screams and the cursing, but now someone was whimpering like a lost puppy. Who? What? Margie was not about to go see. She thought of crawling very quietly into her own closet.

But Diz sat up yawning awake, and she played possum, her feet still in the hall. "Oh *wow!*" said Diz. "Man what are you doin down there?" Margie closed her eyes before she could see him.

"Did I dream guns goin off?" he said. "Are you sleepin?" He *was* looking at her. Where Uncle Bernie had kissed her it still hurt. She closed her eyelids tighter. Diz went away barefoot. In the front of the house someone's loud voice drowned out the whimpering. Margie pushed herself to her knees, closed and locked the door into the hall, crawled and clambered into bed and pulled the covers over her head. It was warm where Diz had been. She snuggled down into a little ball and lay very still.

Her father didn't move, either. To pull the covers of David's bed over his head he would first have had to find them, a test of will and strength as formidable as going out to investigate. One shot, then five more, bangbangbang-bangbang. It had been shooting, all right. Screaming and yelling. His gun? Who else's? Who was shooting? Who got shot? Rasmussen's mind, as if combed free of knots, offered these questions no place to catch. One of the blondes had come back, then Bernie, whose gun? One shot, then two-threefourfivesix. One shot left. If it was his gun. If not, whose? Cops would come. Still loaded. Had he drunk that much? Strange droning in his head. *Three times?* Yes. Six shots? Yes. If his gun, one shot left. Not Rasmussen. Who was shooting? Cops would come. Not Rasmussen. Someone would call them. Not Rasmussen.

Not law-abiding Howard Bunch, either. Several minutes before the shooting started, he had driven off to work, furiously vindicated by the torn fender of his new Mustang, and listening critically to the motor. A general outbreak of guerrilla warfare and the imminent declaration of martial law would not keep him from his appointed rounds, although he had tacitly acknowledged them by ordering Viola to stay home from the UN Day Center. She hadn't even argued.

In the bathroom dabbing salve when the doorbell rang, he had asked, "Who was that?" over his second cup of coffee, swallowed standing up with his hat on, Dagwood Bumstead style.

"Police," Viola said. "Asking about Rasmussens."

"What did you tell em?"

"Didn't have a thing to tell."

"OK, I'm on my way. Don't just sit around watching the TV all day."

Viola had watched him go, invisibly shaking her head. If ever a man believed what you don't know can't hurt you, it was Howard. By now she felt like a one-woman conspiracy to conceal from the whole world the goings-on next door. But even if that policeman had been halfway polite, the very most you could expect, she would not have told him. Like he thought he was Dragnet, except he didn't say "ma'am." Anybody home next door? Notice anything unusual this morning? Last night?

"Minding my own business keeps me too busy to be spying on the neighbors," Viola had said firmly, and not even a thank you out of him. God help Lily and the boys. God help everybody. Howard, of course, had never asked God's help, either as Baptist or as Episcopalian. And when he roared off, Viola just stood by the window with her own cup of coffee, doing exactly what she had told the policeman she was too busy to do.

There wasn't much to see. Something missing. The Volkswagen bus that had been parked in front of Rasmussens? No, there it was across the street halfway down the block. She was about to go fetch in her canary-yellow plastic garbage can when she heard the shots next door, loud and clear, a whole lot of them.

"Dear Jesus!" Was there anyplace they weren't shooting today? Were they gangsters over there after all? That good-looking little man who told her he lived off women? With those shoulders he didn't look like he'd have to shoot anybody. Just squeeze and break your back. The others all blurred together in Viola's mind, all but him, leading her out with his hard fingers. Oh, and the one in black with the hate-stare. He would kill you and never bat an eye. . . .

Well, what to do? Viola ruled out calling the police at once. Stay indoors and mind her own business? She was not that blasé. Take her butcher knife again and go investigate? She was not that brave. She went to the telephone and picked up the directory. She had to find out. What had happened?

No television cameraman trapped in a jungle ambush could have been more intrepid than Richard. Though he had sneered at Bernie's metaphysic of spontaneity, he was not one to pass up what chance might offer his lens, and when Ann came out shooting he stood his ground next to petrified Orange Julius, stood his ground and filmed it all.

Beyond Bernie's turning, gesticulating bulk the door of the master bedroom swung inward and through it stepped a fortyish woman wearing a simple gray-and-white cotton dress whose vertical stripes accentuated her thinness. In her right hand she carried a pistol, and she did not blink against the glare of the Sun Gun. Halfway through an uncoiling movement promising a bump, Donald saw her, screamed, and plunged off-camera into the dark side of the room. The pistol went off. Bernie collapsed on the floor. For something less than three seconds the woman stood motionless, looking not at the pistol, not at Bernie, nowhere but straight ahead toward the figure of Rasmussen in his Dodgers cap facing the television screen. Both hands brought the pistol up at a rigid right angle to her body and she fired it five times, as fast as she could squeeze the trigger. The Dodgers cap flew several inches in the air, the shape beneath it doubled, slumped forward softly onto the floor, and the woman revealed a row of perfect white teeth.

At that instant Richard's cinematic instincts had told him the sequence was over, but he kept shooting, as a voice from the dark came slow, incredulous, full of an awe verging on admiration: "Mom!" His camera recorded the woman turning her head toward the voice, the stiff single beam of her two arms falling slowly, and De Vaughn, springing out of the darkness to take her from the side, trapping her two wrists and the pistol between his hands and swinging her bodily around to face the front door. She did not resist, and in a moment De Vaughn held the gun. Richard stopped shooting. Documentaries made him want to throw up.

"Get some lights on!" said De Vaughn. "She hit anybody?"

"I'm killed, I'm killed," whimpered Donald.

"Wow, is that really your mother?" said Happy.

Still clutching the extinguished Sun Gun, Orange Julius said, "I coulda got killed! Gimme my helmet, man!"

Wondering blankly if De Vaughn had conceivably just saved his life, David switched on the light with nerveless fingers, revealing a floor littered with bodies: Sandra and Wondra, Mitchell, Happy, Donald, Bernie, and the *other* girl. Only Pepe sat black and immobile in his chair. David decided that his own life had not been in special danger, but the blankness persisted as he removed the helmet and returned it to Orange Julius, leaving his head cold and unprotected.

"Jesus Christ!" Bernie pushed himself up off the carpet. "Like I knew she was evil, but wow!"

Ann stood quiescent near the front door. "Please keep your hands to yourself," she said, although De Vaughn was now a yard away, apparently making a body count. "Lady," he said without turning. "You're lucky tonight."

Donald lay on his back, thin and ghostly and faintly pornographic in his diaphanous bikini bottoms, cradling his right hand in his left and whimpering, "I fell on it, right on the burned part. . . ."

"*Hold on!*" Bernie, sitting hatless on the floor, slapped himself hard on the head, as if the thoughts inside threatened to burst out. "Maybe you really made it, too!" he said to Ann. "Got all that evil and poison out in one shot! Wouldn't that be fantastic? All that hate you been storin up all these years? Just gone?"

"You're disgusting," said Ann.

Diz came in and asked what was happening.

"Naw, *listen* to me now!" Bernie sprang to his feet, forgetting SHAZAM. "I mean, nobody planned it, it just came out that way! Old Charley's dead, and you killed him, so your old self is dead now, too! Symbolically. All you got to do is accept your freedom: *you really free.*"

"You're all disgusting," said Ann. "This place is a mess. Why don't you all go away?"

"DON'T FIGHT IT! YOU'RE HOLDIN BACK!"

"Give it up, man," said De Vaughn, offering the pistol in evidence. "Like I say, all that energy got to go somewhere."

"WHAT I BEEN SAYIN!"

"What's *happening*, man?" said Diz.

"She got the TV anyway," said De Vaughn. "Looka there. Man, she got off a lot of rounds in a hurry."

"Beautiful!" said Bernie, jingling with the intensity of his vision. "Him an the TV both! You tellin me *that* ain't symbolic?"

"Aw, Bernie, you crazier than she is," said De Vaughn. "You damn lucky you ain't dead, don't you know that?"

"I was dancin, baby, like the bullets didn't touch me. It all means something, you think about it."

The telephone rang. Ann shivered and hugged herself. "Just let it ring," De Vaughn told Mitchell. But no one stopped Ann when she picked up the receiver and said, "Hello?"

Then, "Nothing," she said. "No. Yes. Thanks for calling. Good-bye."

And no one got in her way when she walked out into the dining room past Diz, who said, "Was it *her?*"

Viola stared at the receiver in her hand, chilled by the buzz of the dial tone. *Hello. Nothing. No. Yes. Thanks. Good-bye.* Exactly like somebody was holding a gun to her head. Viola's duty was clear: she snatched up her purse and ran out the front door. This time she would be on her guard.

Inside Rasmussens' people were arguing. Viola took a deep breath and a half step back, rang the doorbell, and stopped the argument dead. In the corner of her eye she saw the drapes move, and a second later the door opened; it was him in the Malcolm shirt. "Say there, lady-next-door, come on in."

But Viola looked him over from head to foot, and if that wasn't a pistol in his pocket she was *anybody's* fool. "What's that you got there?" She pointed. "Where's Mrs. Rasmussen?"

"We been havin a little target practice here," he grinned. "Anyway, Mrs. Rasmussen did."

"Where is she? She sounded very unnatural over the phone."

"Baby she's an unnatural woman, but it don't mean you got to be, come on in here." With hard fingers he led her back in just as he'd led her out at daybreak. "My name's De Vaughn," he said. Viola told herself she had better take it very very easy, and, having done so, she relaxed a bit.

"So what do you want to stick around for, De Vaughn?" The boy in the blue-jean jacket had both ends of his moustache in his mouth, reminding Viola distantly of a baby's teething ring. "I mean, you got your business done, and this is such a whole lot of meaningless shit. . . ."

"Not to me it ain't," said De Vaughn. "Things are expanding round here, I'm expanding a bit myself. Whole scene is, you know, *fluid*. Richard here's all set to make some more movies, no tellin what might happen."

"You better believe Old Granddad in there is through for the day." This came from a kind of cheap-looking blonde Viola didn't remember seeing before. In fact there were two of them.

"Maybe so," said De Vaughn, without taking his eyes off Viola. "Thing is, we don't get out among the people like this very often. . . ."

"You call these *the people?*" said the boy with the moustache. "Shit, man . . ."

"Aw go read your book," said De Vaughn. "Or go on an split. Do *something*. You wanted to come along, man, *I* didn't invite you."

"Got no bread," said the boy with the moustache, as if he was proud of the fact. "So wake me up when you leave, if it's not too much trouble." He strolled away cool into the dining room. Hippies! For the life of her Viola couldn't see what was so hip about them. Where she grew up somebody hip always looked sharp and knew what was happening. But these new models . . .

"Hey!" said De Vaughn. "Where's your old man?"

"Went to work," said Viola. "Most people can't afford to be partying all night and all the next day."

"Maybe so, maybe so," said De Vaughn. "But that don't mean they *right* necessarily. Anyway . . ." He stretched his arms sideways, showing an inch of flat tan belly between sweatshirt and belt. "*I* got no business can't wait. There's a damn war goin on out there, an this is as good a place to spend the day, right? Got food, got beds. TV's full of bullets but I bet old General Cornwallis here'll dance if we ask him, right, General?" He nodded at the no-good brother, who looked to Viola even more foolish without his hat on. "Say, what's the matter, General? Two minutes ago you jumpin around havin visions an everything. . . ."

"Everything's great, baby," said the no-good brother. Then he slapped himself on his bald spot and dashed out the front door in a flurry of bells.

"Old General had a narrow escape little while ago," De Vaughn said. "Must of affected his mind some way."

As Viola was considering this, she saw Ann Rasmussen come in from the dining room, apparently unharmed. "My teakettle is ruined," she said. "The kitchen is a filthy mess." She sounded as dead calm as she had on the phone, but her teeth looked like she had been eating mud. "Why don't you all just go home?"

"You OK, honey?" said Viola. "David you better see about your mother." But David was just staring at her like everybody else in the room. Then the no-good brother ran back in waving an empty plastic bag and shouting, "Who took my fuckin rice? Richard what you do with it, man? It was in the car an now it's gone!"

The big fat girl laughed out loud and the frog-eyed sissy said, "Don't *yell* at me, baby. What rice?"

"My rice, man, it was *in this bag!"*

"Was that rice? I thought it was like bird seed. We fed it to the seagulls down in San Pedro, didn't we, Pepe? Only they wouldn't eat it."

"That was my rice, you asshole!"

"Say now, General," said De Vaughn. "Don't get so violent, man. It's against your principles, violence, ain't it?"

"Rage is holy," said the no-good brother. "Violence is evil, but rage is holy!"

"You shut your filthy mouth," said Ann in the same dead voice. "It's all your fault."

"My fault? You the one came in here tryin to *murder* everybody!"

De Vaughn began explaining something about a heap of stuff over by the TV, but Viola's sympathies were fixed on Ann, with her muddy teeth and her glassy eyes. She looked completely defenseless, and without waiting on anybody else, Viola led her into the bedroom, soothing her like a child.

"You don't know what I've been through," said Ann.

Viola made her lie down on the bed. Twin beds, but that hadn't kept them from having two children. "I've got to wash my teeth," said Ann. "Margie made fudge. My mouth is filthy."

"Let it all go now, honey," said Viola. "You lay there and rest now, I'll try to keep em quiet." Ann did as she was told.

"Poor woman is dead on her feet," Viola told De Vaughn back in the living room. "People shooting off guns in her house! Give anybody a nervous breakdown!" She didn't see why everybody laughed at that.

"Sit down here, baby," said De Vaughn. "I want to talk to you. . . ." But before either of them could say another word, one of the sissies gave a screech, and Viola looked where everybody was looking, the door into the dining room.

Charley Rasmussen stood there, without his baseball cap on, wrapped up in a bed sheet, like Mahatma Gandhi or somebody from ancient Rome, staring around the room like he'd never seen any of them before. One of the blondes laughed.

"What the hell's goin on out here?" The poor man croaked like he'd been lost in the desert without water. "Guy in my bed . . ."

"*Charley!*" said the no-good brother. "Come forth, baby!"

"By God he looks changed," said De Vaughn. "You girls better see about your student there." A bright bright light like a flashbulb that wouldn't stop went on. That was a camera whirring away. Viola saw the two blondes take poor Charley Rasmussen in charge, like a mental patient who might need restraint.

He shook his head, blinking, and said somebody was in his bed and he had to lie down right now. Walking carefully, like a man taking a drunk test, he started toward the master bedroom, followed by the light and the camera. The two blondes escorted him, one on each side. But De Vaughn went and stopped them. "Say, brother," he said. "I don't know as I'd go in there if I was you. Your old lady just got done tryin to kill you, man."

"You shit, De Vaughn," said the frog-eyed sissy with the camera. The one in the helmet held the light.

Charley Rasmussen just looked completely dumbfounded and exhausted, looking for a place to die. "That moustache one," he said. But De Vaughn led him over to the pile of stuff by the TV. "She put a lot of bullets in *that*, man," he said. "An she sure thought it was you."

Charley Rasmussen only shook his head like it hurt him, and turned back toward the bedroom. "The store calls," he said, "tell em I won't be in."

"Aw well, convoy him on in there, then," said De Vaughn. The blondes did what he said. "I just hope she ain't got another piece hid away someplace."

At the bedroom door, Charley Rasmussen heaved out a long broken sigh. "Jesus H. Christ on a crutch," he said. "I'm still higher'n a kite."

"*Kite*, man!" said the helmeted one. The light went off, and Frog Eye went on complaining to De Vaughn about messing up the scene.

The blondes came back. One of them closed the door; the other said, "Zonked, man. Her, too."

"You know, maybe it's a good idea," said De Vaughn. "When they wake up he may get himself a whole new deal. . . ."

The no-good brother was talking away at a young boy with a big mess of black hair. "Well, you got to *help* her some, baby. She's *shy* is all it is."

De Vaughn was ignoring Frog Eye. "Look here," Viola said to him. She felt like the only sure sane person in the room. "What kind of foolishness is going on around here?"

"*Anti*foolishness, baby," said De Vaughn right back. "You sit down here, an I'm gonna tell you all about everything."

"*Naw,* baby," said the no-good brother. "Like I'm tellin you: *that little chick is ready!*" Without his hat he looked more like the Cowardly Lion than ever.

"Rice paper and bamboo strips," said the one in the helmet to David Rasmussen. "And glue, man. Impact glue. That's all we need."

"For what?" said David, smiling.

"For a kite!"

II. TOO MUCH TUESDAY

EIGHTEEN

Tuesday morning was by now well on its golden way west across the Pacific, the sun arching along its track like a missile and aimed at three-quarters of a billion Chinese. At King Kamehameha Kottages in Honolulu a lady in a hat like a feathered waffle sat down to breakfast. "Oh *really*," she said. "Fresh pineapple *again?*" Her husband, a master plumber from Brawley, California, said you couldn't blame them for pushing the local product.

Tuesday morning had already been survived by approximately half the citizens of the richest and most powerful nation in the world, although the casualties since midnight had been undeniably higher than would normally have been produced by traffic accidents, random murders, lung cancer, and other natural causes. In Saint Cloud, Minnesota, a man in a white nylon robe predicted the end of the world, and ate a hearty lunch of organically grown leeks and walnuts. A senior Senator had put it less apocalyptically to newsmen a few minutes earlier: "The country is in trouble," he had said, converting to extra portent his disappointment at the absence of television cameras. "And I mean *big* trouble."

Tuesday morning had shone none too reassuringly upon Rasmussen's house, too, and had Rasmussen himself been equal to plucking the Times from the dusty oleander outside his bedroom window, he would have been, if possible, less reassured still. WAR IN THE STREETS, announced page one. *Police Battle Guerrillas in Nine Southland Communities.*

The Governor of California had refused to issue an emergency proclamation closing gunshops rather than infringe upon the God-given and constitutionally ensured right of citizens to bear arms. "California is not yet a communist dictatorship," he added. "Thank God."

The Mayor of Los Angeles pleaded with citizens to stay in their homes as much as possible; he hinted that they should resist the temptation to enlist in any of a dozen paramilitary organizations rumored to be in action. "Let's all keep cool," he said. "We're still better off than a lot of places." Asked to name one, he mentioned "off the record" a city of half a million on the east shore of San Francisco Bay.

Indeed, the Oakland Red Cross had received telephone calls from white taxpayers demanding relocation in San Francisco, a project made difficult by the closing of the Bay Bridge to civilian traffic, and the filling of every hotel room in San Francisco by convening members of the National Mental Health Association.

Nor were the panicky Oaklanders unique in their sense of crisis. An Orange County proctologist, spokesman for a prominent veterans' association, called for immediate air strikes against "the seat of the infection," while a Mrs. Himmlicher of Mothers on the March demanded the roundup and internment of all "blacks and beards," including those in the police and armed forces. "Have we forgotten Pearl Harbor so soon?" she wanted to know.

The news from the afternoon half of the country was not much better; so bad, in fact, that it had pushed to halfway down page seven of the Times a heartening burst of lyricism from the Secretary of Commerce, who saw "the end of the inflationary spiral as clearly visible as the sun, moon, and stars."

So perhaps Rasmussen and his family were lucky to have come so far into the day with no more damage done them. Invaded by a band of ex-convicts, sex perverts, and narcotics users; drugged and ravaged, baited and mocked and duped into committing rash acts: were they not all lucky still to be breathing?

A yard apart on their own twin beds, Rasmussen and Ann drew the shallow regular breaths of exhausted sleep. In the half light through the venetian blinds neither looked visibly the worse for their extraordinary performances of earlier in the morning.

Margie caught and held her breath at the first rattle of her doorknob. "Hey, lemme in, it's me." Through door and bedclothes she had recognized the voice of Diz, and only exhaled—inaudibly, like her mother—when her chest threatened to burst. Then someone—*him?*—came into the bathroom next door, and *that* door she had neglected to lock! She held her breath again.

David was breathing remarkably easy, considering the mind-blowing events of the morning. Even Happy's fudge, forgotten in his shirt pocket, couldn't have given his brains such an airing. The Cap's workout with Sandra and Wondra had been more than enough, but leave it to Mrs. Clean to top anything The Cap could do! Their stealing the show from such an exotic cast was a plot right off television: *The Folks Next Door Show the Hippies a Thing or Two.* Sex? Violence? Don't sell Mom and Pop short! But if David's exhilaration contained a trace of warped family pride, it didn't blind him to his own certain place below the 25th percentile. At these games he was a smiling spectator, or he was nothing.

But his attentive inertia was disturbed when the killer in black glanced a laser beam off De Vaughn and caught him smiling. So when Orange Julius asked him where the glue was, David said he would go look, and moved off toward the kitchen as Viola Bunch was saying, "Education field? I can just imagine!"

"True!" said De Vaughn. "Just look at me: I look to you like a rich pimp? You ever *seen* a rich pimp? Rich pimp don't drive no five-year-old Volks wagon bus! Don't go round in a sweatshirt an tennis shoes, baby."

"You can't tell a book by its cover," said Viola. In the corner of her eye she saw one of the blonde twins trying to get De Vaughn's attention.

"Told you girls twice already now," said De Vaughn to the blonde. "We stayin around for a while. Why don't you go do some push-ups, or lie in the sun or something? Got to be a back yard somewhere." Viola readily confirmed that there was a back yard, and a patio, too. The two blondes went out. "They sure don't sass you back much, do they?" said Viola.

"Both very loyal girls," said De Vaughn, and to the figure hovering over the couch: "Say, General, what you want to do, sit down in my lap?"

"No, baby," said Bernie. "Peace." He asked Orange Julius and Happy where they were going. "Bamboo," said Orange Julius. "Groovy," said Bernie, and wandered, like the benign goofy spirit of the place, out to the kitchen. "Hey, David," he said. "You got any kind of rice around? Natural cereals? How you doin, baby?"

David opened a cupboard. In a smooth gaily jacketed façade like novels in a lending library, they filled two whole shelves: Quisp, Quake, and Crackos; Rice Krinkles and Rice Twinkles; Cheerios and Lucky Charms; Crispy Critters and Cap'n Crunch; Cocoa Krispies and Cocoa Puffs; Sugar Pops and Sugar Crisps and Sugar Stars and Sugar Smacks and Sugaroos. "Aw, man," said Bernie.

"Rice is in there," pointed David, and in another cupboard Bernie found it: Instant Rice, Now 50% Faster.

"Go with what you got," said Bernie, spilling out a handful—it didn't weigh anything!—and pouring it through the hole in his beard, head tipped to the side with all six molars. A few moments' unresisted grinding reduced it to fluffy pap. "Wow!" said Bernie. "This shit is *ghost* rice!"

It's what zombies eat, thought David. "Maybe so," he said. Would Fastick Household Cement do, he wondered. Donald came in like a beggar, hand cupped, eyes pleading. He was crippled, he said, and would they please crush him some ice? David opened the refrigerator, hoping he would not excite a misunderstanding.

Diz, standing under the hot spray in the back bathroom, watched the silverfish wriggling between his feet and saw himself come quite autonomously erect. Maybe it was some kind of sign. Bernie had sold him—intellectually, as it were —on the idea of initiating that lumpy little girl into the mysteries of love, and now in euphemistic technicolor he reviewed his own erotic history—four punishing bouts with Happy upstairs in the love room, three whole days before she administered the same blessings to his brother Monk.

Cleaned, refreshed, full of spirit, he watched himself in the mirror using two already damp towels to dry himself and his great black mane. Then, as fully capable as he could wish to be, he let himself into her chamber. Certainly he didn't need the aphrodisiac thoughts of her untutored shyness which flamed through him at the sight of her, coiled and waiting, all hidden under the bedclothes. Here I come, ready or not. "Say, baby, it's me," he said. "Hey, baby . . ."

"Do you call all your students 'baby'?" said Viola. "In this so-called Freedom School of yours?"

"You know," said De Vaughn, "you comin on awful cute an middle-aged for a chick as young as you."

Orange Julius and Happy came in the front door, and left it open. He brandished what looked like, and was, the handle of a bamboo garden rake. "Now all we need's glue and rice paper," he said. "And a knife to cut the strips."

"You still got that blade with you, baby?" said De Vaughn. "How about lendin it to old O.J. there?" More dubious than embarrassed this time, Viola gave her butcher knife to the crazy kid in the Nazi helmet.

He clicked his heels and bowed stiffly. "*Danke schön, gnädige Frau,*" he said. "*Ein gutes Messer um Juden zu schlachten!*" Then, "*Vorwärts!*" and, knife in one fist, bamboo like a drum major's baton in the other, he goose-stepped into the dining room, followed by Happy giggling that she couldn't keep her legs straight.

"Doesn't he give you the creeps?" said Viola. "All that old Storm Trooper stuff?"

"He's just tryin to get it off his back," said De Vaughn. "Like his folks told him about the Nazis *so many times* he finally got enough, understand what I mean?"

"Mmm," said Viola.

De Vaughn shut the front door, and locked it.

But it was too late for Margie to lock the door into the bathroom. *Diz was actually in her bed, naked.* She lay clenched in one terrified knot, hearing nothing, feeling nothing, her consciousness condensed within the huge pounding of her heart. "Hey, baby," Diz was saying. "Don't get uptight, I won't hurt you, hey, gimme your hand."

He found both of them locked together against her chest and began trying to pry one loose. Margie thought wildly of rolling backward off the bed and then slipping underneath it, but Diz had got a purchase on her right hand, and when he wrenched it free she let it go limp.

"Relax, relax," he was saying. "Take a deep breath." That had been Happy's advice, and he needed something to say. He took a deep breath himself; in fact he took two.

Margie did not follow suit, but she risked an instant's peek, saw nothing but a monstrous tangle of black hair, and pressed her eyes shut again. "Hey, you still got all your *clothes* on!" His hands were enormous. Between them her own felt as small and helpless as the paw of a furry little kitty, and to make it worse he began kissing it sideways between his lips, which felt terrifically wide and thick and wet, like he could gobble her up. Then he said the most shattering thing of all:

"*I love you.*"

Happy had said that, too, a whole lot of times.

Now in the kitchen she was saying it to David, who had just found some plain white tissue paper, the kind his mother always wrapped presents in. "But it ain't rice paper," Orange Julius said. "And that ain't impact glue."

"Got to go with what you got," said Bernie, who had attached himself to the kite-building project something in the fashion of a senior statesman.

Donald, his hand in a blue ceramic bowl, trailed the four of them into the dining room, where they sat down around the table and went to work. Bernie produced his yellow oilskin pouch and passed it around. All of them took pinches, David included, and Happy brought a giant bottle of Coca-Cola from the refrigerator to wash it down. Bernie said he'd take plain water, even if it was full of chemicals.

In the living room, De Vaughn listened patiently to Viola's description of an average day at the United Nursery Day Center. "I don't know how much *educating* we do," she said. "What those kids need is love and a little freedom to play."

"That *is* education, baby," said De Vaughn. "Exact same principle as my school." He paid no attention to Pepe, who had finally arisen from his chair and begun to circle the room, testing with stiff fingers the corners of the furniture. When the telephone rang, Richard put down his copy of Look and answered it. "Don *who?*" he said. "Ace Liquors? You mean you lick everybody who comes in?"

"It's his store, man," said De Vaughn. "Tell em he won't be in today."

"I'm terribly sorry," said Richard, "but Mr. Rasputin is indisposed today. . . . I said in-dis-posed. . . . Oh well, if you're such an ace why don't you try licking yourself then?" He hung up.

"Why don't you just leave that thing off the hook awhile," said De Vaughn, and Richard did. "What I don't understand," said De Vaughn to Viola, "is if you so crazy about kids, why don't you have a gang of em?"

Viola looked at her hands.

"Why don't he tell *me* to do something?" said Pepe.

"Who, me?" said De Vaughn. "I'll tell you to do something. Relax. Go punch a wall or something like that."

"Yeah, quit *pacing*, baby," said Richard.

"*What?*"

"You're more terrifying sitting down," said Richard. "That's all."

"That's all, that's all, to me that's all shit," said Pepe. "What in the fuck are we doin here?"

Wordlessly, Margie wondered the very same thing. Diz had moved closer to her, saying, "I love you, baby," seven or eight more times; a few inches backward would put her on the floor. He filled his lungs noisily, and exhaled *right in Margie's face*. "Come on, baby, take your clothes off," he said, Margie pulled her hand free, Diz took another deep breath, said, "Aw fuck it," recaptured her hand and pulled it downward. Margie finally opened her mouth, but her scream came out a squeak. Something shook the house.

"He's got *fantastic* violence," said Richard in the wake of Pepe's slamming exit. "I mean, he's really dangerous, karate and everything. It's the star quality in him."

"He's got spooky eyes," said Viola. "Nothing personal, you know."

"He's got eyes for De Vaughn," said Richard. "I can tell. He's got this fantastic love-hate thing, with the violence. It's what's so exciting. . . ."

"Aw yeah," said De Vaughn. "He probably wants to get beat to a jelly and fucked in the ass all at once, some twist like that. . . ."

"Baby, you're more sensitive than you look about some things," said Richard.

Past her discomfiture at De Vaughn's bad language, it was plain as day to Viola: that little sissy was sitting right there flirting over his Look magazine.

"Lots of messed-up guys around," said De Vaughn. "But one thing I learned in the joint was you prove you a man or you come out a woman."

"Well, I knew that before I went to the joint, baby," said Richard. "But what did you find out?"

"Let that punk make one grab, he'll find out," said De Vaughn good-naturedly. "But I don't mind faggots, long as they ain't tryin to integrate me. Like you OK, Richard, not to mention bein a *cinematic genius* an all. Baby, you ought to see some of the movies this cat makes."

"I'd like to very much sometime," said Viola. She could just imagine!

"Fuckin glue is no good!" cried Orange Julius in the next room. "I told you, you got to have impact glue! This old shit won't even glue my fingers together." He demonstrated this thesis for the other kite builders.

Diz had made wee-wee right in her bed! All over! All over her! Margie had never had anything half so terrible happen to her, never ever. She flung herself out of bed, and into the bathroom, where she thrust her right hand under the hot-water tap. She averted her eyes, looking in the mirror more windblown than ever.

When the hot water got too hot to bear, she withdrew her lobster-pink paw for inspection. Seemingly it was clean. She chanced a peek back into her room, hoping to see him gone. He lay motionless in her bed, with all that damp doggy hair all over her pillow. Through it he said, "Couldn't help it, baby." Nasty wet memories of her own stirred the vague beginnings of pity in Margie. He looked like a big puppy there. And he said he couldn't help it. The trouble was, *she* would surely get the blame.

Maybe the two of them could wash the sheet together.

Maybe, Bernie suggested, if somebody sat on the kite, the pressure would make it stick together. Happy hoisted herself immediately onto the table, settled on the kite, and the drop-leaf broke with a splintering crash.

Happy picked herself up off the floor with surprising grace, but the kite was ruined. "Well, back to the old drawing board," said Orange Julius. "Still got plenty of everything."

"Should've done it on the floor, man," said Bernie. A popping noise somewhere outside the house interrupted his masterminding, he bolted through the living room saying, "Shit, I left the key in it," and got the front door open in time to see Pepe on the little Japanese motorcycle make a banking turn out of Rasmussen's driveway and disappear around the corner.

Into the public world, where the majority of citizens were ignoring the Mayor's advice and going about their everyday business. Civil war be damned, the Gross National Product was headed for a trillion and no one expected a general amnesty for installment buyers. Despite a sudden boom in hijacking, the truck fleets were still rolling. The drivers all packed guns, since private patrols and armed-guard services were fresh out of personnel, and couldn't recruit more. Food and drink deliveries were still keeping pace with the epidemic stockpiling of hoarders, and a good thing, too, for it was getting close to lunchtime, and the Army field kitchens were boiling away in preselected parking lots and playgrounds. Troops patrolled the reservoirs and power plants. True, supermarkets and liquor stores were being robbed in record numbers, but they were taking in the hoarders' money at a rate so much higher that it hardly seemed to matter. Even at Ace Liquors, Don was so busy that he hardly had time to worry about Charley goofing off while kooks answered his phone, today of all days.

Housewives ironing in front of their television sets saw a particularly dramatic event, live and direct, when His Honor the Mayor stuck his head out of his bulletproof plastic bubbletop on his way to an emergency luncheon meeting and told reporters and cameramen that "new steps are about to be taken to secure normalization before the situation can escalate further." Before he could elaborate, an irate pensioner with a little cockscomb of white hair began blazing away at him with a .22 target pistol, and screaming that he had "sold out to the niggers." Bodyguards poured upward of forty slugs of various calibers into him, and His Honor luckily escaped injury, although an unidentified woman was killed instantly by a .22 bullet in the heart, and a passing salesman shot through his sample case, filling the air with an exotically musky scent, which the salesman later told interviewers was "a revolutionary new perfume for men called Love Me Now."

The destruction of the home theater by a more modest

hail of lead spared or deprived the Rasmussens and their visitors of all such evidence of what was going on out there. Rasmussen and Ann slept on. Sandra and Wondra, in their matching gold-mesh panties, and Richard, totally in the buff, sunned themselves on the red bricks which Rasmussen had laid by hand. Viola listened with two minds to De Vaughn's spiel about freedom and energy. In a thickening communal silence, Orange Julius and Happy constructed another kite, watched and wordlessly supported by David and Bernie, by Donald with his blue bowl of ice, and by the *other* girl, who had drifted in from the living room at the crash of the table. Out in the public world the most superbly bizarre things were going on, but everyone at Rasmussens' seemed clearly much better off for not knowing what they were missing.

"Baby," said Diz to Margie, who sat now at the foot of the bed. "You don't know what you're missing. Cause I really love you, man." But Margie just looked at him out of blank little blue eyes and said nothing, so he turned on her little transistor radio and dialed around.

Margie heard nothing, spellbound in a double bind: how could they wash the sheet when Diz was lying on it? And how could he get off it when he had no clothes on?

Diz quickly found the radio a drag: too much news, not enough music. "Baby, what's the matter with you anyway?" Not exactly an unfamiliar question to Margie, yet she had no answer for it.

"Like don't you want to do, you know, what your mother and father do?"

Margie knew the answer to that one. She clamped her lips tighter and shook her head. No, no, no.

While her mother, white teeth still stained by the fudge she had eaten distractedly in the kitchen, the worst Margie had ever made, lay dreaming a most euphoric dream.

She and Howard Bunch sprawled at their ease on red Naugahyde mattresses which covered wall to wall the floor of a spacious tree house. A clear green light filtered through the leafy dome, tinting the air around them and gleaming pure on the shining porcelain bathroom fixtures. But her skin, and Howard's, were one pearly translucent gold, rich and smooth and free of unsightly hair. They had just done it, like a pair of God's favorite movie stars, and in a little while they would do it again, but there was no hurry.

From far below came a faint harsh twittering, as from a flock of angry birds, and, looking down along the magnificent stainless-steel pole which supported the tree house, she saw a filthy rabble milling about, glaring up enviously and shouting what she knew to be filthy insulting words. Someone began shinnying up the pole, and she recognized the shiny red bawling mask of her brother Petey, but stayed perfectly calm in the face of this menace, letting him get within range, and the others who were following his example. At precisely the right moment, she pressed the button on the remote-control panel, electrically flushing the battery of toilets which protected the place, pouring down bombs of excrement upon them. Petey and her father and her brothers and Rasmussen and all of them toppled backward, buried beneath the huge volume of filth, and were swallowed up in the depths of the water, which quickly became pure and limpid and free of infection. She turned to Howard. . . .

On the other twin bed, Rasmussen lay dreamless, hearing nothing at all. Certainly not the door chimes, which rang a few minutes after one o'clock.

Seeing no police cars past the drapes, De Vaughn opened the front door to a tall cheerful young man in a black double-breasted suit a size too large, a starched white shirt and black tie. His face was sweet as a doll's with its clear wide-open blue eyes, polished apple cheeks, and unusually red lips. His blond hair was long on top and brushed straight back, but cropped close on the sides like that of a parolee or a German. In one black lapel gleamed a tiny gold cross, bearing a tinier gold Jesus.

This young man was shuffling a deck of cards like an accordion, and so confidently that his eyes never fell.

"What can I do for you, brother?" said De Vaughn.

The young man snicked a card out of the deck and presented it. Large black printing asked: *Do You Ever Enjoy A Friendly Game Of Cards?*

"I don't gamble much as a rule," said De Vaughn.

Another card said: *Can You Spare Five Minutes To Play Cards With Me?* IT MIGHT SAVE YOUR LIFE! It was immediately supplemented by yet another, hand-lettered in blue ballpoint: *I Am Deaf & Dumb.*

"Well, sure, I guess so," said De Vaughn, ushering the young man inside. "See, baby," he told Viola. "All comes under the heading of research among the people."

Viola didn't see, exactly. "What do they say?" she asked. The young man dispensed another card, and De Vaughn read it aloud: *"I Am A Student Of Everlasting Gospel Bible College. May I Sit Down?"* He sat the young man down on the couch next to Viola, and hipped her toward him as he sat down himself, gathering the three of them chummily together. "Next card?" he said, and took it.

The Game Consists Of 52 Questions. Answer YES *or* NO *To Each Question. At The End Of The Game You Will Receive A* FREE GIFT.

"Got it," nodded De Vaughn. "Deal on, brother."

No. 1—Have You Noticed Lately That The World Is Going From Bad To WORSE?

De Vaughn nodded solemnly, and Viola said she guessed it was probably true.

*No. 2—Have You Wondered About The Terrific Increase
In Crime, Dope Addiction, Divorce, Immorality, Anarchy,
Youth Running Wild, Vice & Sin, Etc.?*

"I give it some thought," admitted De Vaughn, shushing
Viola's comment about "selling Come-to-Jesus door to door
like the Avon lady."

No. 3—Did You Know That GOD INTENDED THIS TO HAP-
PEN?

De Vaughn nodded even harder this time, but put up one
traffic-cop hand before the young man could deal again. He
snatched a ballpoint out of the black handkerchief pocket
and on the back of *No. 3* composed the following message:

We are both SAVED *& accept Jesus Christ as our Personal
Savior. But there are Real Sinners in this house & are you
Man enough to Face Them?*

Disappointment and doubt were chased in succession from
the young man's face by manly resolve, and he nodded
firmly. De Vaughn wrote more:

They are DEEP IN SIN *& maybe hopeless cases. Will you go*
ALL THE WAY *to save them & not give up?*

The young man swallowed. Then he pointed at ALL THE
WAY and nodded, at *give up?* and shook his head.

You may need to Protect Yourself, added De Vaughn, and
standing up he instructed the young man by quick pantomime to take off the brown leather belt which secured his
black trousers. "This is some brave stud," he told Viola as
the young man obeyed instructions, and let himself be led
toward the dining room, whence erupted Orange Julius,
Happy, Bernie, David, Donald, and the *other* girl, disciples
following the kite which Orange Julius carried before him
like a holy object.

The young man looked at them, then at De Vaughn, his
china-blue eyes clearly saying, "Are these the ones?"

De Vaughn shook his head, snapped, "Don't stand round

gawkin" at the kite followers, and guided the young man into the dining room, where he gave him a gentle comradely push toward the bright yellow light of the patio. Viola saw him stuff the belt in his coat pocket, arrange the cards, and begin shuffling them debonairly as he went out into the sun. Then De Vaughn hustled her, too, back into the living room. "Don't want to hang around," he said. "Make the cat self-conscious."

The kite team had gone out, leaving the front door open again. "Well," said Viola. "Time I went home and fixed some lunch."

"Old man be home wantin to be fed again, huh?"

"Oh no," said Viola. "When he goes to work he's gone for the day."

"Well, I wouldn't say no to a bite myself," said De Vaughn.

"Come on, then," said Viola, and they left the living room empty behind them.

The kite team was standing in the middle of Bunches' lawn, blinking around for the best place to launch their project. "Don't go an electrocute yourself," said De Vaughn as he passed.

When Bunches' front door had opened and closed, David smiled. De Vaughn was up in the high percentiles, that was for sure. "What's your name?" he said to the *other* girl. Her complexion, he saw, was almost as bad as Hart's.

"Fuckin wires everywhere," said Bernie. "Get all hung up. . . ."

"Heidi," said the *other* girl.

"Shit oh dear," said Orange Julius. "Where's the string?"

NINETEEN

The President of the United States had declared a National Day of Prayer, and received for his troubles a stinging telegram from the American Association of Soft Drink Manufacturers and Bottlers, sternly reminding him that his own hand had already designated today Pop Goes America Day. Still sulking over the President's unwillingness to allot an entire week to their effervescent rites, the AASDMB minced no words. Their message spoke of broken faith and the credibility gap; it raised the specter of conflicting interests and warned of dangerously eroded rights, without which the nation surely could not stand.

But things were rough all over. In Birmingham, insurgents extinguished the eternal flame flickering atop the Lurleen Wallace Memorial and declared Alabama a free black republic. From the press conference immediately ensuing, white newsmen were barred, but the more enterprising among them picked up leaks committing the new nation to a firm policy of nonalignment with the U.S., Russia, or China. The less enterprising got the hell out, and lucky for them, because minutes later, just after dark, the Alabama Air National Guard leveled sixteen square blocks surrounding the site of the press conference.

Out in California, patriotic organizations were quick to accuse the Governor of shilly-shallying. "Alabama is leaving us way behind," said one spokesman. Another said the Golden State was threatened by a "fatal gap in second-strike plausibility." An electronic poll taken by his own research team reassured the Governor that the majority of his constituents still considered these accusations premature, and who could argue when he told televiewers not to forget that as the most populous state in the Union, California had its own unique problems. "The great majority of us," he said, "are self-reliant, independent citizens, sick and tired of meddling Big Brother government. I am confident in the final triumph of resourceful individualism."

Well, there was the multimillionaire living in a castle near Escondido. Late in the afternoon he bought enough time on a San Diego radio station to recite by memory the entire text of "Paul Revere's Ride," and then to warn fellow Californians of an impending invasion by the Army of Communist Mexico. "All this other bushwa," he said, "is purely diversionary." He called for immediate air strikes at Tijuana and Mexicali.

As he spoke, the White Cross Crusade, an independent patriotic organization headquartered near Bakersfield, responded to intelligence reports of plans to dynamite nearby oilfields by launching its own top-secret Operation Mister Bones: crack WCC troops, disguised with burnt cork, set out on a search-and-destroy mission, only to encounter an itchy-fingered armored battalion between Taft and Maricopa. Not many survived.

And a hundred miles to the southeast, members of Boy Scout Troop 2 of Ocean Park saw an opportunity to do a collective good deed for the day: they volunteered their services to the local police, who issued them nightsticks and MACE guns and ordered them into a disputed area near the Santa Monica Freeway, where rebellious elements were reported sheltering in a pool hall. "Wait, fellas," said their scoutmaster. "Guerrillas or no guerrillas, a Scout doesn't go into pool halls." The police arrested him on the spot, appointed a Life Scout in his place, and sent Troop 2 on its way, pennants flying.

Though somewhat overshadowed by such fabulous group ventures as these, individual enterprise did not betray the Governor's confidence. Take the used-car salesman on South Figueroa Street in Los Angeles, who put up a hastily lettered sign: GUARANTEE BULLETPROOF GLASS ON EVERY CAR. Demonstrating his wares with a blank pistol bought by mail to frighten robbers, he had by midafternoon cleared his lot of all fourteen clunkers but one, a Ford into which he climbed with his takings and headed for Communist Mexico. The main bearing burned out in Long Beach, but with a lapsed Diners Club card he was able to buy a Plymouth, in which he made it to Ensenada, where Mexican police arrested him going the wrong way on a one-way street. He swiftly bribed them, and got drunk on the balcony of a luxury motel suite facing the ocean.

Still more inventive, if less fortunate, was a Pan Am counterman at San Francisco Airport. When his shift ended he carried off a hundred blank tickets, which he sold within an hour from behind a card table set up at the corner of Third and Market Streets, filling in by hand destinations ranging from Las Vegas to Tashkent, and piling up in a flight bag something more than $21,000. As he walked away from his table, a gunman came out of Walgreen's, stuck a Matt Dillon cap pistol in his back, snatched the flight bag, and jumped onto a 30 bus.

Even unluckier was the Coca-Cola man in Sacramento who sold his delivery truck, Cokes and all, to a coffee-colored man in a Red Cross uniform for $1,050 in counterfeit bills, put five hundred dollars in each of two stamped and preaddressed envelopes with identical notes (*Now you can afford that operation. Good-bye. Love, Tommy*), mailed one to his wife, the other to his girl friend, and spent the remaining fifty dollars on an ancient Czechoslovakian automatic, the only pistol left in the store, walked outside, put the muzzle in his mouth, and squeezed the trigger. Nothing happened. The gunshop proprietor refused to exchange it for another weapon. "A deal's a deal," he said. "You didn't ask for no guarantee." The Coca-Cola deserter threw the pistol at him, ran into the street, and flung himself in front of the first approaching car, which stopped inches short. Hands bleeding, green trousers torn in both knees, he dragged himself to a nearby Chevron station, locked himself in the Men, sat down on the toilet, and began sawing away at his left wrist with his pocket nail file. It took him better than fifteen minutes to achieve his objective, since he was interrupted several times by pounding on the white steel door, and bad-tempered shouts of "Why don't you take a laxative, for Christ's sake!"

The surly voice belonged to the attendant of the station, who was anxious to conceal the day's receipts in the paper-towel dispenser, prior to absconding with them after faking a holdup.

A good deal of that sort of thing was going on up and down the Golden State. In Los Angeles County alone, thirty-six bank tellers, twelve supermarket managers, and seven more service-station attendants took all or part of the liquid assets with them when they called it a day. A salesgirl in a Beverly Hills boutique collected one each of everything her size in three cardboard dress boxes, and had them delivered to her apartment. A clerk in a Fresno health-food store smuggled out twenty-five pounds of wheat germ under his clothing, and, more bizarre still, the cross-eyed son of a pet-shop owner in Merced fled a little before closing time with a gunnysack containing his vegetarian father's complete stock of birdseed. He believed he could survive indefinitely in the Sierra Nevada mountains by eating the birds it would attract.

By late afternoon, the strain was beginning to tell, everywhere, on everyone, the young and the old, the rich and the poor, the mighty and the meek. And although Margie's bedside transistor had relayed, between Top 40 selections, only fragments of the local, state, and national news picture, even she was at last to feel the pressure.

At four-thirteen Station KWOW's News Department, Neil O'Neil reporting, broadcast the following News Wow: "WOW! Moments ago a K-WOW Watchbird helicopter was shot down in *flames*—WOW!—near the Interchange—WOW! —killing *both* Pilot Lee Roy Manley *and* Trafficaster Wig Stone—WOW!—making them K-WOW's first casualties in the *fantastic madness* sweeping greater and greater Los Angeles!"

Margie, who, after hours in the same room with a live, naked boy might have been thought past shock, was stunned. She had loved the funny way Wig Stone would report that traffic on the Hollywood Freeway was backed up for miles. Now he was . . . *dead*. It was scary, and for the first time she was wholly glad she had company.

Diz himself had almost forsaken his project. Maybe she was retarded, like his Cousin Nikolai. Brought up by devout anarchists, Diz believed, more or less, in the holy necessity of consent. Rape was out. And his full repertoire of coaxing hadn't brought her any closer than the foot of the bed, let alone out of that fantastic kid's party dress.

"Well, man, why do you think boys and girls are *made* different?" he had finally asked. Her blankness then made him wonder if she knew they *were*. A good thing there was a radio. Even if she was retarded, it was better than going to school.

On that point at least Margie agreed with him, having no way of knowing that except for Everlasting Gospel Bible College, all schools in Westpark were closed, thanks to a jittery School Board. Yes, and it was also better than facing her mother. Margie had forgotten about washing the sheet, there were so many questions she wanted to ask Diz. But that would have meant opening her mouth, so she thought the questions instead. Like how old was he, and was Diz his real name? Like who were his favorite groups, his favorite movie stars? Did he ever go surfing? And when he said, "I love you," did he mean go steady? These questions so engrossed her that she forgot to get hungry. No one had told her this was a symptom of lovesickness.

But the news of Wig Stone's demise—*Shot down in flames! WOW!*—had brought her as close as she had yet come to an inkling of her own mortality. If Wig Stone could die, who was safe? And it didn't help when Diz sat up in her bed and said, "Listen, baby, do you *ministrate* an all that?"

Thanks to Patricia Nunez, Margie knew all about that. It hadn't happened to her yet, and thinking about it made her feel worse than eating a pound of fudge. She shook her head once, in a two-inch arc, and made a sound like "Mo."

For once in his life, Diz regretted his general inability to remember things people told him, for now he couldn't recall whether that made any difference or not. All he could think of was Happy unbuttoning his Levi's and saying, "If you're big enough, you're big enough."

Neil O'Neil came on to promise—WOW!—an exclusive

tape replay of Wig Stone's last words—WOW!—right after a comer on the charts by *The New Animals!* And Diz got an idea. "Say, baby, you dig animals? You know, like pigeons? Cats an dogs, you know?"

He saw her color with pleasure, and nod. Her fat juicy little mouth was even smiling, and Diz was not too seriously offended by the tangle of metal inside. "What kind you like best?" he said.

"Kitties," said Margie.

It had been a long drag of a day. The sun was almost down on the other side of the house, the room half dark and stuffy, but Diz was alert to Margie's enthusiasm, which had been instantaneously matched, indeed surpassed, by his own. "Well, listen," he said. "You know how they roll all round an play?" He made a tent of the bedclothes. "Come on in an play kitties!"

Blind for a moment, he clutched at a handful of taffeta, and pulled, "Take your clothes off, you never seen no kitties with clothes on, did you?" and waited while she actually obeyed, and began groping, with a last fleeting thought that she was practically old enough anyway.

It took him about fifty-five seconds to discover that, practically, she was not old enough. Gallantly, he did not press the point. Fortunately, he did not have to. He was old enough. He was also large and bony enough to hurt her when he fell, like that helicopter whose last roaring moments were resounding in the transistor.

Margie's pain, surprise, and breathless disappointment were nothing to her chill of recognition: *Diz had done it again!* Bruised, half crushed, she squeezed herself violently out from under her fallen playmate and lay drenched with disgust and betrayal for only a moment before dashing into the bathroom, into the shower, where she stood blind, want-

ing the hot spray to shut it all out. But "I love you" meant
wee-wee all over you, and she would know better next time,
whenever that chanced to be.

Her betrayer was feeling a bit betrayed himself. Wait until he saw Bernie. The whole thing had been nothing but
a monster put-on. He paid no attention to Neil O'Neil's
voice, tingling with perpetual climax: "WOW! *Martial law!*"

Indeed, the pressures were beginning to tell. Even as fear-
less a practitioner of business-as-usual as Howard Bunch
would have preferred to be safe at home. But after being
shot at twice, held up and searched at no less than five road-
blocks, he was now the captive of a dozen men, some in
uniform, who had seized him as he left the apartment of
one of his most regular policyholders, a resilient hennaed
widow in Buena Park. While they debated the various mer-
its of shooting, hanging, and cremation, Howard dared not
even scratch. And he itched from head to toe.

"Listen to me, guys," said one of his captors, who wore a
Bell Telephone uniform. "We can shoot him, *and* hang him
up, and *then* burn him!" He didn't mention castration: it
was the one thing they had all agreed on already.

Back in Westpark, Viola was not as concerned about him
as she might have been. De Vaughn had just brought her
out of a deep sweet moist sleep by stuffing a kitten into the
curve of her neck, and it was his silent laughter that shook
the double bed. She rolled toward him, yawning all the way
to her toes, she hadn't yawned like that in ages, and De
Vaughn tried to insinuate another kitten between her breasts.

"How in the world did *you* get in here?" said Viola.

"Talkin to me?"

"I must have left the door to the back porch open."

"Naw, baby, I come in the front door same as you."

"Oh *you*," said Viola. "I bet *you* know *all* about back
doors, man. And windows and chimneys and broom closets."

They had already started laughing when a third kitten tried to clamber over Viola's bare thigh. She gave a shriek, De Vaughn hugged her, crushing a squall of outrage from the sandwiched kitten, and laughing the last breath out of himself. Now Viola began to giggle and, setting each other on in turn, they laughed and laughed, rolling and coughing and crying and groaning for air, until they lay exhausted, shoulder to shoulder among the scattered kittens.

"You went and got em," said Viola. "They could never have climbed up here all by theirself."

"You never heard of flyin cats?" said De Vaughn. "Should've seen em peelin off like dive bombers."

"Great God Almighty," Viola sighed. "Those hamburgers must be good and cold by now."

"Well, go cook up some new ones," said De Vaughn. It was time to be seeing about Sandra and Wondra, but a man had to eat. Watching Viola get up, he said, "Baby, you one hell of a woman, you know that? You must've been goin one hundred percent to waste round here."

Viola just gave him a look over her shoulder as she went out, knowing that one way or another a man *had* to strut a little. But God knows, she thought, it's the truth.

God also knew she didn't get loved like that every afternoon of the week. Or any afternoon, or evening, either, for that matter. Why she didn't feel guiltier, she didn't know. Maybe when she saw Howard she would, and that could be any minute from now to ten o'clock, and she wasn't even worried about *that*. Was it that after eight years she knew in her heart that she had it coming to her? Yes, but not just that: the main thing was she felt *too damn good*, full to the skin, no room left for guilt or worry. No hamburger left, and her in the kitchen without a stitch of clothes on? She put nearly a pound of sliced bacon in the pan at once. She bet De Vaughn could eat it all.

Diz could have eaten it all, and he had the bad judgment to tell Margie he was hungry when she came in from the bathroom wrapped up stiff as a mummy in both wet towels. Without pausing to wonder where she found the nerve, Margie said, "You get out of here! You messed up my bed and it's a filthy mess! You're dirty! You ought to be ashamed of yourself!"

"You mad at me, baby?"

"*You bet your life,*" said Margie. "*You get out of here this minute!*" Diz did as he was told. Holding the towels tight around her with one hand, she was tearing the sheets off her bed before he got his shirt and pants on. He couldn't find his sandals and left without them. Wait till he saw Bernie.

He hadn't long to wait. The kite patrol was on its way back to field headquarters through the tracts of Westpark. Chased from the first promising open space by the B football squad of St. Timothy's High, defying the mainly Protestant School Board by practicing for Thursday's season opener against Immaculate Heart; driven from the second at the point of .22's and Daisy pellet guns in the hands of four unemployed 4-F dropouts being drilled by Bert Hearn, Jr.'s, clubfoot brother Art, they had finally come upon a littered stretch of wasteland roughly the size of two city blocks, claimed only by a peeling sign promising the erection of an ULTRAMODERN OFFICE COMPLEX by PARK WEST, INC., at some undisclosed future date.

Here, under Bernie's executive direction, Orange Julius and a smirking David had taken turns towing the kite on the run through the mustard weed and rusty cans and clods baked hard as concrete until, on the fourteenth or fifteenth try, they got it into the air. For some minutes it hung perilously at an altitude of about thirty feet, borne up by no perceptible breeze at all; then, miraculously, some updraft of smog took it higher, higher, to the end of the ball of string Orange Julius had pilfered from a variety store while Bernie and Happy distracted the squinting lady proprietor with demands for unpolished rice and cigarette papers, for joy buzzers and whoopee cushions and itching powder.

Everyone cheered, even Donald, whose ice had melted, and they all sat down in the dirt to watch. A black-haired teen-age mother pushing a baby carriage stopped to gaze. "Come on, baby," called Bernie. "Bring the kid! This is a love project!" But the girl pointed into the pram, shook her head regretfully, and pushed on.

Not merely undismayed but somehow buoyed up by the girl's faintheartedness, Bernie lay back full length in the dirt, red arms spread. His hat tilted forward. He took it off, nudged aside a big sharp dirt clod, and relaxed again with a sigh of fulfillment, hands behind his head. Looking up at the kite past Happy's bulk, now crowned with the German helmet, Bernie had a vision as familiar as scratching himself, and requiring less effort:

If *only* everybody in the whole world, old and young, rich and poor, black and white and yellow and brown, could be here, in this nowhere vacant lot—in Westpark, for Christ's sake, didn't matter—here in all the junk and weeds and dirt, covered with smog . . .

If everybody in the world was here, just watching that kite floating up there, free and beautiful, costing nothing, hurting no one, connected to everybody, belonging to nobody, and high, high, high . . .

Then! Then it would be like . . . But the most holy truth was past saying in words, always. Bernie toyed with a haiku:

> *White kite*
> *High over Westpark—*

and let it go, settling gratefully for the unspeakable sense of peace, freedom, and well-being.

Then there was a kid standing there looking at the kite while he gnawed on a jelly doughnut. "What's your name?" said Donald. The kid, four or five years old, didn't supply it, but from the edge of the lot a woman did: "Billy? *Billy!* You get out of there and come here to me right now!"

"Ah what the fuck does she want?" said Happy.

She wanted Billy to come to her right now, and after she said so twice more, with no results, she came to get him.

"Christ's sake, he's just lookin at the kite," said Bernie as she came within the perimeter of his vision.

"You shut your mouth!" said the woman. Billy eluded her first grab, and she almost lost her balance on orange plastic high heels.

"We didn't even *touch* him," said Donald. "He just . . ."

"You all oughta be locked up!" said the woman. "Look at you!" She was on the hefty side, her brown hair sprayed and puffed stiff around a thin face. In the skin of her forehead a permanent tuck had been taken. She looked to David like the first half of an ad for a headache remedy.

Billy, seeing no more promising shelter than Happy or Donald, surrendered to his mother. "Now come on!" she said. "Mommy's sick and tired of chasing after you!"

"Hey, what in the fuck is the matter with you?" said Bernie, rolling over in the dirt to take a better look.

"All right," said the woman. "*All right.* You're all under arrest."

"What?" said Orange Julius.

"Citizen's arrest," she said. "You're loitering and creating a nuisance and using obscene language. This isn't your property, either."

Happy laughed so hard the helmet tipped down over her eyes. David smiled and Donald giggled nervously. Heidi focused her cracked blue eyes on the woman, opened her mouth, and said nothing. Orange Julius shut his eyes and stuck out his tongue. But Bernie twisted himself around into a sitting position and began saying, "Peace, peace, peace, peace . . ."

"You *are* under arrest, I'm not kidding," said the woman. "*Any* citizen can arrest *any* criminal, and that's the law. My husband is a policeman, and that's the law."

"OK," said Bernie. He got to his feet, dusting himself off. "OK, baby, then *I'm* arrestin *you*, as a hate criminal."

All but David and Heidi were on their feet now, and while the woman stood spitting out a more complete list of their deviations and derelictions, they surrounded her, Bernie and Happy, Donald with his blue bowl and Orange Julius holding the kite string in a gummy grin. Holding hands, except for Happy holding Donald's bowl, they began to dance around her, stumbling over clods, improvising an unsynchronized singsong of love and peace. Before they had gone around twice, the woman broke out with a cry of disgust at the moment of actual physical contact, and lurched away, towing Billy by one hand. His free paw still clutched a rind of jelly doughnut and his head wobbled loosely back to watch the kite. "If you're not gone in five minutes . . ." screeched the woman over her shoulder. But one orange heel snapped off, and she did not finish the promise.

Orange Julius opened his jaws—"*Schweinhund! Judensau!*"—and for a few seconds the kite string hung free, but Happy caught it, and Julius, drawing Viola's butcher knife from his wide belt, moored the kite securely to its handle and buried it under a little cairn of clods. "Baby!" said Bernie. "Have they got some sickies runnin around loose!"

But then, for more than an hour, nothing disturbed the peace of the kite patrol. Several passersby pointed or waved, and one old man yelled, "Yea, keep er up there!" David, only mildly spaced by his last pinch from Bernie's yellow pouch, decided he had nothing to lose by smiling at Heidi. "Don't talk so much," he said.

She got him in focus, and appeared to think about that for a minute. "On speed I really run my mouth," she said then. "Like now I'm savin up." A bit later she took off and chased a red cat all the way into an apartment block facing on the lot, but lost him there. On her way back, she picked a bouquet of mustard weed. Bernie, lost in contemplation again, ignored a wing of jet fighters which swept northwest toward downtown Los Angeles about four o'clock. The kite hurt nobody; nobody would hurt the kite.

He was wrong. A few minutes later, a man began shooting at it from a third-floor apartment window. They all saw the blue-gray puffs. "Thinks he's Lee Harvey Oswald," said Orange Julius. Bernie wanted to debate Oswald's guilt, but when David got up and left on the run, they all followed him, after hurriedly deciding to cut the kite free to fly, like a talisman, a wish for peace, into the troubled atmosphere over Southern California. It was such a beautiful idea, and they were such sitting ducks, that Bernie forgot about who killed John F. Kennedy.

On the way back to Rasmussens' now, Happy tucked yellow sprigs of mustard weed under the windshield wipers of parked cars, freeing Heidi to run down a lame gray tomcat, which she carried carefully in both arms to avoid its claws. David wondered again what he was doing with this gang. Well, there was nothing better to do.

And getting shot at. He wasn't going to make a very good soldier. But he knew that already, and smiled as he and the rest of the kite patrol pivoted in a ragged column right and headed up the last block home.

TWENTY

De Vaughn found Sandra and Wondra, Richard and Diz enjoying an early supper around the lopsided dining table. "How is every body?" he said. "Got a lot of sun, hey?"

The girls gave him a no-comment look in unison, and went on eating their canned spaghetti Bolognese. Diz finished his and got off to a head start on two-thirds of a butterscotch pie. But Richard stopped chewing and said, "De Vaughn! Baby, did you miss it! That deaf-and-*dummy!* And with a *belt!* I mean, it was surreal!"

"So what happened?" said De Vaughn. "Where is the cat?"

Richard gathered himself for a narrative effort. "Well, he was out in the back yard last time I saw him, then he disappeared. His pants are up on the roof or in the bushes someplace. I mean, Sandra and Wondra just . . ." He shook his head and chewed, at a loss for words, his round eyes bulging wet with good humor.

"Damn!" said De Vaughn. "What you girls do to that poor cat?"

"I made him for some kind of discipline freak," said Sandra. "You know, with the belt. . . ." She went after the butterscotch pie.

"I heard these cards shuffling," said Richard. "Look up and there's just this *huge black shape* against the sun. Then he sort of gropes down at them lying there, but with his head back like he's watching a plane. Somebody says, 'Play cards?' and I think, *What kind of trip is this?* and jump up and go for my camera."

"Hands me this card," said Wondra. "And I sit up to read it, and see him standing there looking straight up in the air, man, and he's got this belt in his hand, and then he kind of sails this other card at me out of his other hand, about can I spare five minutes."

"Like he was maybe about to freak clear out," said Sandra. "All I could see was under his chin, and the belt."

Richard came back, still naked, shooting on the run, and his camera saw the rest, or most of it:

Their breasts white on white, the two blondes in sparkling metallic panties blinked at the young man in the oversize black suit, his legs spread wide apart, his face turned up as if in prayer so urgent as to demand immediate service from heaven. He half dropped, half threw another card toward them. Sandra's lips said, "Deaf and dumb," and Wondra's said, "Wow." Then the young man put the belt in his left, card-dealing hand, and went crouching darkly toward them, eyes shut or almost shut, right hand groping ahead. The girls recoiled and got to their feet; the young man clawed up the newspapers on which they had been lying, and offered them a crumpled mass, demonstrating spasmodically that he meant them to cover themselves.

But Sandra walked boldly past the handful of newspapers, her glaring white breasts aimed like weapons, and tried to seize the belt. In a moment's blind struggle, the

cards flew from his hand and fluttered to the ground, and
the young man leaped backward as if from the devil, strik-
ing out awkwardly left-handed with the belt. But Wondra
had flanked him, and when she grabbed for the belt, Sandra
sank to her knees and seized a handful of his fly. He doubled
up convulsively, evading the tongue Wondra had thrust into
his ear and giving up the belt to her, then collapsing into a
defensive knot around his groin so that his heels came together and his trousers began to slip. In a flash Sandra had
them down around his calves, while Wondra began laying
on with the belt. The young man fell backward onto the
bricks, rocking on his spine in the fetal coil, and Sandra
seized this opportunity to peel off his wide black trousers,
inside out over his shoes.

Even the camera registered his blush as he struggled to
his feet and, on smooth muscular white legs punished from
behind by Wondra with the belt, pursued Sandra and his
trousers slowly across the patio. His face was set in a slit-
eyed mask, as if he meant to let in only the blurred white
shape he needed to stay on course. One hand stretched before him, palm up, half supplicating, half feeling his way.

When Sandra stopped and held the trousers out like a
bullfighter's cape, he charged. Pirouetting, she whipped
them out of reach, and offered them once more. Turning,
the young man seemed aware for the first time of Richard
and the camera. He made a little cramped run at the lens,
his face expressing a fleeting blind peevish distraction from
the main task at hand, to which he returned as Richard
dodged away backward. When the camera found him again,
after a dizzying white close-up of the garage wall, Wondra
was flaying him across his padded black shoulders, a fury
driving him toward Sandra, who no longer possessed his
trousers and now stretched empty hands toward him, beck-
oning suggestively as he stalked her. He whirled to grapple

with Wondra, face turned heavenward again, won a brief tug-of-war over the belt, and took one great swingeing cut at her, missing but gaining the space of a second in which to draw breath and gather his wits.

Wondra retreated halfway across the patio, where she joined Sandra in an immodest pantomime of invitation. Scattered white about their feet, the young man's cards looked like the shed tatters whence their nakedness had sprung. He walked slowly toward them, chin high once more, imploring with both hands, the belt hanging limp and unthreatening. But when from a yard away they pounced, and subjected him fore and aft to an expertly co-ordinated barrage of lewd caresses, the young man's wrath erupted; he burst free and went for them, flailing like a madman, chasing their switching, sparkling tails out of the patio into the back yard, where the camera lost them all for a few moments.

When Richard caught up with them, the girls had counter-attacked: Wondra from behind had hauled the black coat halfway off, binding the young man's elbows to his sides; Sandra had closed with him, twined her arms around his neck, and begun kissing his taut throat in the most abandoned fashion. Thus pulled, pressed, fondled, mauled, and hugged, he lost his balance and fell backward onto the thin dry grass, his white eyeballs rolled up like an El Greco Jesus in a last despairing swoon of entreaty. Sandra rode him all the way down, and immediately set about untying his black tie.

At this point, whether or not by divine intercession, and just as Wondra fell to her part of the teamwork, Richard ran out of film, and by the time he had run cursing inside and fumblingly refilled his camera, the young man's chastity and rage had both been manipulated away. Though not his boundless shame, of course, which left him curled up on his side in the back yard, his face in his hands.

"Man, what a *sound* he made," Sandra recalled now. "Like you know . . . *gargling*. Glug-glug-glug."

Richard had pleaded with the girls to put on their boots and chastise the young man further with the belt: "I bet he'll love it, and we can call it like *Pitiless Creatures!*" But they had said they were tired, so all three resumed their sunbathing. Sorting through the cards, Wondra found the FREE GIFT, a certificate worth ten dollars toward the purchase of a correspondence course called "How To Live With Jesus Every Day." Now she presented it to De Vaughn, who tucked it in a hip pocket and said, "Well, I'm proud of you girls, an on your own time, too."

"Baby, I wouldn't have missed it for *anything*," said Richard. "I mean, it was *pure film*, all perfectly silent."

"Except that glug-glug-glug," said Sandra.

A swollen Storm Trooper barged giggling in the front door: Happy, followed by Orange Julius and Bernie and David, Heidi with her tomcat and Donald with his blue bowl. As Richard tried to tell him his story above their breathless group account of lady maniacs and snipers, the volume rose to a hilarious pitch which woke Rasmussen.

His dependable right hand reached for a Camel. It wasn't there, and memory of the immediate past fell on him like an avalanche. The two blondes. Candlelight and Fourth of July punk burning. Firecrackers. No, a gun.

Under the weight of the avalanche he breathed with caution. No idea what time it was. Evening? The two blondes. Three times. Gunshots. *Three times, for Christ's sake!* His gun? Fired by who? Her, said the nigger. When? Somebody else in his bed, with a moustache. No, David's bed. Couldn't find his clothes. *Never so drunk in his life*. Gunshots. Her, the nigger said, pointing to his Dodgers cap. What time was that? What day was today?

The avalanche was solid enigma, and Rasmussen might have feared for his sanity but for a single memorable certainty, something to focus upon like a candle in the dark: *those two blondes*. Nothing like that had ever happened to him before: not in Georgia, not in North Africa or Italy or Paris, France. And he was forty-five years old! Three times! Thinking of it now, though his dry mouth longed for a Camel, he felt a rich bashful pride spread through him: he wasn't such a dried-up old bastard after all.

His automatic right hand sorted out his genitals with a new respect; despite his awareness of *her* there on the next bed he allowed himself the luxury of a stretch and felt no aches but the delicious stiffness of physical exertion, like after laying bricks in the patio. But those weren't bricks he was laying last night! No, by God! And best of all, he didn't even have to pee.

Her, the nigger said in a corner of Rasmussen's mind, but the rest of him lay at peace, or something that felt like it.

Something like peace, only much better, had irradiated Ann's long day of dreaming. The sequence in the tree house had been only the beginning; from there, gently inflated larger than life, her head transparent and glowing as if filled with neon, she had floated wisely and at ease above warm plains of time; detached, self-sufficient, omnipotent, and benign. People and objects existed, events took place only for her to be supremely independent of them. If she floated, if she flew, it was without the strain of movement, without even the soft abrasion of the air.

And the sound of her dreaming was a rich constant golden hum, only the more reassuring for seeming to come from inside her head, like the light. Perhaps only she could hear it, for her own hyperesthetic skin resonated inwardly: the hum was the sound of her own luminous pleasure. Nothing else mattered at all. So it came as no shock when people and things disappeared from the landscape.

Soft and rich and creamy, more like custard than snow, it covered everything beneath, smoothing the irregularities of the world into contours too gently undulant to cast a shadow. There was no place left for evil to hide.

The change began with the faintest perceptible increase in the articulation of mounds and swells beneath the creamy thick surface. Faint shadows darkened on the periphery. Nothing moved, but the rich overlying layer slowly thinned and melted; the hum began fading and the light lost its warmth.

As the whiteness wore through, dark holes opened like hollow eyes, grew larger, merged, spreading like stains. The coating melted away in tatters, and vanished, exposing the real world that lay beneath: jagged spines of rock and shriveled harsh growths, complex thickets burned or frozen to nothing but thorns and snaggly dry stems, dark tangles of splintered bones, and sharp-angled piles of black rusty junk like dead machinery.

The humming luminosity had faded and gone, leaving a vast silence laden with unbearable desolate loneliness: Ann awoke cold and deathly afraid. In the dream she had registered the change with all her senses; now she still tasted the end of it, her mouth full of dry nettles and a familiar astringent bitterness, like bleach.

A thin frame of light around the bathroom door, and shaving noises: *he* was in there. And the house was still full of people. *Them.*

But before it all melted away, her dream had been so indescribably beautiful. Now the light was all wrong; not morning. But how could a dream gone bad hurt you? How long had she been lying there? The taste in her mouth was no dream. The tip of her forefinger came away from her front teeth smudged.

Rasmussen came out of the bathroom. "You awake?" he said. "I just got up myself. Some party, huh?"

"Let me alone," she said.

That made Rasmussen laugh: *not* letting her alone had been the farthest thing from his mind. He didn't even care if she knew about the two blondes. Rested, shaven, freshly dressed, he went out to join the party without looking back. Christ Almighty, there were more of them than he had remembered!

The smiling of the last fourteen hours had given David's facial muscles an unprecedented workout, but the sight of his father emerging from the master bedroom made him smile again, uncontrollably and long. Minus his cap, and surely smelling of Mennen Skin Bracer, The Cap halted in his tracks; slicked up, on guard, shy, he waited for someone's notice to readmit him to the festivities.

As David hesitated, the narrative polyphony between Richard and the kite patrol died away and Bernie did the office of welcome, a bear hug jingling with sincerity: "Charley! Look at this cat! New man, hey?" David saw his father's eyes above the red shoulder gazing blankly at the blonde twins, right back on the couch where he had been sitting this morning, one reading Look, the other concentrating on unsticking her jacket zipper with a nail file.

De Vaughn added his greetings: "How you doin there, brother? Look like the rest done you good."

"Baby, there's some deep shit gone down here today," said Bernie. "I mean *transformation.*"

Impossible to tell how much of it was due to his uncustomary bareheadedness, but David had to agree that his father did look pretty well, and different. But then a couple

of hours with Sandra and Wondra might change even someone as fixed in character as The Cap.

Like someone starting a cold motor, Rasmussen cleared
his throat and asked the time.

"Half past kissin time," said Bernie. "Time to kiss again!"

Rasmussen spotted his cap and clothes still heaped with
pillows where they had fallen in front of the home theater.
"How'd they get out here?" he muttered to himself, retriev-
ing the cap and fitting it over his skull.

Bernie launched at once into an explanation so mystical
and impressionistic that David watched the incomprehen-
sion deepen like a blush under the bill of the Dodgers cap.
The waters were muddied further when Happy loomed up
between the two brothers wanting to swap headgear with
Rasmussen. "Bullshit!" said Orange Julius. "Gimme my
helmet back!"

Rasmussen gave up on Bernie and turned to David: "Now
what the hell happened? Was you here? Who done the
actual shooting? Was it her?"

David nodded gravely, and noticed Richard and De
Vaughn in sotto voce conversation, significantly not looking
at The Cap.

"And she actually thought it was me?"

"Aw forget it, De Vaughn," said one of the blondes. "I
mean, like once is enough."

"You better believe she thought it was you," said Bernie.
"Man, she had me an everybody else in the room to shoot
at, but she . . ." He pointed at the heap. "The old Charley
Rasmussen there, she really killed him *up!*"

The bill of the cap wagged slowly between disbelief and
outrage, in a cloud of Mennen Skin Bracer. "Son . . . of
. . . a . . . bitch. After all the shit she's put me through all
these God . . . damn . . . years . . ."

"Be glad, baby, be glad," said Bernie. "You a free man now. An she oughta be glad, too, got all the poison out."

But Rasmussen's thoughts were leaping ahead on quite another track, which led, most attractively, to a mental hospital, and not for himself, either. "You know," he mused aloud. "She had a feebleminded brother."

David smiled at this, as if at an old acquaintance: one of The Cap's favorite short monologues, he hadn't heard it since before the Cease-fire. Maybe The Cap was a new man, but he was still hung up with an old script, and the next line was: "That kind of thing runs in the family."

As he said it, the front door opened, Pepe came in, and David stopped smiling.

"Baby you came back!" said Richard.

"Yeah, man," said Bernie. "You still got the bike?"

Vibrating with his negative charge in the spotlight of the room's attention, Pepe smoothed his blue-black hair and said, "Two spades with a sub-Thompson got the bike. I tell you where to go look for it." Bernie didn't ask.

As if a fist inside him tightened all the wires holding him together, Pepe seemed to condense under the questions of Richard and Donald. It was a shit storm out there, he said. He had only come back because he couldn't make it across town to his apartment.

"Well, did you walk?" said Donald.

"Got a car."

"Well, shit, baby," began Bernie. "Like you didn't even tell me you wanted to borrow . . ." One glance from Pepe seemed to appease him.

In the quiet wake of Pepe's entrance, Heidi borrowed some of Donald's fresh ice to soothe the deep scratches on her forearms, and did not deign to answer when Mitchell wandered in with the lame gray tom wedged under one arm and asked her if she had lost it. "And you know there's a little girl doin *laundry?*" he said. "In the bathroom back there? In the shower, for Christ's sake. She wouldn't even let me in to take a piss."

In actual point of fact, he had walked in and relieved himself, over Margie's protests and to her plentifully renewed disgust, standing right there behind her at the toilet and making wee-wee *very loud.* While she knelt in her towel sarong before the open shower stall, trying, and failing, to drown out his sickening noise by scrubbing away harder at the sheet in the shallow tile pool of lukewarm sudsy water, which was sickening enough in itself without someone else breaking in, full of wee-wee, of course, and not so very surprisingly, in the light of Margie's horrid new wisdom, carrying a kitty under one arm, poor thing. But she knew better than to express the slightest interest in the kitty, because if she did she knew exactly what would happen, probably right there in the bathroom, whereas if she didn't look or pay attention, he might just pour all his disgusting wee-wee down the toilet and leave her in peace.

Which was exactly what Mitchell had done, buttoning up his Levi's skillfully with one hand, and proceeding, much refreshed by sleep, his temper somewhat sweetened, back to the front of the house to see what pointless, irrelevant, and quite probably reactionary trips everybody was on now. If De Vaughn hadn't gone off and left him behind, he could at least look forward to a ride back to Marco's.

But De Vaughn was still arguing with Richard, and for a few seconds Mitchell had the unnerving sensation that he had slept for no more than five or ten minutes. Everybody looked just the same, too, as if the house were history-proof, timeproof. But it was dark out now. Had they been arguing all day? About what?

"Say look here, Richard," De Vaughn was saying. "I don't run no sweatshop, man. An you just heard Sandra tell you it's no go."

"Then you've got like no training film," said Richard.

"Aw five minutes ago you were ravin about how great that scene with the Bible cat was," said De Vaughn. "An you got a dummy-killin, too. I'm satisfied, man, why can't you be?"

"All right, all right," said Richard. "But how much longer you want to stick around here?"

"Baby, I ain't keepin you here. The Phantom there say he's got a car, you can split when you want. But if he couldn't get across town on a motorcycle, I don't see what's your hurry. All you know, there's all kind of other interesting shit to come right here. Open your mind, man."

"*Open your ass, man,*" said Pepe, glaring murder at De Vaughn.

"Got it backward, ain't you?" grinned De Vaughn. "That's got to be your bag."

David didn't know which one he would bet on if those two opened fire, but he was sure he didn't want to be in between.

"You want to try me, motherfucker?" said Pepe. "I love to see that, you know?"

"Not right this minute," said De Vaughn, his voice confidently weighted with insincerity. "You look way too bad for me. Bernie, put some of that love-an-peace on the Phantom there, so's he don't escalate no more."

"Yeah, we havin a beautiful day here together," said Bernie neutrally. But if he planned to mount a full-scale benediction, Diz put a stop to it before he could draw his prayer bell. "Man, you really fed me a lot of bullshit," he said. "You know that? About that little chick back there? I mean, there's somethin the *matter* with her, man, or she ought to be in kindy garden or somethin. . . ."

A modest blessing was supplied instead by Rasmussen, of

all people. He had slipped out into the kitchen, and now returned clutching a sandwich improvised out of soda crackers and something pink. He counted the house first, almost genially. Twelve of them, and Jesus! he made it thirteen. But then he said, "Hope everbody got enough to eat. No bread, no eggs, no milk, but just help yourself."

"What are you eating?" said Happy.

"Ffpam," said Rasmussen, with a little shower of crumbs. "No more crackers, though. Say it's time for the news."

"All bad, brother," said De Vaughn, but not convincingly enough to keep Rasmussen from discovering the mortal damage to the home theater, and relapsing at once into slow, head-shaking outrage. "Two . . . thousand . . . God damn bucks," he said. "Shot."

"Shot is the word," said De Vaughn.

"Be glad, baby," said Bernie.

"Shouldn't be runnin round loose," said Rasmussen, and as if mentally drafting a crew to help him subdue her for commitment that very night, he glared balefully among the crowd.

It added up, all right. Trying (she thought) to kill him *and* shooting up the home theater certainly outweighed the two blondes, *if* she knew about them (and besides, he'd been loaded). What's more, the shooting was double evidence of inherited insanity, while there was nothing so very crazy about his own little escapade. It seemed he couldn't lose.

"Believe me, brother," said De Vaughn. "News tonight ain't gonna make anybody feel good. Ask the old Phantom there, he's been out checkin the action. . . ."

"Some fuckin nut even took a shot at us, baby," said Bernie. "It's some evil shit goin on. . . ."

Rasmussen disregarded them both. But neither he nor anyone else in the room could disregard Viola Bunch, who opened the front door, her stricken face seeming to take in the roomful of people for a moment before cramping into a mask of grief.

David couldn't understand what she was wailing through her tears. It sounded like *Killed White! Sister called up said they killed White!*

De Vaughn got to her very quickly and had an arm around her shoulders, but there was as much anger as grief in her and she shook him off. "With a *machine gun!* Said they cut him in *half!* And he's *fourteen years old!*" De Vaughn, still saying nothing, took her gently in charge again, seemed to reject the front yard, and led her through the silent audience into the dining room. "And Howard hasn't come home," she was saying.

Above the muttering in the living room, a woman's sudden crying made Ann instantly curious. Far from expressing some submerged need of her own, the sound made her feel superior: she herself had never been further from tears.

A shower, a vigorous brushing of hair and teeth, a fresh dress: these had completed what a day's sleep had begun in the way of restoring her physically to normal. Last night she had not been herself, but even that was normal in such a houseful of degenerates. Now she felt equal to them again. The worst dreams couldn't hurt you, and everything that had happened since Bernie came had been like a dream.

Grinning whitely into the mirror, she *looked* normal. They hadn't touched her. If they didn't leave, and fast, she would go to a motel. She had kept her part of the bargain, now let him keep his. Fair was fair. It was them or her. The woman's crying had gone away. Good. Let them all go away.

Her entrance into the living room commanded silent attention; they all simply transferred it from Viola Bunch to Ann, who looked around and saw no one but a lot of bums and beatniks and perverts, and Rasmussen, X-raying her with nothing she hadn't seen before in the way of sneaky suspicious hatred, and David, who said in that phony solicitous voice that never fooled her for one second: "Hi, Mom. You OK?"

"*You bet your life,*" said Ann. But she hadn't prepared anything else to say—it must be perfectly clear to them where *she* stood—and before she could say or do anything at all, an ugly little one with orange hair and a big mouth said, "Hey, lady, I'm very hungry, what's to eat?" A wise guy; Ann knew the type. "Hey, no kidding, lady, I been out getting shot at all day and I'm starving."

"Come on, how about it, lady?" said a disgusting big fat boy-girl thing in a steel helmet. "What are we having for supper?"

Sensing her command at the moment, Ann took her own sweet time inspecting them. One of the two blonde girls on the couch was openly smirking at her, and something she was about to remember was displaced by a brilliant idea going off in her head like the bell on the electric timer. "Why certainly!" she said with her whitest smile. "Right away! I'm sure you're all hungry."

David recognized the mealtime quickstep at which Mrs. Clean left the room, and only he seemed to notice the vibrant sarcasm of her exit speech. His father had thought of something, too. "She use my gun?" he asked. "The automatic?"

David nodded.

"Where the hell is it, then?"

David remembered the floodlit struggle. "I think De Vaughn took it away from her," he said.

Wouldn't you know it? To Rasmussen it seemed a natural frustration: the one person in the whole gang who was out of the room, not counting Viola Bunch, who'd had somebody killed. But Rasmussen had his own problems, which he preferred to ponder rather than go looking for De Vaughn, with whom he felt himself in somewhat ambiguous relation. No, it was *she* who had to be settled, and fast.

Richard, too, had an idea, and began expounding it guardedly to Donald and Pepe.

"He'll go absolutely *bobo!*" said Donald. "He'll kill you!"

"Let him try to kill me," said Pepe.

Rasmussen marched past them toward the kitchen and his final solution to the problem of Ann. When that was done, he would see about what he owed De Vaughn.

"You mess around with De Vaughn you'll be sorry," said Sandra. But neither she nor Wondra saw fit to warn their principal, perhaps out of a conditioned respect for his freedom and self-determination.

David, smelling trouble, decided it was time for a breath of fresh air, and went outside onto the front lawn.

TWENTY-ONE

However purposefully he had set out for the kitchen, there was still room under Rasmussen's cap for a fragment or two of habitual self-doubt. But these dissolved when he saw her, in a travesty of her customary brisk efficiency, flinging an incredible miscellany of ingredients into her largest aluminum pot with an air of divinely controlled inspiration, an insouciant gaiety which could only be mad.

She had already opened, electrically, a dozen or so cans—Campbell's soup, Del Monte peaches, Hunt's tomato sauce, Hershey's chocolate syrup, Dole pineapple chunks, Chef Boy-ar-dee ravioli. Now, while her left hand maintained a steady autonomous stirring with a large steel spoon, her right was emptying the cans one by one into the pot, interspersed with other items from the open cupboard—prunes, dried beans, foil-wrapped bouillon cubes. With an empty soup can she dipped flour, then sugar, then salt, each from its steel canister. A whole bottle of A.1. sauce. A can of apricot nectar . . .

Poor bitch, thought Rasmussen, in spite of himself. What

he said was: "*Je-sus H. Christ!* All these years I been livin with a God damn lunatic an I never knew it!"

Ann spared him a bright glance. Her left hand went on stirring. "Mash for the pigs," she said. "All your friends say they're hungry."

"Not satisfied tryin to kill me and wreckin two thousand bucks' worth of TV set," said Rasmussen. "Now you want to poison a whole houseful of people."

"People?" Ann had to wait while chocolate syrup drooled slowly into the pot. "I know pigs when I see them. I know what they like. I was brought up on a pig farm."

"Well, now you're goin to the *funny* farm," said Rasmussen, and laughed dryly, and coughed, and drank a glass of water, refreshed by which, he recited an up-to-date list of her qualifications for commitment, ending, with a relevance purely emotional, in the phrase, "cold, skinny, dried-up, tight-assed bitch from hell."

"Not like your two blonde friends," said Ann, in a dangerously conversational way. For a terrible moment, Rasmussen saw the score tied at two-all, and had to make himself think of the bullet-riddled home theater before he could continue.

"That's right," he said. "That's right. Not one God damn bit like them. You thought you made an old man out of me, but you got another think comin."

"Well well well," said Ann, and dropped five Lipton's Flo-Thru tea bags into the pot.

If she had no more to say than that, Rasmussen certainly had: "Listen to me for a minute. I want you to get this one thing through your head. Are you payin attention?"

Ann turned to face him. Her left hand went on stirring, and her eyes seemed focused on the bill of his cap. Crazy. "Crazy," he said. "You're crazy as a coot. You're a God damn homicidal maniac, and *I*"—tapping the second button of his shirt—"am gonna put *you*"—pointing at her nose—"away forever. I got me a dozen witnesses out there. And I'm gonna do it. And, well, there it is."

"I see," said Ann. But she didn't look as if she saw, her eyes were too bright and know-it-all. She really *was* crazy! It came now as something of a shock, almost as if she were not the woman he had intended to threaten.

"First thing in the morning," Rasmussen said. The thought of the missing Pontiac stung him like a gnat. But there must be a padded wagon you could call.

Ann turned her attention back to the pot. Slowly she let a handful of split peas trickle into the mixture. "I did one crazy thing in my life," she mused. "And you know what that was."

Indeed Rasmussen knew: it was her invariable answer to his charge of feeblemindedness in her family.

"But you don't know *how* crazy I was to marry you," she went on in the same mild voice. "Because I didn't have to. I got the curse going back there on the train."

Shouldn't Rasmussen have been delighted to hear at last confessed something he had conjectured over the past years in so many thousand cramped private rages? Perhaps so, but instead he was furious, and the fury was a relief, for things had been going much too chattily to produce a really satisfying climax.

"Ah, you bitch!" he howled. "You got the nerve to stand there an tell me that now? After all these years?"

"All these years, all these years. Don't you talk to me about all these years." She was saying it into the pot like a witch's malediction. "You don't know a *thing* about all these years!" She turned to face him again. *"Because you're a stupid pig!"*

That was more like it! "I just wish I had a picture of you right this minute," said Rasmussen. "Standing there out of your God damn mind, cooking up that crazy mess of shit!"

"For *pig* you and your *pig* blondes and your *pig* brother and all your other pig friends!" She had stopped stirring. *"Now get out of my kitchen, you pig, while I cook your mash!"*

Rasmussen was right about one thing: she did make a memorable picture at that moment. Unfortunately for him, the parties who could have done the job were otherwise occupied, poised outside the shut door to David's bedroom, Richard holding his camera, Donald holding the Sun Gun, Pepe holding himself cocked like a weapon. And despite Richard's express wish that the crew be unaccompanied, Orange Julius and Happy and Diz had trailed them, and were now strung out along the hall at intervals of about a yard.

No light showed beneath the bedroom door, and they could hear De Vaughn, comforting or seducing in a voice too low to be understood. Pepe turned the doorknob gently as a thief, Donald switched on the Sun Gun, Richard started shooting, and in they went.

Perhaps they should have waited a little longer. As it was, they barely had time to be disappointed. Where he and Viola sat, fully clothed, on the edge of David's bed, De Vaughn turned to face the glare. "What the fuck is this?" he yelled. "Shut that thing off!"

"You're on Candid Camera, baby," said Richard. "Do your thing."

De Vaughn stood up, shielding his eyes. "G'on an get out of here, Richard," he said.

"I want to see you make it with your clothes on," said Richard. "You must be *fantastic!*"

De Vaughn's right foot flew up and punted the Sun Gun

flying from Donald's hands to shatter against the doorframe, and in the sudden darkness Pepe missed his first leaping karate jab. Before he could get off another, De Vaughn was out of range, and ready. "Get on out of here now," he said. "All of you. Fore I boot your ass."

"Me first," said Pepe. "I want you." He sniffed the incense staling in the air as if it were blood.

"I mean you specially," said De Vaughn. "You chulo cock-sucker."

And no doubt the two antagonists would go for each other in the next instant. Viola could hardly restrain De Vaughn, and neither Richard nor Donald even wanted to hold back Pepe. The chips, it seemed, were down, the irrevocable challenges issued, the hostilities escalated past any settlement short of mayhem. David's room, so recently the scene of one extraordinary collision of bodies, would now be shaken by another, conceivably even less merciful than the first.

Incredible, then, that one syllable, transmitted by Heidi in the living room, and relayed at near-electronic speed to David's room, should have forestalled, even momentarily, the outbreak of hand-to-hand combat between Pepe and De Vaughn. But it did just that.

"Fuzz," said Heidi, when she saw the blue uniform and the gun come through the front door. "Fuzz?" said Bernie in the dining room, halted jingling in his tracks en route to make peace between his brother and sister-in-law.

"Fuzz," said Diz, having held his place outside Margie's locked door when he saw the Sun Gun explode. "Fuzz." The word leapfrogged Happy and sounded in the wide mouth of Orange Julius.

"Fuzz?" said Richard. "You killers better cool it."

Perhaps because Pepe had in his pocket the keys to a stolen Dodge Dart, license number CVS 514; because De

Vaughn still had in his pocket a 7-millimeter Italian automatic pistol, not quite empty; because being arrested while in possession of these items would almost certainly send them back to a place they didn't want to go; perhaps for these reasons, among others too complex to guess, they cooled it, and settled for an exchange of heartfelt promises to be kept at the earliest opportunity.

Pepe, Donald, and Richard, quite understandably considering their shared handicap in dealing with the law, slipped out the back door with no more said. But De Vaughn, who might have been thought comparably handicapped, or worse, told Viola he must see about the girls, and asked her if she would mind returning the pistol to Mr. or Mrs. Rasmussen when she saw fit. Viola, her grief unallayed but temporarily eclipsed by the rush of events, simply nodded, and watched him go, thinking she should slip out the back door and go home herself, but not doing it.

Heidi's vision, to say nothing of her mind, had been blurred by the strain of peering through the magnifying lens of Bernie's Swiss Army knife at the sexual apparatus of the lame tomcat she had finally pinned between her knees on the floor. The man had looked like fuzz to her, and she had reacted accordingly.

David was still out on the front lawn, or he could have told her that it was not in fact a real policeman, but only Bert Hearn, Jr., in the blue uniform of Hearn Security Service, Inc., a firm which ostensibly offered to supply armed guards and day-or-night watchmen for the protection of anything from a presidential aspirant to a warehouse full of lettuce crates. At a time when most such enterprises were working around the clock and charging double, Bert Hearn, Jr., had turned away from profit to answer a higher call. Bert, Sr., founder of the Hearn S.S., had been living in Camarillo State Hospital since 1954, tirelessly unraveling a communist plot to infiltrate the power companies and poison the electricity in American homes. Bert, Jr., cheated out of an FBI career by astigmatism, had picked up the flickering torch and borne it ever since, at no small cost to the health of the already moribund company: no one, it seemed, paid cash money for security against the international conspiracy of Jews, Negroes, communists, beatniks, Eastern bankers, and psychiatrists. But as yet no one had tried to strip the Hearn S.S. of their blue uniforms, or take away their guns.

So David, on the front lawn inhaling what passed in Westpark for fresh air, had recognized Bert Hearn, Jr., and his brother Art while they and two other men were still over at Farnum's on the opposite corner. He could hear the sound, if not the sense, of Bert Hearn, Jr.'s, terse urgent phrases, and Farnum's querulous responses from his front doorway. Bert Hearn, Jr., had a rifle slung over one dark-blue shoulder.

And a holstered pistol belted around his waist. But David only noticed that after Bert Hearn, Jr., had led his men, now including Farnum with his eight-iron, straight across the street and onto Rasmussen's lawn. Except for Farnum's complaints about missing something on TV, none of them spoke until Bert Hearn, Jr., made out David and barked, "Say, fella, your dad home?"

As David's loyalties raced around his skull in search of an answer, he saw Bert Hearn, Jr.'s, glinting eyeballs shift upward. "*Hey, you!*" he bellowed in a thick authoritative voice, and drew his pistol, a giant Colt automatic, with the speed of much practice. "See that?" he asked one of his men from the target-range crouch into which he had dropped. "Man. On the roof. No pants on. Gone now." David turned and saw nothing.

"Something funny going on here," said Bert Hearn, Jr. "Better reconnoiter round back, Art."

His brother, also in Hearn S.S. livery, slipped off up the driveway, his speed only a little impaired by the specially built shoe on his left foot. "We expect grillas and saboteurs in here any time," said Bert Hearn, Jr. "That one on the roof had white legs, but we expect they'll paint theirself." He brought an oversize luminous wristwatch up to within three inches of his face. "Nineteen-forty-nine," he said portentously. "What's your dad got for weapons, boy?"

David was spared having to answer by the screeching arrival of a new Ford Galaxie, which ejected into their midst Bud Cronk, a member of the Ace Liquors bowling team, like Horst Schmidt, who stayed at the wheel of the idling sedan. "Charley ready?" said Bud Cronk to David. "Know your phone rings busy? Don said he didn't get his car back so we figured we better stop by for him." Two dozen words seemed to have left him breathless.

"Hold on there, buddy," said Bert Hearn, Jr. "You live in Westpark?"

Bud's answer was lost in the gunning of the Ford's engine. "Get the lead out!" yelled Horst. "You wanna forfeit?"

"There's a war on, fella," said Bert Hearn, Jr. He shouldered past Bud Cronk, mounted Rasmussen's front step, and made two dents in the door with the muzzle of his Colt. Then he walked in. "Fuzz," said Heidi.

David's curiosity made him crowd in after Bert Hearn, Jr., along with Bud Cronk, Farnum, and the two other members of the original party. One of these was a maloccluded grocery checker recently fired from the Westpark Super for failing to give out Blue Chip Stamps; the other, a former salesman of plastic dog turds.

Sandra, Wondra, Heidi, and Mitchell: Bert Hearn, Jr., knew none of them, and of course it was mutual. But they must have looked suspicious enough to him, for the Colt stayed in his hand, pointed at the dining-room door. "Charley Rassmussen here?" he said, and, when no one answered, added, "There's a man on the roof."

Rasmussen, fresh from as clear-cut a decision as he could hope for over that certifiable mental case, heard his name called clearly, a moment after Bernie told him the cops were here. Perhaps they could take her along right now! And he could sign the papers tomorrow! With that in mind he strode into the living room and looked down the barrel of an enormous pistol in the tense right hand of Bert Hearn, Jr. Jesus Christ! Nuts on every side!

"Now what in the hell do you want?" said Rasmussen. "Are you pointing that God damn thing at me?"

Bert Hearn, Jr., holstered his pistol, but swept the room once more with narrowed eyes, as if checking for booby traps, or perhaps midget snipers lurking behind chairs. "There's a war on, Charley," he said. "Or didn't you notice? Example Number One: there's a grilla on your roof."

"Charley we got about five minutes, you ready to go?" From his place behind Bert Hearn, Jr., Bud Cronk couldn't help looking up the skirt of one of the two sexy blondes on Rasmussen's couch. "Horse is out there waitin. . . ."

Rasmussen had completely forgotten this was Tuesday night, and an important Tuesday night, too: Ace Liquors and Kleenrite fighting it out for the lead of the Westpark Bowl Majors. "What's on the roof?" he said. "Waitin for me?" Hell yes, he would simply grab his ball and shoes and Ace Liquors shirt and get clean away from these loonies.

"Pull yourself together, Charley," said Bert Hearn, Jr. "We got a war on our hands, fella. Now what kind of weapons you got?"

"Weapons?"

"Charley, it's exactly four minutes to eight."

Bert Hearn, Jr., consulted his watch again. "Sorry about that, fella," he told Bud Cronk. "It happens to be nineteen-fifty-three. Exactly. Better get synchronized. Charley, in case you didn't get the message, there's a war on. Poisoning the reservores. Shooting. Burning. Raping. Grilla raids everywhere. Now what kind of weapons you got? Wasting a lot of time. Could of painted his legs white."

Enough of this. Ignoring Bert Hearn, Jr.'s, admonition to *bring his own ammo*, Rasmussen ducked into the master bedroom to fetch ball, shoes, and shirt. Ah Jesus Christ! They were in the trunk of the Pontiac! Well, then, the hell with it: he'd rent them at Westpark Bowl.

But when he bolted back into the living room he was again covered by Bert Hearn, Jr.'s, Colt, swinging in a tight arc to include him along with De Vaughn, who had come in from the dining room, followed by Diz, Happy, Orange Julius, and Bernie, in that order.

"Hold it right there," said Bert Hearn, Jr. "Looks like you got your own little grilla force right here, Charley." The grocery checker had produced a shiny nickel-plated revolver, which he held in his small right hand. The ex-plastic dog turd salesman had drawn a hunting knife with an eight-inch blade, and Farnum gripped his eight-iron in both hands like a baseball bat.

"I guess you know this is gonna cost us a forfeit," said Bud Cronk, and Horst Schmidt, grown tired of gunning his Ford, had come to peer in the door and ask, "Say what the hell kind of party is this, anyhow?"

Bert Hearn, Jr., wanted to know the very same thing. "Hands behind your head, all of you," he commanded the other side of the room. "And you." He pointed the Colt at De Vaughn. "Come a little closer where I can get a look at you." De Vaughn did not move.

"Fucking Gestapo," said Mitchell. "Pig motherfucker."

Rasmussen saw the lead in the Westpark Bowl Majors go a-glimmering. "What do you think you're doin?" he said.

"You God damn silly gung-ho son of a bitch." He had taken just about all he meant to take. The others, not counting *her*, had at least waved no guns around.

Bert Hearn, Jr., let the insults pass, merely nodding slightly as if they confirmed the evidence of his own eyes. "Now I'm gunna count three," he said to De Vaughn. "One . . ."

De Vaughn began taking soft steps toward the eye of the Colt, hands folded behind his neck, elbows pointing straight forward. Folds of the sweatshirt made the letters across his front read MCMX, like a number in Latin. His freckles looked darker.

Beneath set lips the front teeth of Bert Hearn, Jr., appeared to be biting at high speed on something about the size of a grain of rice. The motion towed forward his blunt manly jaw, and the eyes above it, narrowing into a squint. A little jab of his Colt stopped De Vaughn two yards from its muzzle. "Well, well, well," said Bert Hearn, Jr., through his teeth. "Black power." He strained an inch closer as if trying to make out the faded letters on the sweatshirt, and a number of things happened, not all at once, to be sure, but in very rapid succession.

From the doorway Horst Schmidt's wheedling falsetto said, "Thay, girlth, don't run awa-ay!"

Another voice, like steam escaping, said, "Kee-*hah!*" and Horst Schmidt disappeared backward with a rich yelp of visceral pain.

De Vaughn punted Bert Hearn, Jr.'s, pistol hand with a force which might have sent a football half the length of the field, fell to his right as if escaping an onrushing tackler, and recovered quickly enough to find Bert Hearn, Jr.'s, groin with his knee while reaching with both hands for Bert Hearn, Jr.'s, large blue-black pistol. De Vaughn's eyes met Pepe's for a fraction of a second, past, between, or through the grocery checker and the ex-plastic dog turd salesman, hard-pressed and seemingly uncertain of whom to shoot and to stab, respectively.

Pepe had to content himself with breaking the grocery checker's right wrist, and De Vaughn had to dodge a wood-chopping swing of Farnum's eight-iron as he bulldogged Bert Hearn, Jr., over one hip and down onto the floor, the Colt exploding once in transit and digging a fist-sized divot out of the plaster ceiling.

Pepe picked up the grocery checker's shiny revolver.

Farnum and the ex-plastic dog turd salesman beat a quick tactical retreat into the nearest unoccupied corner, eight-iron and hunting knife trembling at the ready.

Mitchell came forward to stamp his right cowboy boot hard upon Bert Hearn, Jr.'s, pinioned pistol fist.

Bud Cronk recoiled backward away from the gun in Pepe's right hand, and almost knocked down Rasmussen, who about now would have liked to pop almost anyone, but not Bud Cronk, at least not from behind.

Mitchell picked up the Colt, seemed surprised by its weight, and pointed it at no one. Certainly not at Pepe, who had the drop on the whole room.

Now Donald appeared in the front doorway, and Richard, who said, "*Pepe!* Baby you look like Bonnie and *Clyde!*"

But Pepe seemed for the moment disinclined to shoot anyone, unless it might have been De Vaughn, sitting astride Bert Hearn, Jr., and catching his breath. Pepe stared intently at De Vaughn.

And now across the room the terrorized subjects of a few moments ago were rising from their various postures of humiliation, like the insulted and injured, the despised and oppressed losers of the world, to revenge themselves upon those oppressors still on their feet: Happy pitched a small ceramic ashtray which shattered a foot above Farnum's head; Orange Julius, beginning with A, hurled one brand-new red-and-gold volume of the All-American Encyclopedia after another at the besieged pair, telling Diz, who reached for XYZ, to find his own stuff to throw; Heidi ran forward almost to within range of Farnum's eight-iron and two-handedly flung her tomcat upon the ex-plastic dog turd salesman, who failed to skewer it on his hunting knife and took its eagle-spread talons full in the face. Books, cushions, ashtrays, table lamps: anything small enough to pick up and throw: the intensity of the barrage would surely have driven the two out the front door, had not the black figure of Pepe, made twice deadly by the shiny pistol, blocked that escape. As it was, the ex-plastic dog turd salesman sank to his knees, touched his torn face, and looked in plain horror at his bloody fingers, while Farnum cowered behind one upthrown elbow.

As well he might, for Happy, finding herself empty-handed, took off her helmet and flung it point-blank at him. Farnum somehow found the wits, and barely the time, to put it on, backward, before the charge, led fullback fashion by Happy, bowled him into the corner, and buried him and his bleeding compatriot under the combined weight of herself, Orange Julius, Diz, Heidi, and Mitchell, who began pounding the butt of the Colt on the helmet as if it were a gong in a Peking Solidarity parade.

Donald ran over to the pile but couldn't find anything to kick. Richard shrilly blamed De Vaughn for ruining his Sun Gun and making him miss all *this*.

De Vaughn picked himself up off Bert Hearn, Jr., saw Pepe, and took a step away from him. "G'on, man," he said, weary and a little condescending. "You don't want to be shootin me now. We sort of on the same *side*, more or less."

"With my hands, baby," said Pepe, and handed the pistol to Richard. He and De Vaughn had just begun to circle each other when Viola walked in and cried, "*Stop* it! *Stop* it! Stop all this fighting!"

But Mitchell did not stop beating time on the helmet, and Happy did not stop methodically bouncing up and down on top of the ex-plastic dog turd salesman, and neither Pepe nor De Vaughn stopped his stalking.

Their breaths exploded simultaneously, the four stiff fingers of Pepe's right hand flashed, De Vaughn's left forearm flew up to block and slashed down at Pepe's neck, missing as Pepe spun away and Viola fired the last bullet in Rasmussen's pistol into the ceiling.

The gonging and bouncing ceased in the corner. "I'm too fast for you, man, take my advice," said De Vaughn, but postponed proving it for the moment.

"You're both *fantastically deadly*," said Richard. "But . . ."

"Stop it," said Viola. "Stop it now." She took two steps forward. "That's enough now. De Vaughn you stay over there." The gun in her hand seemed to lend her a certain authority. "Bodies lying all over. . . ." She began to cry.

"Yeah," said Bernie rustily. His principles had kept him on the sidelines, along with Sandra and Wondra, who had been denied the opportunity—and perhaps lacked the will—to bring their own weaponry into play. "Yeah, man," said Bernie. "I mean, what does violence prove?"

"You rooned my helmet, you bastard," complained Orange Julius, as the shock troops began unpiling. "Where am I gonna get another helmet?" But he put it on again, and called Farnum and the ex-plastic dog turd salesman a pair of *Judische Schweine*.

Mitchell disregarded the accusation, and told Heidi no she couldn't see the Colt. "It must still be loaded," he said. "I could have shot myself."

"Well, now let's clear the God damn area," said Rasmussen. "These sons of bitches ought all be locked up, or at least get em out of here."

Easier said than done: coughing and blinking, Bert Hearn, Jr., had rolled onto his side, and was nursing his pistol hand in his crotch; the ex-plastic dog turd salesman pushed himself up onto hands and knees, trying to clear his throat; Farnum was not moving at all.

Rasmussen began hauling at Bert Hearn, Jr.'s, uppermost shoulder, but he needed help. "We ought to frisk them," said Donald. "I've been frisked so many times." And he ran his unburned hand ingeniously over the sagging blue uniform, lingering over the most unlikely places for concealed weapons, but eliciting from Bert Hearn, Jr., no more than a thick blurt about "niggers," choked off by a phlegmy paroxysm of coughing.

"Disgusting!" said Richard. "Baby if *that's* your idea of trade . . ."

But when Rasmussen and De Vaughn had hauled and pushed Bert Hearn, Jr., in a stumbling crouch out the front door, Donald did as thorough a job of frisking the ex-plastic dog turd salesman as he exited crawling, and then made similarly free with Farnum, who had to be picked up and carried by Rasmussen and Happy and Orange Julius. "That weapon isn't even worth concealing!" Donald declared, giving Farnum a last contemptuous tweak, at which the body focused bleary eyes on Richard and creaked, "You're not from no CBS."

As they set Farnum down on the concrete front step, Bud Cronk snapped out of his glazed trance to listen for a moment. "Horse must've left!" he cried, slipped between Rasmussen and Happy, leaped out the front door, tripped over the groggy Farnum, and cartwheeled through the air to land roughly on the front lawn a few feet from where Horst

Schmidt still lay, half paralyzed by Pepe's first lightning attack.

David, who had witnessed that blitz from the corner of his eye and quickly put a distance between himself and the action, had been thoughtful enough to turn off the idling Ford when it was clear that its driver had no immediate use for it. Only now that the tumult had died down, and the casualties—one-two-three-four-five, and Bud Cronk made six —lay thick on the lawn, silent except for groaning Bud and the grocery checker hunched moaning over his broken wrist; only now did David risk a look inside. Two shots had been fired: there might be more bodies. He wasn't smiling.

But "Come on *in*, baby!" cried Faggot One, the movie maker. "You missed all the exciting part!" And David saw that everyone visible was still in one piece. Somehow or other the good guys—if you counted the spook in black leather—had won. Even if Mrs. Bunch was crying, David had to smile. The Cap looked normally troubled. Probably worried about how to get the rest of them out. "Hi, Dad," said David. "How's it going?"

"OK, OK," said Rasmussen, shaking his head instead of nodding. "Sons of bitches," he said, not sure of whether he meant Bert Hearn, Jr., and his vigilantes, or everybody in the world. A muffled comprehensive rage had backed up in his chest like heartburn. He should have popped somebody, even Bud Cronk, even from behind. And now Ace Liquors had forfeited the lead in the Westpark Bowl Majors, and the house was wrecked into the bargain. "Well," he said. "Well, now what?"

Then David remembered the other one, clubfoot Art Hearn, dispatched to reconnoiter the back yard. He must still be somewhere about.

He was in, fact, lying dead to the world in the back yard,

lying where Pepe had struck him down, with a primed fury meant for De Vaughn, a moment after he and Richard and Donald had slipped out the back door. Margie, stealing out to hang up the wet bed sheets she held at arms' length in front of her, tripped over his orthopodiatric shoe, and very nearly fell. Almost having to go in and wash the sheets all over again so distracted her that she carefully pinned them up on the plastic clothesline before she noticed Art Hearn.

A dead body! All bodies which lay so still were dead, she knew that much. Especially if they were in uniform. And she had heard more guns going off just now. She had never seen a dead body before. And one sheet was dripping in his face. But if she went in and told, the sheet would be discovered, and she would catch it. Well, she would catch it anyway, even if it wasn't her fault, but that didn't mean she had to practically ask for it. He wouldn't feel the dripping anyway; dead bodies didn't. She hurried back into the house, locked herself in her room—both doors this time—and got into bed.

"There was another one," said David. "His brother, the one with the clubfoot. He went round back."

But Rasmussen was distracted from answering by a scream like a fire siren: Donald had been the first to see in the front doorway a lean brown man in a torn and bloody white shirt, a large white Band-Aid striped over his upper lip, and a nylon stocking wound round his head like the piccolo player in "The Spirit of '76." Howard Bunch had come back alive.

"Honey, what did they _do_ to you?" Viola ran to him, and everyone heard him stammer out a disjointed, harelipped account of a miraculous escape from lynching when a pickup truck spraying submachine-gun bullets had scattered his captors long enough for him to make a run for it. His Mustang was full of holes, he said. Who were all those people lying out in front? And what was Viola doing here?

However shaken by emotion, and distorted by the Band-Aid like a Groucho Marx moustache in white, Howard's voice traveled recognizably through the silence to the kitchen. Ann added Rice Twinkles to the complex mélange which she had not yet stopped stirring, and smiled to herself. Him, too, with his little curly hairs like pigtails. Pig hairs.

The pot was within an inch of brimming over, but the Rice Twinkles made the mash a little too dry. Pigs liked slop. Ann knew just the thing. She stopped stirring and went to find it.

Everybody had lost their minds, Howard was saying. The police had stopped him five times before the lynch mob caught him, and twice after! Your life wasn't worth a nickel out there!

Viola told him his nephew Dwight had been killed, but Howard seemed incapable of taking it in. "Who are all those people out on the lawn?" he asked again. "And what are you doing here?"

"Well, brother," said De Vaughn. "Sounds like you had a pretty rough day, but it got pretty wild around here for a while, too."

Howard's eyes bulged beneath the nylon headband as he read the front of De Vaughn's sweatshirt. "Brother!" he said. "Huh!"

Ann couldn't find it anywhere on the back porch. In the bathroom, then? No, she remembered now. She had poured it all down the shower drain to kill those filthy little animals in the nest. But it didn't matter. She could thin the slop with whiskey, or beer. But she wished she had some of those disgusting little bug bodies to mix in, or some flushings from the toilet. Pigs, pigs . . .

"Better take the old man home an feed him somethin, baby," said De Vaughn. "Bein hungry always makes em cranky."

"Who are you supposed to be?" said Howard. "How come you're not out with the rest of the troublemakers?"

"Me?" said De Vaughn, with a tilt of his head. "Aw, man, I'm your mama's back-door man. I'm your *father*. Bet you ain't played the dozens in years, have you, brother?"

"Well, if we're going, let's go," said Donald.

Pepe released a sigh like air from a pressure cooker. "Fuck all this shit, I'm goin," he said, as if he had thought of it himself.

Richard pointed Donald at his black suitcase, picked up his camera, and went along airily, saying, "OK, later on, all you people. De Vaughn you behave yourself, baby. And everybody's invited to the premiere!" He tucked the shiny revolver in one hip-hugging brick-red pocket, as if he might find some use for it, and followed Pepe and Donald out. David, closing the door after them, saw Pepe swing one last kick into the obstructing body of Horst Schmidt.

"*Soooeee!*" From the dining room Ann called them to eat. She appeared in the doorway carrying the big aluminum pot on one hip like a child. "*Soooeee!* Everybody good and hungry? Come and eat, there's plenty." She caught sight of Howard Bunch, and flashed a dazzling intimate white smile at him. "Look at you, Howard," she said. "You're a disgusting mess!"

No one, not even Happy, moved to accept her invitation.

"Howard's got little kinky black pig hairs," Ann told them. "Howard's just as good as anybody else. Howard's got a big . . . *thing* like a pig."

It couldn't have been easy, but Howard looked even more stricken than he had when he walked in. "Come on," he ordered Viola, and turned to leave.

"Better do what the man says," De Vaughn advised her. "We gonna have to be movin on pretty soon anyway. But I'll be seein you around."

Viola couldn't argue with both of them. Dwight dead, maniacs with guns every way you looked, Ann Rasmussen standing there evil and crazy and talking dirty. *And what did she say about Howard just now?* It was too much for Viola. She handed the gun to Charley Rasmussen and let Howard lead her out.

"Howard don't run away, come and eat!" called Ann. "That's my Sunday husband, Howard Bunch," she confided to the room. Even that didn't stop Viola from closing the door behind her. Bud Cronk sat looking up at them from the middle of the lawn, where he had been trying unsuccessfully to revive Horst Schmidt. "It's your fault," he said. "All of this mess. Why don't you people stay in your own part of town?"

Howard took two steps and on the third syllable of "Motherfucker!" kicked Bud Cronk in the left kneecap hard enough to send a delicious pain shooting up his own right leg. From inside the Rasmussen's, Ann's piercing soprano rose again: *"Soooeee!"*

"Don't pay no attention to her," said Rasmussen. "She's crazy as a coot. She's just talkin out of her head." Howard Bunch her Sunday husband?

But as De Vaughn's party gathered itself to depart, Bernie could not resist sharing with his sister-in-law, and anyone else who wanted to listen, a fresh new batch of insights granted him during the last few minutes.

"Man don't you *see?* It's all out now, you an Charley an everybody, we're *free!* An what it means is like if everybody alive got together—you know, gay an straight an spades an Mexicans an white—everybody *living*, man, we could just kill up all those sick poison zombies an have it the way we want! You know, not really *kill* em, but like *overwhelm* em, like we just did. Because shit they got nothin goin for em but hate. . . ."

"You're the biggest pig of all," said Ann.

"*Now you shut your mouth!*" said Rasmussen. "Is that all you can say? Pig this an pig that an the other?" Compounded by what she had said to Howard Bunch, and by the sight of the two blondes getting ready to leave, his rage almost strangled him, and he turned it upon its natural target. "*I had enough!*"

"Naw, she's just gettin the last pieces of it out," explained Bernie. "It's good for her, you just be patient." But when he saw Orange Julius going out the door in his helmet, and Happy and Diz and Mitchell and Heidi, he hesitated only enough longer to tell Rasmussen: "Listen, baby, it's been a groove seein you but I'm gonna split with these people now. . . ." In the doorway he paused to hitch up his blue-and-white overalls and set his Stetson more firmly on his head. "An David," he said. "You better not wait till they catch you, either, baby."

Rasmussen saw De Vaughn's eyes on him as he shepherded Sandra and Wondra toward the door. "Say wait a minute," he began, and De Vaughn waited.

"Ah, well, ah . . ." said Rasmussen.

"Pigs, pigs, pigs, pigs," said Ann.

"You better get clear of her while you can, brother," said De Vaughn. "Ain't gonna get a better chance."

"I'm gonna do that, but . . ." Rasmussen reached into his pants pocket, which was empty.

De Vaughn took in the gesture and dismissed it. "Naw, don't worry about a thing, man," he said. "We even. You a real honor student, tell the truth." He followed the two blonde ponytails out and shut the door behind him.

"Jesus Christ," said Rasmussen. They were gone, all of them. Ann had disappeared. David was looking at him.

Rasmussen let go with a sigh. "Son of a bitch," he said. "What a . . . You know, she's really got to be put away this time."

Still pondering the latest development, Mrs. Clean's words about Mr. Bunch, David said nothing. But Rasmussen, unaccustomed to his son's support, did not miss it now. Already he was beginning to feel like a man who had come through a perilous battle by dint of his own toughness and perspicacity. There was more to come, no doubt, but for the moment he had surely earned the right to sit down and draw breath.

A breath full of Camel smoke, and he drew it in deeply. He wouldn't even mind watching TV for a bit: *that* flashed home to him again, and he exhaled with irritable force. "Ah hell," he said. "Well, anyway, they're gone, I guess that's the main thing."

"Supper's on," came Ann's voice. "Come and swill it up, it's ready."

David said he was going to bed. Rasmussen was on his feet. "Got to do something about her right now," he said. Together they went into the dining room. She had laid out a dozen or more plates and soup bowls; they covered the entire top of the table, minus the leaf Happy had broken off, and now, with the hearty impersonality of a kitchen helper in a public institution, her busy ladle dumping one load after another, she was sloshing them full of the glutinous reddish-brown conglomerate.

Nausea stirred in David's solar plexus, and the sound nausea made, disembodied and amplified, came from the open French doors into the patio, framing now an apparition in a white-smudged black coat and an oil-stained gray tarpaulin. His cheeks burned red in his blanched face, but his chin was high over his convulsing Adam's apple, and his blue eyes rolled disdainful accusation down upon the Rasmussens. "Glug-glug-glug," he said. *"Glug-glug-glug."*

"Jesus Christ Almighty!" said Rasmussen. "Where did *he* come from?"

From the shelter of the garage, where, except for a single fruitless sortie onto the roof, just after dark, he had spent the last seven hours in repentant prayer. So to him the Rasmussens were strangers—loathsome ones, evidently.

But this did not keep him from presenting them with a message, painstakingly hand-lettered in leftover white enamel on a dusty piece of gray-brown cardboard.

JESUS CHRIST DIED ON THE CROSS FOR YOU

YOU ARE ALL DOOMED

WHERE ARE MY TRUOSERS PLEASE

"I think the girls pantsed him," David explained. "That's what they said anyway. He's deaf and dumb. They made movies of it."

"Tell him I don't know where the hell his trousers are," said Rasmussen, as if David's knowledge carried with it the gift of tongues. "Which girls?"

The apparition pointed energetically at the last line of his message.

"You know," said David. "The two. They hid his pants somewhere, I don't know. . . ."

"Ah for Christ's sake!" said Rasmussen. But he hurried into the master bedroom and brought back an unclean and rumpled pair of gray cotton-dacron slacks. These he handed to David, who handed them to the apparition, who withdrew into the patio.

"Is there one God damn nut case in the area we didn't

get here today?" said Rasmussen. "That's what I want to know."

Ann had filled every plate and bowl, but the pot was still half full. With only a moment's pause to reflect, she leaned over the center of the table and emptied it. The stuff began spreading slowly, like lava.

The apparition returned, now wearing the gray slacks, which fit him rather well, though perhaps a cuff's width short. He glanced once at the table, pointed at the middle line of his message where it lay on a chair; then, individually, at Ann and David and Rasmussen. "*Glug-glug,*" he said.

"What's he say?" said Rasmussen.

The apparition, as if commanding some imperishable dignity, walked into the living room, out the front door, and away into the night.

"I'm a son of a bitch," said Rasmussen deliberately. And to David, who had accompanied him into the living room: "You mean they gave it to him, too?"

"That's what they said. I wasn't here then."

"Jesus. I don't know." As much to be moving as to go anywhere, Rasmussen went back into the dining room, where the viscous red-brown tide, still lumpy despite an hour's patient stirring, had flowed over and between the brimming dishes and now dripped thickly onto the carpet. "Will you look at that?" he said. "I bet there's nothin fit to eat in the house!"

David said he wasn't hungry, and went to bed.

"Aren't you going to eat?" said Ann, and Rasmussen was dizzied by how perfectly *normal* she looked, as if something was the matter with *him* for not falling on his face and gobbling up that slop!

"You . . ." he said. "What was all that about Bunch?"

"You and your pig blondes. You'll never catch up with me."

"Are you kiddin? You? An that *nigger?*"

"Every Sunday. And he's more of a man than you'll ever be. Even if he has got pig hairs."

Uncoordinated as ever, present when he couldn't use it, absent when he could, Rasmussen's anger seemed to be deserting him once again. Her and Bunch? He should be choking her, but he felt more like laughing. After today, what did it matter anyhow?

"Hell with it," he said, and he meant *all* of it.

"Fuck it," he said, and spit at the table.

But on his way to bed again—where else was there to go? —he noticed Bert Hearn, Jr.'s, abandoned Lee Enfield rifle on the floor. Somebody had taken the big Colt; it was the moustached kid. And Rasmussen had his own empty automatic. He took the rifle with him into the master bedroom. Nowhere to lock it up, so he emptied it, stood it in the corner next to his bed, and put the clip under his pillow. Just to be on the safe side, he locked the bedroom door. Let her sleep on the couch for a change. Where she was going, the beds would be hard. He lay down on his own bed, on the rumpled sheet, still smelling faintly of perfume and the Fourth of July. In seconds he was asleep.

Some time before midnight, when Art Hearn painfully recovered consciousness in the back yard, he was so relieved to find the wet on his face wasn't blood that he forgot to look for his pistol in the dark weedy grass. And when he stole away to look for Bert, as fast as his bad foot and his shattering headache would allow, the Rasmussens' house was all in darkness.

III. MORNING AFTER

TWENTY-TWO

Wednesday morning brought pronouncements. The Governor of California and the Mayor of Los Angeles patched up their lovers' quarrel and held a joint news conference before a battery of network and independent cameras. Calling each other by their first names in a manner reminiscent of Huntley and Brinkley, they took turns revealing the latest steps taken to "normalize the situation," as the Governor put it. These included the opening of a massive EDA, or Emergency Detention Annex, on the southern edge of the Mojave Desert.

"Ron," the Mayor said, "I think our viewers might like to see the exact location of EDA 1, don't you?"

"Right, Sam," said the Governor, and with the tip of a classroom pointer he described on a large wall map a circle several miles in diameter just north of Pearblossom. "Accessible by State Highway 138, you see?" he said. "And I've just had a call from our State Engineers down in, ah, down in, ah, Death Valley, saying EDA 2 will be ready by tomorrow night. But, Sam, you might like to mention the TAC plan, which has already been activated this morning."

"Sure thing, Ron," said the Mayor. "Folks, the Governor was referring, as some of you know, to our Total Air Control Plan. . . ." He nodded off-camera, and his image was replaced on several million screens by film clips of large helicopters being loaded with boxes marked .50 CAL and racks of small bombs. "These babies," said the Mayor's voice, "are already airborne, and fifty of them will be aloft at all times, nonstop, until this mess is cleaned up. Same principle as the Strategic Air Command, you see. Now, Ron, I think you've got that list of the various private organizations we've designated as AMP, that is, Auxiliary Military Personnel. . . ."

The Governor had it, all right, but before he could read it viewers saw him, one amazed eye still bright, flip over backward and disappear, swivel chair and all, to the faithfully reproduced sound of a gunshot from a weapon marvelously concealed in a camera operated by an employee of an independent UHF television station which specialized in Fundamentalist religious programs.

Before the assassin could fire again, he was swarmed to the floor by fellow newsmen and security guards. "Talk to my lawyer," he snarled, when dragged to his feet to face half a dozen quickly converging lenses. "I'm innocent before God."

Luckily, however, the Lieutenant Governor was on hand, already made up, and as the putative assassin was hustled out of the Mayor's Press Room, he stepped into the vacancy before the cameras. "This terrible and horrible tragedy," he said in a trembling voice, "shall not and will not and must not impair us from normalizing the situation at the most immediate possible time."

Then he picked up his fallen superior's list of deputized organizations and began to read. "The Minutemen," he said.

"The Southeast Asia Combat Veterans' Association. The Christian Ranger Guardians. The Napa Valley Mutual Defense League. The White Cross Crusade. . . ." For even that organization, undeterred by the 70 percent casualties suffered the previous morning between Taft and Maricopa, had declared themselves ready, to the last survivor.

The Rasmussens, of course, neither saw nor heard any of this. David, up earlier than he had been for months, wandered in and out of the house, here and there picking up odd relics of the night before. Margie, lying on a bare mattress and wondering if her sheets could be dry yet, kept her transistor tuned to KWOW but deliberately refused to listen to any News Wows. And Rasmussen, though he awoke to the dependable thump of the Times against the front of the house, would find no news of the Governor's mishap in its pages.

It was late, the Times. Sun was up already. His right hand plucked its first Camel of the day, his gas jet set it afire. The pressure was there. Had he got up in the night? But she wasn't there. With the first deep chestful of smoke, Rasmussen felt his capillaries constrict with dread of the day to come.

Everything had changed, and probably gone on changing while he had slept. Everything was falling apart, out of control. But he had to pee: at least that hadn't changed and, smoking tensely, he stalked into the bathroom. Among all of yesterday's fantastic events, his mind played hide-and-seek with his ultimatum to Ann, and lost: last night's tomorrow was right now. The sun was up. Impossible that she would go peaceably.

He had slept soundly for the better part of twenty-four hours, but standing now before the toilet, he felt himself draining dry, empty of vitality. He flushed with a sense of loss, drew a hand along his jaw and was unnerved by its smoothness. Years it had been since he had shaved at night: his scarcely bearded morning face suggested some diminishing of physical process, and robbed him of a morning ritual he needed more than ever today.

Hell with it, he would shave anyway, and get back on his trolley. Today of all days he couldn't afford to show any sign of being under par: she would take it as failure of nerve.

But the razor didn't feel right. For lack of normal resistance, it failed to give him that scraped toughness he needed. He bore down, and sliced himself along the edge of his lower jaw; the cut instantly sweat blood, and Rasmussen stung it white with styptic pencil. Musn't show a crack. It was all out there waiting for him, and he must confront it seamlessly, smooth and resolved beneath his protective skin.

His razor hand stopped, as he apprehended a dangerous contradiction: the more normally he went out to face her, the harder it would be to carry through his plan. Rasmussen grew cagey, and resumed shaving with a lighter touch, eyeing himself distrustfully in the mirror. He needed to rehearse, and this meant carefully reexamining the evidence which had led to his ultimatum in the first place.

All right then.

1. She had tried to kill him, or what she believed to be him.

2. She had destroyed a two-thousand-dollar home-theater complex.

3. She had cooked up an indescribable mess—only someone crazy could have done it—and poured it all over the place.

4. She had confessed to having fraudulently forced him to marry her.

5. She had confessed to having committed adultery with Howard Bunch, a nigger.

At this point, as he washed away the traces of instant menthol lather, Rasmussen sensed in the evidence a confusing overlap: part of it led to a mental institution, part to divorce court. And if part of his purpose in going over his grounds had been to arouse himself anew, that part had succeeded so well that he now found himself hard put to sort out the evidence coolly. That bitch! She deserved both divorcing *and* locking up, not to mention being cooked alive by napalm! If only he had a spray can of that!

What he lacked in rehearsal he would make up in feeling, then, and when she actually had the guts to knock on the bedroom door and call, "Charley are you coming out today?" he roared back at her: "God damn right I'm comin out! An *you're goin in!*"

He blotted his angry face on a hand towel, hurried into his clothes, pulled the Dodgers cap aggressively down over his forehead, and like Walt Alston emerging from the dugout he charged out to get it over with fast.

No one was in the living room. Last night's wreckage had all been cleared away, although across the room the broken picture tube was plain to see, and welcome.

The phone rang. Rasmussen jumped, and grabbed the receiver before it could ring again. "Yeah," he said, feeling weak in the knees for no reason at all.

"Don, Charley," said the voice in his ear. "Hope you're comin in today, place got busted into last night, don't know what all they got away with yet, but it's plenty."

"Jesus H. Christ," said Rasmussen. "Yeah, OK, soon as I can."

"Falstaff didn't come yesterday, neither," said Don. "Got hijacked."

One thing at a time, one thing at a time. Rasmussen felt like saying please, but didn't.

When he walked into the dining room he felt like saying he would be a son of a bitch, and did. There she was sitting in her usual place, with her usual Well-what-took-*you*-so-long? look on her face. There was David, there was Margie, there was cereal, sugar and milk, toast and coffee, his already poured and probably cold already. No trace of last night's crazy slop. Rasmussen had to restrain himself from stooping to inspect the carpet.

And luckily, for he would have found nothing. Ann, inheriting the gift of an unprecedentedly messy house (or almost so; there had been Bernie's last visit), a house empty but for sleepers, had spent a good part of the night restoring it as nearly as possible to its normal pristine state. Indeed, she had quite enjoyed herself: the resumption of her favorite daily pastime had allowed her to work off most of her tension. When she had swept up every shard of broken ashtray and lamp, put all the encyclopedias back in their glass case (a miracle it hadn't got broken); when she had scraped up and disposed of her culinary whimsy, washed and dried and put away every last dirty dish, cleaned the stain-resistant plastic fiber carpet and pressed it dry with her steam iron on an extension cord, *then* she had fallen quickly asleep on the living-room couch, so returned to sanity (if she had actually so very far to come) that she didn't mind the faint scent of perfume left by two of its recent occupants. Getting up with the sun, she had ducked out to borrow the necessaries of breakfast from a yawning Mrs. Coffman, and to note with satisfaction her blue Volkswagen, apparently no worse for wear, across the street. She had her own solution to the main problem firmly in mind, and besides, there were still all three bedrooms to be cleaned.

"You don't have to start the day by swearing," she said now. "Your coffee's getting cold."

So that was her game! Rasmussen saw through it in a flash. "*No you don't, God damn it!*" he shouted at her. "I want a few words with you."

But that wasn't half strong enough, and if he lost control of the situation now . . . "*Right this God damn minute! Out here!*" He went booming through the swinging door into the kitchen. It was spotless.

"Are you completely out of your head?" He heard her through the door. She wasn't coming. "Haven't we all had about enough around here with your brother and his little friends?"

Oh no. Oh no. Not so easily. Rasmussen boomed back into the dining room and let go at the nape of her neck with all five rounds of his evidence, point-blank, rapid-fire, and in plain enough English for even a mental case to understand.

"So?" she said, still without turning.

"*So I'm gonna put you away!*"

"You are? Better watch out they don't take you instead."

"Where's your keys?"

"What for?"

"Store got looted last night, I got to get over there."

"I thought you were going to put me away."

"Don't you worry about that," said Rasmussen.

"Where are your witnesses?"

"All over the place," said Rasmussen, as his mind's eye watched their farewell parade out the front door: the queers and the one in the helmet and the big fat girl in fatigues, Bernie, the son of a bitch to blame for it all, and the blondes, the two blondes, and De Vaughn. "I know where I can find em when I want em," he said, and looked at David. But the little traitor was looking into his bowl of Quisp, and, as it happened, toying with a little plan of his own. But would he have the nerve? Probably not.

"Fine," said Ann. "That's just fine, because I need them myself. I'm divorcing you." She drew breath. "My keys are in my bureau drawer, my spare ones, and don't you dare touch them, because somebody's still got a set, and the lock will have to be changed. Go get your own car back."

"Seventy-seventh Street Station," David remembered into his Quisp. "They called. . . ." He looked up in time to see the Dodgers cap torn from the skull and swatted overhand at the back of her head, as if to kill a wasp. Or perhaps he was just trying to get her to look at him.

She stared straight ahead. "That's just fine, keep it up," she said. "Hitting me in front of the children. It'll all count." She smiled. David did not.

Rasmussen yanked the cap back onto his head at a dangerous rakish angle, and ran out. Not to seize and load Bert Hearn, Jr.'s, Lee Enfield rifle; no, only to get out, out, out of the house before his head exploded.

"It's only fair," said Ann. "Margie eat your cereal."

Committed to a course of impartial neutrality between them, David sensed himself now to have been left, tacitly or by default, a seeming partisan of Mrs. Clean. He had his reasons for avoiding any such suspicion, particularly during crisis. So to even it up with The Cap he went to the telephone, looked up and dialed the number of the Seventy-seventh Street Station.

They took a long time to answer, and when they did, David heard heavy breathing, then, "What you want?"

"Is this Seventy-seventh Street Station?"

"Not no more it ain't, motherfucker," said the voice. "Now what you think of that?"

David replaced the receiver, and saw the Los Angeles Times standing on his father's legs in the open front door, its edges clamped tight in his father's fingers. "What's new, Dad?" he said. Nothing good, from the look of the front page, a black broadsheet of disaster.

"Christ Almighty," said Rasmussen. "It's a real civil war." His eyes roamed over the rich meal of death and destruction spread before him on pages 1A and 1B, finding no place to begin. His head was pounding, he felt dizzy. His fingertips registered the uncommon thinness of today's emergency Times, only sixteen pages; a once-trusty shield gone flimsy in the hour of need. He sat down in the nearest chair, shook his head, blinked, and looked for a morsel small enough to sneak past his headache for a starter.

A name caught his eye. "Hey, what's that buddy of yours name? Eric B. Hart, that him?"

"Where?" said David, leaning down past the cap. That was him.

Rasmussen's left forefinger stabbed at a small box wedged between large chunks of stories jumped from the front page, one of those brief "human interest" items employed by makeup editors to break up too-heavy concentrations of important news.

SAXOPHONE CASE MAY HAVE
CAUSED MUSICIAN'S DEATH

A black leather case containing a soprano saxophone may have proved fatal to a young Westpark musician early yesterday morning.

Police who discovered the bullet-riddled body of Eric B. Hart, 21, of 352½ Williams st., speculated that his slayers may have mistaken the instrument case for one containing a rifle or machine pistol.

Hart was found near the corner of Firestone blvd. and Juniper st. There were no witnesses.

"That the guy?" said Rasmussen. "What in the hell was he doin runnin around over in that neighborhood?"

David thought the rest of his life would not be long enough to explain that to The Cap. He went out onto the front lawn. Everything seemed bright, everything had hard edges. Across the street a brown dog lifted a leg to water Farnum's lawn.

Well, Hart didn't care. If he could read that little piece in the paper, he would probably think it was funny. It was so completely wrong and so completely right. It just completely missed the point, that was all. But Hart was used to that. He didn't care. You want to play jazz you play with spades, or it's nothing. Zero bullshit. If anybody expected him to stop doing that just because there was a war on, they didn't know Hart.

But who was left in the whole world for David to think about and feel good? It was nothing to smile at. It seemed to settle something. He went back into the house and approached The Cap. "Dad?" he said.

At the moment Rasmussen wanted only a respite from the problems hanging over his head, but he looked up at David, and seemed to recognize him.

"I know this is a bad time to ask," David said. "But I've been thinking. I mean, I'll be going in a week about, and I thought I might take a little trip somewhere. You know, *first.*"

"Trip?" said Rasmussen, blinking beneath the pounding of his headache. "Trip where?" He rattled the Times. "Christ Almighty, can't you read?"

"I thought maybe Mexico for a couple of days."

"Mexico? That's the God damnedest thing I ever heard of in my life! Mexico?"

"Just for a couple of days. I'm going in the Army." It didn't hurt to remind him; he had a lot on his mind.

"Sure, but . . ." The Cap nodded at the dining room. "Christ, I'm gonna need some help with, ah . . ."

"But that'll take a while, Dad. There'll be papers to fill out, and a hearing. I mean, I'd be back. In time."

The bill of the cap fell an inch: thinking. "Well . . . well . . . I guess you're old enough to do what you want. But you could get killed before you get out of the country."

"I don't have any money," said David, hoping that all the times he had not asked The Cap for money wouldn't prove more hindrance than help now. "I'll pay you back," he added.

"On Army pay?" said Rasmussen. "You're nuts." He thought some more. "OK, go get the checkbook. On the dresser."

David went and got it. That wasn't all he got, either.

"How much you need?" said The Cap.

Better not name a sum. "Oh, whatever you can spare."

"Hundred be enough?"

Let the tone be just doubtful enough. "Sure . . ."

"Aw hell," said The Cap, and scribbled a check for *Two hundred and no/100 dollars,* and signed his name. "Guess you want a little ah . . . before Basic, huh?"

David took the check and nodded, bashfully man-to-man.

"Just watch out you don't pick up a dose down there," said The Cap. "Them Mexican girls are crawlin with it."

David promised to watch out, and headed for his room.

Rasmussen went back to the paper as if he had just bought himself a bit more reading time, but his headache spoiled it, the print swam, the God damn headache had dropped on him out of nowhere, and everything was out of control, here at home, out there in the streets. . . .

He closed his eyes until they would read again, found the item about that poor dumb bastard of a kid, forced himself to start with the front page. Head ready to burst, chest cramped tight, he meant to read every word, but his concentration kept lapsing.

Although his own private rage seemed to relocate itself piecemeal in the public sector, where it should have been a

viable source of satisfaction, what he went on feeling remained personal, and physical. As he painfully conceived a
more public-spirited vision of the relation between his personal trials and those of the world at large, still his brain
and body ached for vengeance. He asked himself: what was
the problem of a crazy homicidal wife but a drop in the
bucket when the niggers were trying to blow up the city,
the state, the whole country? But God damn it to hell, somebody had to pay!

And the sons of bitches were sneaky, they came at you
every which way, the Times was solid with proof. Out of
nowhere, like his headache, came a surging gut conviction
of the conspiracy between the two Green Berets and De
Vaughn; it struck him with such stunning clarity that he
broke off his reading in the middle of a story about blowing
up a Molotov-cocktail factory in Pacoima.

And Howard Bunch, too! Christ, didn't that cinch it?

He dashed into the dining room. She and Margie were
still at the table. "Get in your room!" he cried, in such a
voice that Margie obeyed before her mother could defend
her.

"What is it now?" said Ann. "Can't you go for five minutes
without hollering your head off?"

"Was that true what you said last night? About you and
that black son of a bitch?"

"Try and prove it," she smiled. "You just try."

David had his bag packed. It contained toothbrush and
razor, clean socks and underwear, and a loaded .38 Police
Special he had picked up an hour ago in the back yard. In
one pants pocket he had the check, in the other the spare
keys to the Volkswagen. He still had the chunk of fudge
saved from yesterday's party. So that was it, and he'd better
hurry before he started smiling at himself.

No, one thing more. He made a little ceremony out of it,

first lighting one of the gutted stumps of candle on his dresser top, then starting to read the fine print:

> The law requires you, subject to heavy penalty for violation, to have this Notice, in addition to your Registration Certificate, in your personal possession at all times and to surrender it upon entering active duty in the Armed Forces. . . .
>
> Your Government Appeal agent, attached to your selective service local board, is available to advise you regarding your rights and liabilities under the selective service law.

That last sentence made him smile and, without reading the rest, he inserted one corner in the candle flame and tilted the card until the flame caught and spread. Before he burned his fingers, he dropped it and watched the last corner char to ash. He blew out the candle. In his wallet he replaced the card with the one he had picked up in the patio before breakfast. It was the size of a playing card, and he had to fold it in half to fit it into the plastic window. *No. 39*, it said. *Will You Be Saved From The* ALL-CONSUMING FIRE? That was a tough one, all right, but it, too, made David smile.

Bag in hand, he went by Pig Bird's door and saw her deeply concentrated on cutting out the head of a beautiful blonde, whose hair spread out in goddess-like rays all over a scarlet pillow. Bye-bye, Pig Bird. Be a good girl.

Through the open kitchen door he saw Mrs. Clean's narrow back as she rinsed the breakfast dishes in a cloud of steam. All clear so far.

In the living room all he saw of The Cap was the Times, lying on the carpet in a loose tangle, and the front door standing open. *Chim Chim Cheree* began playing in his head like a scratched LP; nothing so creative as the Coltrane variations, of course, just the first eight bars of the melody, over and over and over.

He had to get to the bank before they could stop the check, that was the main thing. So he loped through the open door, *chim chim cheree,* and straight across the lawn and the street to the blue Volkswagen. He had the key in the ignition before he saw The Cap, apparently trying to batter down Bunches' front door with the rifle butt.

The motor caught, the door opened, Howard Bunch in a green kimono sprang out at The Cap, hugging him, knocking him backward onto the lawn, the rifle locked between them. *Chim chim cheree,* David couldn't wait around to see who won. As he drove past he saw them rolling over and over, first one on top, then the other. *Don't look back.* That made him smile. From the bank, Canada was north, a right turn at the first signal. *Chim chim cheree, chim chim cheree,* by nightfall he would be a long way off.

Design by Sidney Feinberg
Set in Caledonia
Composed and printed by York Composition Company, Inc.
Bound by The Haddon Craftsmen, Inc.
HARPER & ROW, PUBLISHERS, INCORPORATED